TRUE GRACE

KAREN E. OSBORNE

Black Rose Writing | Texas

The author grants the final approval for this literary material.

First printing

This is a work of fiction based on real people, places and events

ISBN: 978-1-68513-267-5 (Paperback); 978-1-68513-435-8 (Hardcover)
PUBLISHED BY BLACK ROSE WRITING
www.blackrosewriting.com

Printed in the United States of America
Suggested Retail Price (SRP) $22.95 (Paperback); $27.95 (Hardcover)

True Grace is printed in Minion Pro

*As a planet-friendly publisher, Black Rose Writing does its best to eliminate unnecessary waste to reduce paper usage and energy costs, while never compromising the reading experience. As a result, the final word count vs. page count may not meet common expectations.

PRAISE FOR
TRUE GRACE

"*True Grace*, by Karen E. Osborne, will hold you captive by its tragic and uplifting journey . . . of true grace."

–P. L. Jonas, author of Hall of Deception

"If Edith Wharton chronicled early 20th century white upper-class society, Karen E. Osborne does the same for Black middle-class society."

–Carolyn Geduld, author of The Struggle

"A compelling and suspenseful historical family drama, about a woman with intelligence, courage, heart, and of course–grace."

–J. Ivanel Johnson, author of the JUST (e)STATE Mysteries

"A courageous young mother must make the ultimate sacrifice to keep her children safe in 1920's Harlem. Gripping, heart-breaking and inspired by the author's grandmother, *True Grace* by Karen E. Osborne is a true delight."

–Gail Olmsted, author of Miranda Writes and Miranda Nights

"With its wicked-fast plot and stunning heroine, *True Grace* immediately snags and immerses readers in the colorful nineteen-twenties Harlem of speakeasies, gangsters, and flappers. A propulsive family saga with vivid historical detail."

–Jill Caugherty, author of The View from Half Dome

"An inspiring story of courage and inner strength immersed in richly constructed historical detail."

–David Rabin, award-winning author of In Danger of Judgment

To my best friend and lifelong partner, Bob,
and to my grandmother, who endured and overcame so much.

TRUE GRACE

PART I

CHAPTER ONE

The first time my husband died, I felt fear, shame, and guilt. The second time he died...

April 1924, Harlem, New York
I hurried up the stairs to our Amsterdam Avenue walkup. Thousands of dashes up and down wore narrow steps to a grooved shine. I'd forgotten three envelopes on the kitchen table, stamped and ready to mail, and I was running late. Waist-length hair, white since age twenty, sat coiled on top of my head. Held in place by hairpins, it wobbled as I climbed. Despite the warm spring day, heat pumped from the radiators in the hall. The cotton blouse clung to my back.

"Morning, Missus." My second-floor neighbor, her housedress covered by an oversized apron, swept in front of her door. A welcome mat sat propped on its side against the wall and a bucket of ammonia-smelling water and stack of rags stood nearby.

"Good day, Mrs. Thompson." I waved, huffing a little. She seldom called me by my name. Perhaps she found Herbert, my husband's Portuguese surname, odd. In America, it was often a first name and Henry's given name–Henriques–used by others as a last name.

Although in a hurry, trying to complete my errands, and return home in time for Henry to get to work, I slowed a bit to catch my breath.

"Good thing you're young," Mrs. Thompson said, her Jamaican accent reminding me of home. The dull ache in my gut sharpened from the memory.

"That's the truth," Mrs. Salmon said from the third-floor landing above me, her Georgia intonation thick.

Tottering on the edge of the stairs, Mrs. Salmon held her fat purse in one hand and a woven-wood shopping cart in the other. Gray hair poked out from her ill-fitting wig.

It took time for my neighbors to accept me, especially those like Mrs. Salmon, who migrated from the south. The hair, British accent, light eyes, and fair skin made them cautious at first. I enjoyed being different, but not always. As often as possible, I used American English, rather than British terms. I tried to fit in.

We moved to Harlem from the north Bronx where we experienced fresh air and room for the children to run. But Henry's work was over an hour away. Although we paid a higher rent in Harlem, we enjoyed every convenience, and Henry reached work in twenty minutes.

"Let me help." To prevent tripping, I lifted the hem of my ankle-length skirt with one hand, grabbed the cart with the other, hefted it down the stairs, and then sprinted back up.

"God bless you," Mrs. Salmon said.

Mrs. Thompson asked, "Are you going to the post office this morning?" Every Saturday, I made the trip. The ladies of the building studied my movements, but I didn't mind. They were kind and their gossip harmless.

I paused and walked down one flight. At this rate, I'd never retrieve my letters, get to the post office, purchase groceries, and return in time for Henry's commute to work. "I am. Do you need something?"

"Stamps. I'll pay you when you return." Her smile squinted her eyes.

"My pleasure."

"How are all those children of yours?"

"Fine, thank you." For once, everyone was healthy at the same time. No sniffles or earaches, no coughing or tummy pains. I picked up my pace again, rounded the stairs, and reached our fifth-floor apartment. It would take only a minute to retrieve the letters.

Managing my household required precision. The one crowded water-closet housed a toilet, bathtub, sink, and narrow hamper overflowing with clothes ready for scrubbing. A washboard leaned against the wall behind the hamper. Although grateful the seven of us–Henry, five children, and me–didn't have to share a hallway bathroom, I still longed for a house like the one we'd owned in Jamaica. There, one bath was ours and the children used the other.

Shame on me. I had no reason to complain. We lived well and even though my marriage dashed my dreams for a different life, my plans for my children's futures lived and breathed.

Weekdays, Sylvie, and Patience helped me get the little ones cleaned, dressed and fed. Sylvie, an almost young woman at fourteen, applied herself. She'd attend college by the time she reached sixteen. What a joy she was–reading to the boys and entertaining her little sister, five-year-old Irene. Sylvie created paper dolls and sewed clothes for Irene's rubber and cloth dolls. Pink-cheeked white babies with yellow hair and brown rag dolls with yarn hair kept both girls busy. Irene combed their tresses with vigor. The dolls looked like bald old women.

Patience, who of late insisted her name be a modern Patricia, just turned thirteen. My age when Henry married me. A quiet girl, Patricia, appeared sad of late, a puzzle for me to solve.

Eight-year-old George and Irene attended a primary school run by the Catholic Church, even though we were Episcopalians. The older girls, Patricia in the eighth grade and my scholarly Sylvie already in tenth, escorted them before walking to their own classrooms. That allowed me to spend time with the baby, Andy. At three, he was a chubby handful who spoke in complete sentences. He counted to twenty in English, Portuguese, and Spanish. His favorite words were, "No" and "Why."

On Saturdays, my complex routine changed. Sylvie and Patricia walked ten blocks to their piano lessons provided by a strict and gifted Trinidadian. George and Irene took part in Bible Study at nearby St. Luke's, where we worshipped every Sunday. My friend Beryl and I took turns picking up all the children. I'd left Andy in Henry's care while I ran errands. Work started at noon for him on Saturdays.

I turned the key and pushed opened the door.

The familiar sounds made me stop. At first, I couldn't place them. I expected Andy's laughter, toys banging, the Victrola Henry purchased playing a new jazz or ragtime recording.

Instead, I heard guttural groaning. My body stiffened and skin prickled. I recognized it. The grunts were the sounds Henry made when he did his business inside of me.

I walked past the kitchen and living room to the first of three bedrooms–two for the children and ours at the end of the hall. The baby napped in his big-boy bed. Toys lay scattered on the floor.

When I reached our bedroom, I pushed open the door. Henry lay on top of Patricia, his overalls, and briefs around his ankles. His naked derrière moved up and down.

"Few minutes more," he said, breathless. "That's a good—"

I don't remember if I screamed aloud or only in my head.

CHAPTER TWO

My legs trembled and knees sagged. What? How? The pain in my throat made it difficult to swallow. He peered at me without turning his head, slipped out of Patricia, pulled a handkerchief from his pocket, dabbed her vagina, and then wiped himself.

Books and a glass of water crashed to the floor as I stumbled into the nightstand. He pulled up his overalls and hooked the suspenders on his shoulders, then faced me. "I have to go to work."

Patricia, whimpering, drew her knees up to her chin and curled into a ball. Andy wailed. His cries filled the apartment.

In a what's-for-dinner, matter-of-fact voice, Henry said, "We can speak tonight." Then he brushed past me. "This is not how it looks."

Not how it looks? I remained unable to move or speak, but my mind whirled. What father could do such a thing? Was this the first time? For how long?

Andy ceased crying. "Papa going bye-bye?"

He must have lifted the baby. I found my strength, my will, and ran to the bedroom Andy shared with his siblings.

"Leave him alone." I snatched him from Henry's arms. "Get out." With one arm holding Andy, I pummeled my husband with my right fist. "Get out, get out."

"Calm down."

The flatness of his tone conveyed an order and a threat, causing me to pause for the barest of seconds. I shook my head, my balled fist at my side. "No," I said, my voice shaking. "Leave. Now."

I moved only when the door slammed shut. After bolting the lock, I searched for something to create a barricade. Andy wriggled down. I shoved a dining room chair over and blocked the doorway. Still shaking, I picked up Andy again, put him on the scatter rug and piled wooden cars and trucks within easy grasp. Then I cranked the music box key. "Twinkle, Twinkle, Little Star," piped out.

"Enjoy your toys. Mama will be right back."

Tears streamed. I swiped at them and swallowed the bile in my throat and mouth. I wept for both my daughter and thirteen-year-old Grace in our marriage bed. Cold sweat coated my face both then and now. Not wanting to upset Patricia further, I arranged my expression and walked into my bedroom.

My darling girl appeared asleep. Wet eyelashes and flushed cheeks hinted at how much pain she endured. At thirteen, she possessed her woman's body. Her large breasts heaved with each breath.

A terrible thought struck me. The first time Henry took me, rough and urgent, I became pregnant. I gave birth to Sylvie at age fourteen and Patricia at fifteen. What if my girl was pregnant? Once again, I wondered if this was the first time and, if not, why she didn't tell me. The possibility that he also hurt Sylvie sucked my breath away.

Patricia stirred and rolled onto her back. Her hiked dress wound around her waist and molten brown eyes clouded. "Don't be mad at me, Mama."

"No. I'm not angry." I sank down on the bed. "You did nothing wrong."

She wept and hiccupped, making a plaintive sound that buckled my soul. I lay down next to her and stroked her hair and back. No words came. So, I hummed the music box song.

CHAPTER THREE

For a long time, Patricia and I lay spooned together.

"Mama." Andy appeared in my room and stood next to the bed, sucking his thumb. "I'm hungry."

What a terrible mother I am. "Yes, of course. Mama will make you lunch." I glanced up at the wall clock. One-thirty. It was my turn to pick up the young ones at St. Luke's. Worse than terrible. The Deacons knew us. The protocol stipulated a phone call first, but I didn't hear the operator ring. I knew how blessed we were to live in New York. So much of the country had yet to own phones. But, in Harlem, many, if not most, households owned one, and our church did as well.

If the Deacons failed to reach me, they'd contact Beryl Moore, my dearest friend, and she'd gather everyone and bring them home. I trusted her and breathed easier.

Patricia was asleep or unwilling to open her eyes or speak. Careful not to disturb her, I inched off the bed, pulled the coverlet up, kissed her cheek, took Andy's hand, and headed for the kitchen.

All my movements seemed unreal, like practice for a play. Make a cheese and tomato sandwich, pour a glass of milk, sit Andy in his chair, and pretend everything was normal.

Except, I couldn't let Henry back in the house. I weighed my options in case he tried to return. I thought about my neighbors hearing a commotion. Everyone found Henry the epitome of a gentleman—gracious, smart, and hardworking. And he was. But there was another side and despite others finding him handsome, to me, Henry was ugly.

He kissed too hard. His tongue, thrust inside my mouth, tasted like his last meal. I tried not to think about him kissing Patricia, but the image lodged in my mind.

The seconds clicked by on the wall clock and the electric icebox hummed, underscoring the quiet. I tried to think.

He raped Patricia. This was not the first time. I felt it in my bones, like some universal truth. He raped Sylvie too. I knew it, just as I understood why he'd seldom touched me since Andy's birth. Grateful for this, I failed to see.

With trembling fingers, I dialed the operator and asked for the police.

The overwhelmingly white police force had a contentious relationship with the people of Harlem. As the Italian and Jewish families left and the hold of the Mafia lessened, both legitimate and illegal Black enterprises flourished. The white crime bosses grudgingly yielded business to Black men who fashioned their operations after the successful Mafia. Bribes kept officers looking the other way. Speakeasy owners, bootleg liquor distributors, illegal gambling runners, all paid for protection. Police brutality was rampant for ordinary, colored citizens and those crooks unable or unwilling to pay.

Calling the police, therefore, was a huge and scary step. But I didn't know where else to turn to protect my girls.

It took over an hour for two officers to knock on my door. Their eyes swept the room and then scrutinized me. I still had on my skirt and blouse, each rumpled and stained with tears and butter.

The tall one asked in an Irish accent, "Something going on between you and your man?"

The way he asked turned my breath hot. I wanted to say, "He's not my man, he's my husband," and declare, "I'm Mrs. Herbert, a respected homemaker." Instead, I pressed my lips together.

The shorter one said, "Is he here?"

"No."

"Okay. So, what's the problem?"

How do I say aloud my husband is a rapist? "He hurt my... our daughter."

Sylvie and the rest of the children would be home soon, and I'd have to explain. Andy stood close by, listening, but not understanding.

"Beat her up?" The tall one asked. "What'd she do?"

Fury boiled. The local police were quick to judge colored folks and immigrants. "Molested her." The words hung in the air like dialogue balloons over cartoon characters' heads in *The Herald Tribune*.

"Whoa, now. How do you know?" the shorter one asked, his hands up, palms out. "Is that what she said?"

"I witnessed it."

"You *saw* your husband," he paused, as if searching for words. "*With* your daughter?" The disbelief and disgust in the tall one's voice sent an electric jolt down my spine.

"Yes."

"Is she here?" He took several steps into the living room.

"Stop. No."

He spun around, his right hand on the grip of his gun.

I looked up from his pistol into his eyes and lowered my voice. "I sent her away."

Not true, but I couldn't let them question her, make her re-experience the trauma in front of these men, strangers, who already doubted and disrespected me. I'd left a cup of peppermint tea on the nightstand. Patricia swallowed two Aspirins, but only a spoonful of rice and peas. I prayed she was asleep.

"Maybe it was her idea," said the shorter one, shifting from one foot to the other.

Sweet Jesus, please help me. "She's thirteen years old."

The shorter one had a ruddy nose and cheeks, and thick eyebrows that made an unkempt line across his brow. "If we go after him, he'll end up arrested. Do you want that?"

Did I? Out of the house and never able to return, for sure, but in jail? My thoughts bounced around. How would Sylvie get to college with Henry in jail, or the children finish school, happy and healthy, with no father to provide? Surprising myself, I said with surety, "Yes."

He shook his head as if disagreeing or not believing.

"What if we were discussing your daughter?"

His mouth twisted. "Not possible."

The taller one, slim with bright red hair under his cap, asked, "Why don't you let him sober up and make amends?"

Amends? "He wasn't drunk."

The shorter officer rolled his eyes.

"You're gonna ruin his life," the taller one said. "Yours too. And the girl's." He paused. "They'll say *things* about her." His eyes bore into mine.

Holding his gaze, I tried to swallow the bitter saliva filling my mouth again. I didn't want any of those outcomes. "My children's safety is what I desire," I said before lowering my eyes.

CHAPTER FOUR

The police left, promising nothing, and I knew they'd do nothing to help me. Their tone and words washed over my body. Shame and anger clouded my mind. I tried to breathe more slowly, deeply, but my breaths came in gulps.

Beryl, her twin boys–Josh and Nick–and my two, arrived a few minutes later. I forced a smile and a projection of calm. Tales of their day bubbled from four small mouths. When I failed to show, St. Luke's office contacted Beryl. She'd used the respite, she explained, to run errands, so it took extra time for her to arrive at the church and bring the children home.

Irene glared and pouted. I cuddled her and apologized. "Patricia is sick, so I stayed."

"Does she have the sniffles?"

How to answer? "We must take care of her. Let her rest."

That explanation was enough for Irene, who ran into her room to find her favorite doll.

Sylvie arrived, and after greeting everyone said, "I'm hungry."

"Fix yourself a sandwich." In my ears, I sounded normal and composed. "There are sweet biscuits for the children."

"What's wrong with you?"

I tried harder. "How did your lesson go?"

"Where's Patricia?" Sylvie's crumpled brow conveyed suspicion or worry. "She stayed home. Said her stomach hurt."

This sent another shock of pain through me. If Patricia stayed behind at the request of her father… I couldn't finish the thought. It pained me to think about my negligence and failure to notice she hadn't gone to her music lesson. "Why didn't you tell me?"

Sylvie's voice faltered. Her eyes darted. "I told Papa."

I pressed my hand against my abdomen and slowed my breathing. "She's ill. In my room," I said, modulating my voice to project calm. "Please. Mind the children."

Beryl eyed me. "Come on, Sylvie, I'll help you get the children settled," she said in her melodic Jamaican accent. "Your mom needs a moment."

Bless her. Like so many Jamaican women I knew, Beryl stepped in and acted without quizzing me first.

The apartment wasn't big enough for me to hide and gather myself. When Sylvie came into the kitchen to make sandwiches and retrieve the sweets, I stood at the stove, preparing tea. Happy children-sounds helped me regain my equilibrium.

Beryl returned. The children's door shut behind her.

With deliberate and well-practiced movements, I placed the china teapot, cups, creamer, and sugar bowl on the table before sinking into a chair. "I've asked Henry to move out."

Henry and I converted the space meant to be the dining room into a third bedroom to accommodate our growing family. The table, once the centerpiece of the dining area, now covered with a white-lace tablecloth from my English grandmother, served as a cooking workspace and the setting for meals.

"Why, on earth?" Beryl asked. "What happened?"

I never told Beryl about my wedding day at age thirteen, the day all my girlish dreams came to a crashing halt, or the first time Henry came to my bed. Secrets are bits of life-carnage tucked away, hidden from the light. To people rude enough to ask, I reported I was thirty-two rather than just celebrated my twenty-seventh birthday, preventing them from working out how young I must have been when I gave birth to

Sylvie. I pretended I loved my husband and lied, even to myself, that I forgave Mother.

"We had a fight."

"Mend it." She shook her head and waved her hands. "Husbands and wives—"

"Not like this."

Beryl was a dear. Coppery skin and hair, wide nose, and mouth, and always a smile and kind word. We met the first year I came to New York from Jamaica. Pregnant, two little girls in tow, I almost bumped into her. Beryl and I supported each other across the cobblestones. We navigated motorcars, bikes, pushcarts, and horse-drawn carriages. She was pregnant with her first. Two immigrant women heaving swollen bellies. We became friends.

"What kind of fight?"

"The kind that after it's over, you ask your husband to leave and never return."

Beryl sipped her tea. She blew out a puff of English Breakfast infused air. "How will you support yourself?"

Gratitude welled up. She didn't ask what he did. She took me at my word.

"Will he give you money?"

Although he squandered most of his inheritance before sailing to New York, he brought some funds with him. Once here, he earned well and sent for us. The move from the Bronx gave the children access to better schools and all of us a bigger and nicer flat in opportunity-rich Harlem. Lots of jobs, commerce, new businesses, and packed jazz clubs frequented by colored and white couples created a vibrant community. As a family, we enjoyed many comforts. I made all our clothes on the Singer Sewing Machine we'd ordered from the Sears Roebuck catalog. Our apartment included beautiful parquet floors and a spacious ice box–a new electric one. Yes, I budgeted with care, but I served wholesome food, and we had enough money to pay for Catholic School for four children and give to St. Luke's Church when the plate came around.

"I'll find work." There'd been no time to figure out how we'd survive, but this seemed a reasonable step.

"Doing what? You told me your British school only taught you what a lady needed to know." Beryl snorted. "Not anything useful."

The teachers at Walthamstow Hall, a school in Kent, England, for missionary's daughters, taught me how to read, write, play both the violin and piano, excel at needlepoint, sewing, and making lace. I wrote with beautiful penmanship. The schools in Harlem taught my children math, science, and geography. George knew every capital city in the US.

"I can work as a seamstress from home."

Beryl frowned. "You don't think he'll take care of his children?"

Not likely from jail, I thought, but of course, didn't say. How long would they keep him there? I realized, sitting with my friend, that I wanted him locked up. Not just arrested, but imprisoned, so he could never hurt Patricia or Sylvie again. Protect Irene. Never touch another young girl. Then what?

"He's such a good provider and father," Beryl said, echoing my neighbors' judgment.

Secrets weighed you down, cobbled you to stories you shared, but then forgot. I told no one, not even Mother, that every time Henry touched me, I felt raped.

Beryl must have noticed my wobbling chin or the moisture clouding my vision, because she reached across the table and squeezed my hand.

"Whatever unforgivable thing he perpetrated… can he right it and still support his family?"

"I cannot rely on him," I said.

"Should you go home to Jamaica?"

Images of Mother in her tiny cottage, living on a paltry pension, filled my mind. Whenever I thought about home, the first place I pictured was Gram's grand house outside of Birmingham, England, not the brick and wood house in Bolobo, Congo where I was born, not Kingston, Jamaica where the British Baptist leaders exiled us after Father died, not Henry's and my home in St. Catherine, but Gram's manor in the country. Which was silly because no one invited us to live there. "No," I said with a smidgen of truth. "I can't burden Mother."

"What then?" Beryl asked.

"I'll figure something out. We'll be all right." I prayed this was so.

CHAPTER FIVE

The banging on the front door brought me awake. Still in my skirt and blouse, I'd fallen asleep despite the day's tragedy, drifting between drowsing and wakefulness, riding a wave of distress. I stumbled out of bed, careful not to make a sound.

The hammering started again. "Open the door, Grace. You're embarrassing yourself."

It was Henry.

"Let's talk," he said. "You're behaving foolishly."

"Go away. I'll contact the police again. They're looking for you." Of course, they were not. I pressed my ear to the door, hoping to detect receding footfalls. When the next bang came, I jumped backwards.

"Don't do this."

I covered my ears.

"At least let me come in and get my kit and pajamas."

I clutched my fingers together, my blunt-cut nails dug into my palms. His request made sense. Wherever he stayed, he'd need his toothbrush and shaving paraphernalia. Plus, the less he kept here, the better.

"Mama, what's wrong?" Sylvie stood in our hall, rubbing her sleep-filled eyes, her robe cinched tight around her small waist. "Why is Papa yelling?"

"Go back to bed." I hurried to her. "This is for grownups."

"The police are coming for Papa?"

His key scratched in the lock. "I'll be quick. Let me in before the neighbors hear us." I prayed the chair, once again leaning against the door, would hold.

"Yes," I said to Sylvie. I waited to see if she would say something, ask a question. Did she suspect why her father was banging on the door because it happened to her as well?

Henry pounded again. Sylvie stumbled backwards as if feeling the force of his fists. I stepped toward her, but the thought he might wake the neighbors, and I'd have to explain, terrified me. Mrs. Thompson already asked about her stamps and my health. No. Embarrassed or not, he'd have to manage sans his kit. "Go away. Leave us alone."

Once again, I pressed my ear to the door. This time, I heard his footfalls walking away. I faced my daughter's wide eyes–gray-green speckled with gold. Her lower lip quivered, and tears gathered.

"Did Papa hurt you, too?" I asked in a whisper, fearful of the answer.

With both hands, Sylvie wiped the water from her cheeks. "Good night, Mama."

By not answering me, I understood the truth.

She turned and moved towards the room she and Patricia shared, stopped, and pivoted. "Are we going to be, okay?"

"Yes, my darling. We are." I vowed this to Sylvie, to Patricia, to my babies. A promise I had to honor.

. . .

Sunday went by with Patricia in my bed. There was no word from the two officers. Nor did Henry contact us. The children asked about Sunday school and church, but neither Patricia nor I had the strength to leave our flat.

Sylvie, pale and not eating, looked as ill as her younger sister. "When is Papa coming home?"

It was Sunday evening. We sat in the kitchen sharing a cup of tea and sweet biscuits. Sylvie only nibbled on hers, but she drank. The children were all asleep, the house quiet.

"He's not," I said. The heaviness of the words crushed my chest.

"But he'll still take care of us?"

"No."

Her cat-like eyes stared into mine. "Because he hurt Patricia?"

I waited to speak, choosing my words with care. "And you."

Sylvie shook her head, as if disagreeing. "How will you pay for things?"

How indeed? The risk loomed, but my options were nonexistent. "I'll work," I said. "We'll be fine."

She shook her head again, put her cup, saucer, and spoon in the sink. "We won't." She left the kitchen, feet shuffling like an old woman with worn out legs.

"You're wrong," I said, but I whispered it, speaking more to myself than to Sylvie.

Monday morning, I walked to the police station to press formal charges and force the police to act. I wore a cloche hat and a long, mauve dress with buttons down the front. Brown gloves, matching the lightweight coat, covered both shaking hands. I wanted to look prosperous and therefore taken seriously.

A three-story brick building with the words POLICE engraved in stone above the front double doors reminded all visitors to enter with care. Some people took me for white–my skin the color of cream, according to Henry. Beryl asked me once if I ever considered passing, but I saw no point. Henry, browner than I was, and George and Andy browner still, made passing impossible. And until now, I saw no advantage. But here, alone, and afraid, it occurred to me I should. White men worked in the same factory where Henry labored. White people still lived in Harlem, although fewer each year. The neighbors in my building were all colored since the last white families fled. Just as the officers who came to my door guessed I was Black because of my address, perhaps these police officers would as well. I stood in the entranceway dithering, my mind in a jumble.

"Can I help you, Ma'am?" The officer stood behind a desk that was elevated above people who approached.

The way he asked made me believe he assumed I was white. "I'd like to have my husband arrested," I said, in my posh accent.

"What'd he do?" asked the tall man with a barrel chest and a high-pitched voice.

I explained.

"You're sure about this?" His question reminded me I didn't know what I was stepping into. "You're better off not pressing charges."

Head held high, I said, "I understand, but this is what I must do." The night before, I had a fitful sleep, and whenever I drifted off, doubt plagued my dreams. Each time footsteps clomped in the hall, fear gripped my insides, wondering if Henry returned. No, in answer to the officer's question, I was not sure, but I had to forge ahead for the sake of my girls.

He slid papers across the desk. "Fill these out." He pointed to a spot where I could sit and write.

Race was one of the questions on the paper. I hadn't thought of that.

"Thank you," I said, handing in the forms.

The officer looked over my written complaint, his face grim. "Niggers," he muttered under his breath, and dumped the document in a pile to his right. He neither looked at me nor responded.

As I turned to leave, instead of anger, the appropriate emotion, I felt afraid and humiliated.

To my surprise, they found Henry at work on Tuesday and arrested him. I learned this from the attorney who contacted me. Henry belonged to a fraternal organization. Lawyer Booth explained they hired him on Henry's behalf. The solicitor didn't ask about my needs or share his next steps. Would the organization, or brotherhood, as the solicitor called it, hire another lawyer to protect my children and me? I didn't understand the judicial system or know what questions to ask.

CHAPTER SIX

For the rest of the week, I moved as if sleep walking. Shopped, cooked, avoided conversations with the neighbors, and gave evasive answers to the children's questions just as Sylvie did to my inquiries. Patricia withered in my bed. No word from Lawyer Booth. What was happening?

We spent the weekend at home. There were no piano lessons or Bible study, no trips to the post office, and no music on the Victrola. Instead, we huddled together and spoke in hushed tones, as if someone had died. The small ones kept their eyes on me, as if waiting for a signal, an explanation, a return to normal. I found it difficult to think past getting Henry away from the girls. But they were counting on me to navigate our lives without him.

All my dreams for each one of them must come true–Sylvie graduating from college and becoming a teacher or even a school principal. Patricia safe and loved by someone like Father, doing missionary work here or abroad, or working in a library. George, Irene, and Andy were too young to think about their future-selves other than receiving an excellent secular and religious education. Mother and Father drilled that into me.

"Become a teacher, like your sisters," Father said.

"Study hard and you will always be able to take care of yourself," Mother said.

Well, that didn't work out.

During the week of waiting, Sylvie avoided me, her nose in a book or reading to the little ones. Although few households read to their children, Sylvie enjoyed doing so. She acted out the stories to the delight of George, Irene, and Andy.

Sunday evening, the attorney called and summoned me to the courthouse the next day at 9:00 a.m.

I packed George and Irene off to school. Sylvie stayed home with Andy and Patricia, and I walked east and then south.

The Harlem Courthouse on East 121st St. and Sylvan Place, between Lexington and Third Avenue, was an imposing brownstone. Dimly lit hallways and ornate staircases helped you forget for a second about the cells in the basement. Henry sat in one of them.

The attorney, a dark-skinned colored man sporting a gray-flecked beard and kind eyes, greeted me in the lobby. I'd never met a Black solicitor before.

Lawyer Booth touched my elbow, and we descended the stairs. "He wants to speak with you alone. The officer will only give you a few minutes."

We reached the bottom step.

"Mr. Herbert told me you're a foreigner," Lawyer Booth said.

"I intend to become a citizen." I'm sure I sounded defensive. It took time and a shift in thinking to shed one's identity for a new one. At least it felt that way to me. Leaving the Congo, then England, and Jamaica, required discarding pieces of me. In England, I lost the safety and nurturing of my parents still in Bolobo. Not an orphan, but adrift from parental anchors at a tender age. In Jamaica, I lost my childhood, my future, and became a married girl and mother. Arriving in New York, I thought I'd blossom, gain rather than diminish.

"No disrespect," Lawyer Booth said, "but perhaps you don't understand our laws."

Dank and smoky air filled the hall. Portraits of imposing white men hung from the walls. My eyes fixed on them, I waited for the attorney to explain himself.

"The courts convict very few men of molestation."

"You said we only have a few minutes." I didn't understand the law, but he didn't understand rape. "Shouldn't we go in?"

"Now, for our people," he said, ignoring my query. "More convictions happen, but still..."

Aware of his scrutiny, I continued to stare at the lengthy line of portraits of past police commissioners and mayors, but my mind and pulse raced. Blood pounded through me at an alarming rate.

"Your daughter will suffer from the experience with no victory to make it worth the grief and shame. Are you hearing me, Madam?"

Lips folded under and right hand pressed against my stomach, I nodded.

"For Mr. Herbert's arraignment, there must be no doubt of his guilt. The District Attorney's office will grill both you and your daughter. A trial may be a year away. The legal process allows for a vigorous defense that will challenge your veracity and motives, paint your daughter as the instigator, label her with vicious words."

"You're his lawyer. Is that what you plan?"

"It's what must be done."

I sucked in air.

"Should you be the exception and a jury convict him, you will still lose. Your family, neighbors, people you call friends, will heap scorn, even shun you both."

The police said the same, but this description was more vivid, more frightening. I believed them all.

CHAPTER SEVEN

The stench of body odor and fear filled the closet-small room. Henry, disheveled and slumped forward, sat shackled to a narrow table and chair. He was the son of a well-to-do family in Jamaica, descendant of a prominent Jewish merchant and freed-enslaved woman. Henry carried himself like an educated man of means. Ten years older than I was, he had broad shoulders, straight back, and wavy brown hair brushed back from his face.

Now he appeared old. Stubble covered his cheeks. His hair stuck out at angles. Skin crinkled under his eyes. It had been a week since his arrest, and yet the extracted toll marked him.

When he saw me, he tried to stand, but the chains held him to a crouch. "Where have you been?" His voice rasped.

"Taking care of our heart-broken family."

He looked down at his imprisoned wrists and drew audible deep breaths.

"Sit." Another in-and-exhale. "Please."

"I'm fine where I am."

Standing over him on the other side of the table gave me a bit of confidence. I reminded myself that I'm the daughter of missionaries who fought the Congo River filled with crocodiles and mountainous rhinos, doctored the ill, built schools and water-wells in the middle of the bush. I came from tenacious British and African stock. As the days unfolded and I thought about my actions, my family's jeopardy, I banished fear and the pull to quit.

"We can't have a trial." This was my new goal–no jury of white men believing slanderous things about Patricia, blaming my girl the way the police did. If Henry's acquittal was a possibility, I needed another path.

Henry's sunken eyes stared at me, his mouth working but not speaking.

"Plead guilty for Patience's sake." To add more weight to my argument, I used the name we gave her at birth. "They'll make her testify."

"How is she?"

"Lawyer Booth said you could plead guilty. He'd strike a deal with the prosecutor, and they'd send you to a hospital." With reluctance, the attorney offered this possibility after I pressed him for alternatives to a jury trial. The decision, he explained, belonged to Henry alone.

"What did she tell you?"

Some of the terrible smell in the room came from Henry. A fastidious man, he bathed every other day and only wore the clean clothes I scrubbed and rinsed in the tub, hung to dry, and ironed smooth.

"Sylvie broke down and shared everything." Which was a partial truth. She'd not admitted as much, but everything about her behavior told me he'd started with her before moving on to Patricia.

Henry winced.

"If you plead guilty, no one will witness your shame." Our shame. And I could not give a jury a chance to set him free. "A psychiatrist must agree, of course." I was unaware of how Lawyer Booth would arrange this. "You'll need to engage a doctor." Would the fraternal organization pay a physician? Must I when I was already struggling to feed my family?

"I want to speak with both girls."

"No, never again."

"They're my children."

"Not anymore."

"You don't have money to live on. The family is going to starve." He spoke these words as if he were still in charge. "Get me out of here. Tell them you made a mistake."

The possibility of my family going hungry became real over the last week. When we lived in the Bronx, I planted and harvested herbs and vegetables in a tiny plot at the front of the house. In the back, we had peach trees and a chicken coop for fresh eggs. Our Italian neighbors grew grapes, made wine, and shared both. Local farms provided milk and cheese and fresh produce. City living required depending on the tiny pots of herbs that lined my windowsills, the offerings of the local grocer, and the vegetables men hauled in horse-drawn wagons. I sank into the chair facing Henry.

"Listen to me. Our rent is high. All the fancy things you enjoy, they cost too."

I blinked several times, willing any show of emotion away.

Henry leaned forward and grabbed my hand, his voice rough with urgency. "How will you pay for the children's school? Be smart. This will not work out for you."

The words sounded portentous. I pulled my hand free.

He sat up as straight as the chains allowed and spoke with clipped authority. "They'll take your babies from you."

Of course, I'd thought of this. I knew it happened to women with no men and no way to support themselves and yet my breath caught in my throat hearing it.

"Being a wife and mother are your only skills. Think."

I braced my shoulders. "I'll work as a seamstress."

"You'll never earn $4,000 a year making drapes and sewing ladies' dresses. You're upset. I understand." He lowered his voice to a whisper. "It won't happen again. I give you my word."

"You hurt Sylvie too." When did it begin? When was the last time I heard her laugh?

"You have my solemn promise," Henry said. "As God is my witness."

"I asked Patricia how often, but she's stopped speaking. She says nothing all day long."

"Booth assured me I can return home tomorrow if you recant. I lost my job, but I can talk my way back in. The plant requires my skills." His tone turned from pleading to hard. "Explain the mistake. Tell the coppers you were angry because I stepped out on you. You made it up for revenge." He leaned in as far as the chains and table would allow. "Apologize."

"How long?"

He slouched back against the wooden chair. The chains clanged.

"You're not hearing me," he said, shaking his head. "You were always smart." He tugged on the tip of his nose. "When we walked into a room together, people noticed. They admired you. Do you want to lose all that?"

"Never mind. Don't tell me." Why would I want to know how long he'd raped our daughters? Now, I must save my family. I'm the daughter of brave and mighty people, I repeated in my head. My English and African blood saturates me with strength. "Plead guilty. Let a doctor testify to your insanity. No trial, no sordid tales, no public embarrassment, or disgrace." I lifted my chin. "They'll let you out once you're cured." I had no way of knowing if this was true, nor did I want him free.

I rose and walked to the locked door before twisting around. "It's the right thing to do." I paused and then repeated his words. "As God is *my* witness."

He stared at me, unblinking, before speaking. "Don't do this to me, to your family. You'll regret this for the rest of your life."

Once again, the warning rippled through me, sounding like a prophecy.

CHAPTER EIGHT

Tuesday morning, the sun warmed the late April air enough for me to throw open the windows and let our laundry flap in the breeze. Patricia got out of bed for breakfast and bathed. Sylvie and the young ones went to school without a fuss.

I washed the dishes, tidied the house, and then sat at my writing desk, a roll top secretary where I kept letters, pens, pencils, and paper.

Just as I realized we couldn't have a trial; I knew it was time for Henry to die.

I understood the pain and consequences of death.

The first death I experienced was my sister Patience for whom we named Patricia, a prankster who played harmless tricks and made the family laugh. She died of Yellow Fever soon after her eighteenth birthday and my fourth, right before Mother and Father sent me to England. Often, the sorrow of the two events melded into one.

I had two pregnancies, one on top of each other–Sylvie and Patricia. The twins, who followed Patricia ten months later, lived for three days. They died hours apart in my arms. I begged Henry to wait, to not demand we couple again until my body and heart healed. He slept alone for six weeks. I became pregnant as soon as he returned to my bed. Three months into my pregnancy, Henry left for New York and sent for us four months later. Olive was the first to be born in America. She blessed us for two years before succumbing to Scarlet Fever the same year George was born. I was nineteen-years old and, overnight, my black hair turned silvery-white. Although I was a stoic woman in body and spirit, losing Olive left me broken.

Father's death cut the deepest. Malaria never left you. If fortunate, you mended, but it lived within you and often returned. In Father's case, it did many times, and the last bout changed everything. The Baptist Ministry Society forced us to move to Jamaica rather than return to the home Father left us in Bolobo, the deed in Mother's name. It stood two-stories high with exterior steps leading to the main-second floor. An entrance on the first floor led to Father's workspace. Angled around two sides of the house, a veranda gave us cool places to sit, and lots of windows let breezes blow through.

"It is unsafe for a widow with children to carry on missionary work," the man in charge told Mother, not acknowledging all she'd accomplished at Father's side.

Ten-year-old me asked, "Why can't we live with Gram?"

Mother explained Gram didn't want Father's Black family, the family she'd hosted every Easter and Christmas. When Father died, we died. Mother lost our Bolobo home, our freedom to live as we pleased, and I lost my childhood and future.

It was time to write to mother. In my note, I explained why I could no longer send her money. Henry fell ill and we don't know if he will live, I penned.

I paused and stared at my words. What evil might Henry's invented demise bring?

• • •

Clothes, dishes, and the apartment sparkled. The children were in school, and Patricia still swaddled in my bed, the duvet wrapped around to her chin. The icebox held little for dinner. I had to find work.

Pushing Andy in the pram, my samples and sketchbook packed in a cloth bag, we made our way downtown. The tailors in the posh neighborhoods would appreciate the care of my stitches and beauty of the garments. I chose three of Irene's dresses, an evening gown made for a church celebration, and lace curtains taken down from the windows in the living room.

We crossed the avenue, careful to avoid a mound of steaming horse dung. Its pungent scent mixed with the choke of car fumes. Fresh growth shimmered green on the trees. Despite the throbs of fear and guilt inside of me, a seed of hopefulness sprouted.

I parked the pram outside the first establishment on my list, lifted the bag of samples and, holding Andy's hand, walked in. A hanging bell jangled.

Bolts of cloth and sewing machines filled the tailor shop. The spools of thread unwound as the men worked the pedals, feeding muslin to jackhammer needles. Scraps lay on the floor. The dingy, tobacco-stained walls held yellowed photos of women in wedding gowns and men in fine suits.

An ancient woman approached me. "What do you want?" she asked in a tone as sharp as her pointed nose. I saw no colored men or other women. Some of my hope seeped out.

In my poshest British accent, the one I learned at school, I said, "May I speak to the proprietor?" My intonation gave people pause long enough to consider my words.

Not so with this one. She looked at Andy, and then me, in a put-you-in-your-place way. "He's busy."

"I'm an excellent seamstress," I said, and tugged the gown from the bag, offering it to her for inspection. "My name is Grace Herbert."

The woman didn't take the dress.

"If you look, you'll see I'm accomplished."

She eyed my brown Andy. "We don't hire niggers."

My cheeks flushed. I heard these awful words before, but always as part of someone else's story. In England and Jamaica, people treated us with respect because we were the family of gentry. In America, I was a mother and homemaker, married to an educated provider and church member. Images of the police officers looking me over, smirking, flashed through my mind. Gram's rejection of her son's family. No, racial hatred also wove through my story.

I knew I should leave, walk away, head high. Before I reached the door, a man approached me, took the gown, and examined it. He was tall with a large, sword-like nose resembling the ancient woman's. Coffee or nicotine stained his teeth.

"You're good. I can see that," he said. "But our patrons won't accept a colored girl." He handed the garment back to me. "Even one as fair as you."

"I can work from home."

"What about fittings?" He shook his head. "Sorry."

The ancient woman stared hard at him. His eyes flicked from her to me. "Might do better with your own people."

I had started there, of course. Began uptown near home. Harlem enjoyed only a few tailor shops. Many people in the neighborhood made their own clothes or bought them from the Sears and Roebuck Catalogue.

"No need to pay at first," I offered.

Andy tugged on my skirt. "I have to pee-pee."

"On a trial basis." I couldn't afford to work for free, but after a week or two, they'd see my worth.

"Mama." He pulled harder and pressed his knees together.

If I asked for a restroom, they'd refuse me. "We'll go home in a minute. Hold it in like a big boy," I whispered.

A customer walked in with a suit draped over her arm. She stopped short when she saw Andy and me.

"I can't use you," he said, turning a yellowed tooth smile on the waiting woman.

I scooped up my bag and then Andy, balancing both on my left hip. He smelled like fresh urine, damp against my side. My humiliation complete, I still had to try one more time. Determined, I thrust a folded paper into the tall man's hand. "That's my information, in case you change your mind."

He took the white-linen sheet, my name embossed on the top and address penned beneath it. He crumpled it into his vest pocket.

The ancient woman crinkled her nose. "Don't bother coming back."

I attempted to walk out with dignity, but my head was too heavy to lift.

"I wet." Andy said. Tears dribbled.

"It's okay, my darling. We'll washup when we get home."

I looked at my list of shops, but going to the next carrying a wet, crying three-year-old made no sense. We trudged toward home. Four blocks away from the tailor shop, a young boy rushed up to me. "Miss, Miss." A jumble of curly black hair covered his head, forehead, and ears.

"Yes?"

"Here." He proffered an envelope.

"Thank you." I searched for a coin for his trouble, but before I dug it out, he turned and dashed away. I tore it open.

Dear Mrs. Herbert,

Please come by this evening at 7:00. I have work for you.

Owner

The Louis Tailor Shop

No name. But it must be the man who'd taken my note. He liked the quality of my stitches and seemed embarrassed by the ancient woman's attitude. Unable to hire a colored woman in front of customers, he might secretly. It didn't matter. He had work for me.

My mouth and lips were so dry, I couldn't show the smile inside.

CHAPTER NINE

At six-fifteen, I was ready to go. I'd noticed the men working the sewing machines wore white shirts, black pants, and vests, and the ancient woman dressed in black, so I donned a white blouse and an ankle-length black skirt.

"Why do you have to leave?" Sylvie stood in front of me, hands on her narrow hips–a new and unacceptable behavior. I tugged both down to her sides. She scrunched her face and crossed the rebuked arms under her breasts.

"I have a job, so your responsibility is to take care of your sisters and brothers."

"What about my homework? Plus, Maggie's coming over to play chess." She gave me an accusatory glare. "You said everything would be okay."

Irene asked. "Why can't Papa work and you stay home like before?"

"He's sick. We must manage on our own," I said, my tone soothing. "Can you be strong for him?" Lying came easier, I'm ashamed to admit.

"Until he's better," Irene said.

"Yes," I agreed, cementing the untruth.

Secrets and lies–treacherous twins working in concert.

In a few weeks, I'd announce he'd died. Although pitied, people respected widows. Sylvie could still attend college and Patricia finish high school, something I didn't achieve. The alternative was people blaming the wife of a man convicted of molesting his daughter. "Why did you let this happen?" "Weren't you satisfying him?" "How dare you prosecute your husband?" As the lawyer said, scorned and shunned. And Patricia. Ugly whispers behind her back, and some to her face, adding another layer of lifelong scars. Her future ended and Sylvie's in jeopardy. Henry wasn't wrong. Destitute women also lost their children. The city or state took them. I must become a widow and support my family.

I still had to work out the details. The church members would expect a service and funeral. How might I explain things to Henry's sister? I never hinted at his critical condition. The lies piled up, like Andy's building blocks, in my sorrow-saturated gut.

"When can we visit him?" At five-years-old, Irene was bright and persistent.

"Soon."

"What's wrong with Patricia?"

"I've explained," I said to Irene. "She's ill, but she's getting better. Sylvie is in charge. Be a good girl and listen to her."

I grabbed my sewing basket, a sweater, a butter sandwich, and an apple. "Sylvie, there's a pot of stew on the stove. Make sure Patricia eats some and don't forget to line the bowls with bread first before spooning it in." We had to fill bellies with less. The meal contained no meat, just beef bones for flavor. "Give the little ones a glass of milk."

"The milk isn't real," Sylvie said, her face as tight as her crossed arms, reminding me of Mother. How alike my first born and Mother appeared in expressions and attitudes.

"It is," I said, screeching a bit. The milkman used to deliver six quarts a week, but the previous Monday, I cut it back to three and added water to make it stretch. Eighty cents was too dear a price. "I must go."

Irene, with bright ribbon-bows tied to the end of each braid, gave my legs a hug.

"Bye my darlings. Be good."

Eight-year-old George said, "Can we get a puppy like Rin Tin Tin?" George had never watched a silent movie, but everybody talked about the hero German Shepherd in films.

"Mama will be back…" Just not sure when or how late. I was hoping for a proper job, but this might be only for tonight, a garment needed in a rush. "If you're in bed, I'll kiss you goodnight."

"I'll take care of it," George said. "I'm going to name him Ruffy."

"Soon." I kissed the top of his head. "Maybe."

The brisk walk downtown took me thirty minutes. Despite the cool night air, perspiration beaded on my cheeks and forehead and trickled from my armpits.

The shop looked dark. A closed sign dangled from a cord on the other side of the glass door. I knocked and waited.

The man with the long nose opened the door. He didn't smile, only dipped his head forward. The bell swung and clinked. He stepped back and let me walk in.

"Good evening," I said.

He didn't speak, only motioned for me to follow.

The place was silent, with all the sewing machine seats vacant. I hurried behind him to a storage space in the rear. Bolts of cloth stacked on top of each other made a tunnel to a desk and chair. My breath quickened.

"Thank you for asking me to return," I said to his back. The hairs on the nape of my neck rose. My basket clutched to my chest, I said, "I'm eager to work. Can you tell me the pay?" I prayed he didn't remember my offer to labor for free until I proved myself.

He didn't respond.

"What's your name?" I asked.

He stopped, turned, and unbuttoned his vest.

"Is someone else here whom I should meet?" My voice quavered.

He slid his belt from around his waist.

I took two steps back. "There has been a misunderstanding. I'm here for a position as a seamstress."

Flashes of the night Henry and I first had sex, his suspenders hanging as he hovered over Patricia, imagined pictures of him with Sylvie, all blinked, and whizzed. I took two more steps back.

He dropped his pants and underwear. His penis, flushed at the tip, bobbed erect. "You're a beautiful woman." Holding his penis in his hand, he said, "Suck it. I'll pay you well."

I turned and ran to the front door, fumbled with the lock, checking over my shoulder every other second.

His voice came from behind, but close. "Five dollars this time."

The lock yielded. My bag slipped.

His breath on my neck made my nape hairs rise again. He reached out and grabbed my shoulder. "More than a night's work sewing."

I shook free, snatched up my belongings, swung the door open, and sprinted into the night.

CHAPTER TEN

Empty budget envelopes lay stacked on my writing desk. Only a few coins rolled about in my purse.

Andy, Irene, and George asked for their father. Once again, I explained he was too ill for visitors. Sylvie knew the truth, that Henry was in jail for molesting Patricia, but she kept our secret. I told Beryl Henry cheated on me with a young girl. A partial truth is just another name for a lie. I hated all the subterfuge. I felt trapped and anxious all the time. Bile churned in my stomach and my head ached.

Patricia refused to go to school. Most days, she lay in bed curled in the fetal position. I tried singing to her. I brought the phonograph into my room. Louis Armstrong, Duke Ellington, and Joe "King" Oliver's jazz filled every corner. Andy and I danced and clapped, but Patricia only stared. Just as I did when she was a baby, I hand-fed her soup or porridge. Nothing succeeded. Dry-eyed, she withered in my bed.

A visit to our family physician was impossible. Too many questions to answer and more lies to tell. Tea, soup, kisses, and rest–a sure cure. I thought it best not to ask or to say anything about what happened. Let the memory fade. But, based on my own painful past, I understood the memories might recede while still lurking beneath the surface, ready to bubble up unsummoned and at inconvenient times.

Daily, I checked our supply of Kotex, looking for evidence of Patricia's menstruation. All three of us bled the same time every month. In a few days, we'd be due. I looked for other signs, but only two weeks had passed. Too soon to know if a fetus grew inside of her if that was indeed the first time. Just the thought of it made me dizzy.

During the first months of my marriage, Mother never asked me questions or offered explanations. She stayed by my side, hugged, and loved me. But we never spoke about sex. When I became pregnant, I didn't understand what was happening to my body. I had to do better by Patricia.

Mae, Henry's sister, wrote to him. Of course, I didn't open the letters. But the longer his silence, the more she'd worry. My neighbors inquired about his absence. I told them he contracted a deadly strain of pneumonia and lingered at death's door.

Dressed and ready to go, I spoke to Patricia from my bedroom doorway. She lay inert, surrounded by unopened books the nuns sent home. "I will be back in an hour."

Vacant eyes looked through me.

"I'll bring you ice cream." I'm not sure why I said that. We needed meat, not treats. But if I could access our savings account, then maybe ice cream was possible.

She gave me a flicker-smile.

"Strawberry." There had to be some joy in all this misery. "Can you take care of Andy? He'll probably nap until I return." It scared me to leave him. Like an old person in her dotage, Patricia either stayed silent or hummed under her breath, a repeated sound like a Monk's mantra. "If he wakes while I'm gone, give him a slice of bread and butter. I'll be back soon."

I'd never been to a bank. In fact, our neighbors didn't use banks. But Henry enjoyed being equal to white folks. Mulatto like me, he said, "I'm as much white as I am colored, and my white self is going to the bank."

In the 1920s, Harlem exuded a renewed sense of pride and purpose. A'Lelia Walker, daughter of the hair product and salons entrepreneur, Madam Walker, entertained colored and white artists and dignitaries in her Harlem brownstone. Black men bought real estate from fleeing white owners as more immigrants from Caribbean countries arrived and more colored southerners migrated north. Used to wealth and privilege in Jamaica, Henry opened an account in the only Harlem branch.

The bank lobby looked palatial. Light bounced off the brass and mahogany. Mirrors hung like paintings on the walls. Only white men and a few women stood in line. Most likely local merchants with homes in Westchester and along the Hudson River in the north-west Bronx. Everyone behind the gilded cages were Caucasian men dressed in suits and ties.

A burly man in uniform eyed me as I walked toward a line. This gave me pause. If discovered, they might arrest me. I pushed that thought away, nodded, and smiled at the guard, hoping I didn't appear guilty since I looked and felt out of place.

I queued up while I rehearsed my request in my head.

"How may I help you?" The bank teller had an oval face and no facial hair. The collar on his white shirt looked tight against his Adam's apple. A sheen of moisture edged his mouth where a mustache might grow.

I pushed our savings book under the cage opening. "I'm here to make a withdrawal from our account."

He studied the entry-filled booklet. At my urging, every payday, Henry deposited two dollars. I witnessed how he'd squandered money in the past and therefore insisted we save for a *rainy day*. Well, it was pouring now.

"How is Mr. Herbert? We've not seen him."

I gave a wan-non-committal smile. After the disrespectful manner of the police officers, the cordiality surprised me.

"Is he well?"

"He suffers from pneumonia."

"Not serious, I hope."

Since I wanted to empty the account, I couldn't make it too dire. "On the mend."

"I'm glad to hear it."

"But, he's unable to work while he recovers, and his *five* children are hungry."

"Do you have the required paperwork?"

This caught me by surprise. "No, I'm afraid not."

"I can give you a withdrawal request to take to him."

Oh no.

He reached down and retrieved a yellow and white rectangular form. Carbon paper separated each sheet.

"I can't get to the hospital today. It's downtown and my ill daughter and baby are waiting for their lunch." That didn't sound ominous enough. "Plus, the rent is due, and the landlord is quite threatening. I'm afraid." I found it easy to let my lips quiver since I was, in fact, terrified.

His skeptical expression cleared, and a worried one took its place. "You will need to speak with the manager." He pointed toward an office to the right.

With the forms in my gloved hand, I tried to gather myself as I walked over. The man behind the desk wore a navy-blue suit with a matching vest stretched across his belly. His pipe-tobacco smell reminded me of Father. The brass nameplate read *Reginald Wells, Manager.* He offered me a seat, and I took it, back straight, knees pressed together, gloved hands and the form on my lap.

"My husband has pneumonia," I said, exaggerating my upper-class-British accent. "Since he can't come into the bank, he asked me to collect our savings to help his family until he can work again."

Mr. Wells frowned. "Quite impossible."

White men ruled my adopted country. I understood that, but surely this one would offer compassion to a lady in distress.

The manager spoke again. "Mr. Herbert must sign that withdrawal slip in your hand."

A kernel of annoyance pressed up, replacing a bit of the fear. I repeated the plight of my children and the imaginary threatening landlord, something that would be true soon enough.

He clucked his tongue. "A letter from his doctor on the physician's stationary would do." He nodded his head. "Husband or doctor's signature. No exceptions."

I stood. "I will return," I said to the top of his balding head. "With the document."

Colored, female, and an immigrant. Add convict's wife, committed for a heinous crime, and our exposure to more hate and danger would grow. But that wasn't the most urgent concern. Our rent and food on the table were at the top. There had to be a way to get our money.

I could ask the lawyer, but he might want the money for his fee. Was the brotherhood the lawyer told me about still paying him? The thought of visiting Henry again and asking him to sign the forms overwhelmed me. He loved his children. My breath hitched. It was hard to reconcile both thoughts–that Henry loved his children but molested our girls. I wasn't sure he loved me, so I never asked, and he never said.

I hoped he loved us all enough. My family needed our savings.

CHAPTER ELEVEN

I sat at the kitchen table with notepaper and a pen, staring at my botched efforts. Henry's handwriting was quite distinct from mine. He'd learned his penmanship in Kingston while I mastered mine at a British girl's school where ladies were taught how to form perfect letters. Tiny scratches had to replace slanted loops. I tried again. And again. Would it pass muster at the bank where they had Henry's signature on other documents? The blank withdrawal form mocked me.

Henry kept his important papers in a box under our bed. On my hands and knees, I crawled forward until I reached it. If there was a document that had his signature on it, using the withdrawal form's carbon paper, I could trace his scrawl well enough. At least better than my poor forgery.

The cardboard box cover sagged. Henry used to keep it in the wardrobe under a pile of memorabilia from Jamaica. I pulled the box free, sat on the floor, pressed my back against the bed and lifted the lid. Birth certificates, our crossing papers, and Henry's citizenship decree lay among a Bible and a knife I'd never seen. A wooden barrel held the long blade, its decorative handle marked with an arrow. It looked old and well used. Unsure why, I slipped the knife into my skirt pocket. Before Henry's departure, I never feared for the children's or my safety, but now the man in the tailor shop, the police officers, and Henry himself, left me anxious. What good would a knife do? Yet I kept it and returned to my search for a signature I could trace using the carbon paper of the withdrawal slip. The only useful samples I found were the children's birth certificates. Would one of them do? I chose Olive's and slid the box back into place.

My stomach rumbled, reminding me how little I'd eaten. I decided to work on Henry's signature later. Now I needed to get to Mr. Cohen's. Except I had little money with which to purchase food and necessities. I pushed myself up, pinned a cloche hat to my coiled hair, and left.

. . .

Grocery bags in both hands, I trudged up the steps to home. Mr. Cohen let me shop with a promise to pay next week.

"How are you today?" Mrs. Thompson waved as I passed her floor. "You don't look yourself."

I straightened my back and willed a polite smile. "Are you well?"

"Oh yes. Thanks for asking." She met me on the stairs. "It has to be hard for you."

If I spoke, I might cry.

She patted my back. "Is your church helping?"

Until now, my pride kept me from asking anyone for aid. We assisted others and didn't require support. "We're managing."

"If you need some work," she said in a stage whisper, "I have a church-friend who is looking for a dressmaker. I thought of you, but then…" Her voice trailed off.

No thank you, sat on the tip of my tongue. Too painful to have my neighbors pitying me. Instead, I said, "Until Mr. Herbert can return to his position, I'd welcome any opportunities you may have."

She beamed. "Let me print her name and telephone number. It's a shared number in her hallway. Ask for Denise and someone will fetch her." Mrs. Thompson handed me the slip of paper. "She's not someone like you, but she's a good person. We both attend St. Ann's on a hundred and tenth."

Unsure of what she meant, but grateful, I took the information.

I contacted the recommended woman the minute I reached the apartment, and we agreed to meet the next morning while my children were in school. The appointment would mean leaving Andy and Patricia alone again, but I had no choice because Mr. Cohen and our landlord required payment.

. . .

We sat on a bench in the park a few blocks from my home. Miss Denise fidgeted. Her heavy makeup failed to hide old scars and fresh-looking bruises. "I need a gown, and Miz Thompson told me you sewed."

The May sun warmed my neck and shoulders. "What do you have in mind?" I kept my expression neutral, trying not to focus on the tight yellow dress decorated with appliqued oranges covering each of her breasts.

"Can you make me something pretty?"

"Is it for a special occasion?"

"My sister's birthday party." She hiked her shoulders and let out a whoosh of air. "She's classy like you."

"Oh, I'm not so—"

"Yeah, you are. You dress nice and talk proper. She's like that." Long fingers, their nails painted blood red, several cracked and chipped, rubbed each arm. "I'm a hooker, in case Miz Thompson didn't say." She used the street term for women who men paid to have sex with them. Not a word heard in decent discourse. Her gaze held mine. "Is that a problem?"

Shock rippled through me, but I didn't change my expression. The possibility of earning money was too important. "No." This explained my neighbor's comment. "Tell me about the event."

"She's turning thirty and having a big bash at the Rennie." Miss Denise shook her head, a tiny movement, and smiled.

The Harlem Renaissance Ballroom, known as the Rennie, opened three years earlier. Colored men built and owned the square block complex that held prize fights, dance marathons, film screenings, concerts, and stage acts. It was also a meeting place for social clubs and political organizations in Harlem. Henry and I went to several balls there. Last year, we danced the new Charleston. Henry didn't love dancing as much as I did, but he danced with me because he knew I loved to. My shoulders drooped at the memory. We were happy in our way.

"You alright?"

I re-focused. "Your sister is lucky to—"

She interrupted me again. "She's smart is what she is. Got out of the life five years ago."

"The life?"

"That's what we call hooking. Anyway, she married this John who made it big in the numbers business. A king." A frown wrinkled her brow. "You understand?"

"Yes, of course." *Numbers* was a gambling activity that many of my neighbors took part in. The "kings" in Harlem, wealthy colored men, ran the illegal rings. "I don't know any regular people who did well playing." Owners rather than bettors seemed to succeed.

She made a dismissive sound.

My cheeks flushed. "So, a formal affair?"

"Yeah."

"Gloves?"

"Huh?"

"Are you planning on wearing opera gloves?"

"Not going to an opera, and it's in July. Gonna be hotter than a hooker's titties in the eyes of a John."

I laughed a nervous twitter.

Miss Denise joined me. "Pardon my French."

I explained long evening gloves, worn to enhance a strapless or short-sleeved ballgown.

"Short sleeves sound good," Miss Denise said. "Better to hide my arm jiggle." She flapped her flesh to underscore her point.

A group of school children ran by, holding armloads of books, reminding me I needed to get home. "I'll bring you sketches of dresses and swatches of material. Once you decide, we can meet for a fitting. May I come to your home?" Fittings in my apartment in the mornings were possible, but the thought of letting strangers into my home left me uncomfortable. My mind flashed on Henry's knife, which I now kept in my purse.

"Not right for a proper lady, but I got a friend who lives in a decent place."

I felt hypocritical and unchristian. "If you'd rather come to my home…?"

"Nah. That's okay. My friend's apartment has enough room for fittings. She may even want a dress."

"Brilliant." Tension I was unaware of seeped out. I wondered if she sensed my embarrassment. Now for the tricky part. "A down payment will make it official." I hoped I sounded businesslike rather than desperate. "Plus, you pay for the fabric once we choose it."

Without hesitation, Miss Denise dug in her bag and pulled out a stack of rumpled bills.

"Ten dollars total for the dress, not counting the material." I held my breath.

"How much up front?"

"Five now and five when I'm finished."

She thrust a ten-dollar bill into my hand. "I trust you. Miz Thompson says you're okay."

It took concentration to keep my hands from shaking. I slipped the cash into my purse. My first time earning. Perhaps taking care of my children was possible. They wouldn't starve, as Henry predicted. "Thank you." I waited a beat. "If you have other friends who might need my services, I'd be most appreciative of a recommendation."

She cocked her head to one side. "They dress more like me," she said, running her hands over her body, emphasizing her point.

"Yes, that would be fine. I sew a wide variety of styles."

She nodded and then snapped her fingers. "One more thing." She grabbed her orange-covered breasts. "Can you make these look…" She paused as if searching for the right adjective. "Modest, like yours?"

I surprised myself again and laughed aloud. "You have a lovely figure."

"You know what I mean."

"Yes," I said, still smiling. "I will do my very best."

Walking home with ten dollars in my purse, and hope in my spirit, I tried to remember the last time I laughed. Somewhere along the way, I lost the ability. The exact moment, month, or year eluded my memory. Well, it was back. I laughed aloud at nothing and almost skipped the rest of the way.

CHAPTER TWELVE

May 1924, Harlem New York

Friday evening found me facing the ire of Henry's sister Mae.

"What do you mean, you buried him? Without me? When was the service?" Mae's fury came at me like a wounded beast. "I traveled by bus from the factory and walked for at least a mile to visit and pray with my brother, and you tell me he's dead and buried?"

Mae worked in a rare silk factory in the Bronx, unusual since most silk came from Japan, and few ordinary people could afford to buy it.

With eyes wide, she shook her head and stepped back. "I don't believe you. Where? Show me his grave."

I rubbed my hands along my thighs, then pressed them against my stomach. "It happened quickly."

Right after receiving the money from Miss Denise, I implemented my plan and announced Henry had died. Still in jail awaiting trial, he'd yet to agree to a guilty plea as I requested, nor had I returned to the bank with the forged withdrawal slip or asked Henry to sign the form. But putting people off became too difficult. The three youngest children fussed and pestered. Friends from the neighborhood and church asked pointed questions. So, I told them he died, and we transported his body to Jamaica for burial. I'm sure my lies colored my face and tone. Like a belly swelling with a baby, soon it would be obvious to everyone.

"We thought he had pneumonia and would recover." I swallowed the guilt. "That's why I didn't send for you."

Her eyes blinked hard. "And?"

"It turned out to be something else–a contagious disease."

Silence.

"Tuberculosis." This change of illnesses was risky, but doctors let relatives visit pneumonia patients. Besides, Mae still lived in the Bronx, went to a different church, and socialized in separate circles, so I felt safe enough she'd not heard the first diagnosis. "They quarantined him." I raised my hands, palms up, to underscore my helplessness. "We had to bury him right away."

Shame washed over me. Besides the children and me, Mae was his closest relative. His other four siblings lived in Jamaica. I sank down onto the sofa.

Mae flopped next to me. "You told no one? You didn't write to our sisters?" Her tone and expression made her continued doubt clear.

"I'm sorry," I said, and meant it.

Mae's eyes filled up. She pulled out a handkerchief from her bag and dabbed her eyes. She looked a lot like Henry. Same strong features, wavy hair, brown skin, and small hands. "What did I ever do to merit such treatment from you?"

Heat suffused my cheeks. She'd always been kind to me. Although not a close relationship, we spent Christmas Eve and Easter together. A maiden lady and a generous aunt, the children loved the presents and sweets she gave them. Mae deserved the truth.

"He's not dead."

"I knew it." She crossed her arms. "What then?"

"He molested Patricia."

Mae's mouth flopped open, and her eyebrows shot up.

"And Sylvie. I petitioned the police, and they arrested him. He's in jail, awaiting trial."

"Trial? Jail?"

Her tears dried, and mine flowed. My linen handkerchief sopped up the moisture from my eyes, cheeks, and nose. "Yes."

Mae stayed quiet for a long time. I felt judged, misunderstood. This was why I told everyone Henry died. Her shoulders rose and sank, and her small eyes searched my face.

With nothing to add and an unwillingness to explain further, I waited.

Mae said, "Some claimed Father acted the same way. I remember grownups whispering."

"What?"

"Our mother was thirty or more years younger than our father." Her voice sounded sandpaper raw. "I was the oldest girl, born right after Henry. Nothing happened to me but…" Her voice trailed off. "Nothing I remember."

Her words made me think of Sylvie. "Tell me about the whispers."

"Elder relatives, not family we saw often, claimed he'd hurt girls before he married our mother." She shook her head as if saying no to an unasked question. "My memory is foggy. I was quite young."

This news staggered me.

"I remember how sad our mother seemed most of the time. I thought her melancholy was a consequence of growing old even though she was younger than I am now."

"He never hurt you or your sisters?"

"We didn't discuss such things." Mae looked up at me and then her eyes darted away.

I waited, but she stayed quiet. "Why didn't you say something to my mother before Henry married me?"

In an aggressive, defensive tone, she said, "I just told you why."

The room swam and blurred. Cold, clammy sweat bathed my face. I attempted to stand. Waves of dizziness sent me back on my derriere. I put my head between my legs and sucked in air.

Mae jumped up. "I'll get you some water."

When she returned and after a sip or two, I said, "Tell me about your father." I remembered meeting a big man whose square jaw and dimpled chin thrust forward when he spoke. Stories about sea adventures entertained me while I waited for Mother.

"I shouldn't have brought it up," Mae said.

"What else did you hear?"

"Nothing."

Was there something defective in the Herbert family, something passed down from generation to generation, and brewing in mine? I thought about my George and Andy and shuddered.

"Thank you for telling me," I said. How might I stop a generational curse? The water glass now empty, I stood, this time without dizziness. I shifted my focus. Mae was a good person and perhaps a victim unable or unwilling to remember. "Would you like to visit Henry?"

"Prison isn't a good idea." She sounded like her old self again, the tears dried, and empathy gone.

"Not you too." Anger pricked.

"I think the price you will pay—"

"Stop. Please. I know what I'm doing." Whatever the consequences, they had to be better than letting him hurt my girls. "What about Irene? Will she be next?"

Mae made a sucking sound through her teeth, lifted her chin, and straightened her back. "How are you managing?" She looked around the apartment. Her gaze landed on my living room windows. The lace curtains were gone, bought by a neighbor, and replaced with unadorned cotton.

"I've found work here and there," I said. Plus, I sold the china tea set, a wedding present from Gram, along with two gowns I'll never need again. One of them had swirled while we danced at the Rennie.

Mae's eyes lingered on the windows.

"What I need," I said, "is help convincing him to plead guilty." I explained by painting the same picture the lawyer laid out to me.

"Exactly," she said. "They won't convict him, but it will destroy his reputation and your home life." She shifted in her seat, looked away from me. In a softer voice, she said, "He's my brother. The only one left."

She'd lost her two younger brothers, years before. Still, she had to help me. I reached over and touched her forearm. "At the prison hospital, he'll have treatment and the possibility of a cure." Although, I said this, I didn't want it to be true.

She clenched her fingers together. "I have to think about it."

I wanted to scream. "Thank you."

Long after Mae left, I sat, replaying our conversation. People didn't speak about such evil, much less address it. Stopping this horror fell to me.

I walked over to my desk and took out fresh sheets of stationery. It was time to write Mother, tell her the truth, and request honesty in return.

CHAPTER THIRTEEN

Mother's letters were as light and soft as the scones she baked for afternoon tea. Dappled with buttery snippets of her day, she inquired about our health, the children's schooling, and my church activities. In my letters, I did the same, sharing only positive news. Worrying her served no purpose other than unburdening myself at her expense.

In one of my earlier missives, I included the photograph we'd taken on Easter Sunday in G. G. Studio on 125th Street. Each of us wore new spring outfits. Henry purchased his at Al & Joe's Men's Wear. I made my dress and the children's clothes from remnants I bought at the Cotton and Woolens store. Thinking back sent a shudder through me. We celebrated Easter before... The photo of us presented a deceptively happy tableau.

I wrote a different letter now. While I still did not want to distress her, I had to share and unearth what happened.

Dearest one,

Thank you for your last correspondence. I smiled when I saw it, hungry for your news. I read your funny story to the children, about the vicar at St. Mary's, making them laugh. Now that your cold has passed, and summer days at the shore lay ahead, your health will improve.

I paused, trying to think how to move from our usual to the terrible.

I'm writing today to share grievous news. It's good you can lean on your friends, Rowan and Eloise. I fear you will need their comfort and support.

I pressed my hands together to stop the shaking.

Henry is not ill. I lied to you, and I beg your forgiveness. I came home to find him molesting our sweet Patricia.

My tears smudged the ink. I took another sheet of stationary and started over–included the police, the jail, Lawyer Booth, and my deception to protect Patricia and our standing in the community. *"Henry must plead guilty because of insanity,"* I explained. I ended my letter with a plea of my own.

"Henry's interest in a young girl must have caused you some worry. Why did you allow him to marry me? I remember asking you. Feeling abandoned, even betrayed, you never gave me a genuine answer. You only said, 'It's for the best.' You said I would learn to love being a wife and mother.

The thought of taking Patricia and Sylvie from school and wedding them to older men is abhorrent to me.

"You said, 'I had no choice.' Please help me understand."

I stared at the letter. For years, unsatisfied with her responses, I wanted to ask again, "Why?" But I was afraid of the answer, or frightened the reply would cause emotions I didn't want to experience.

. . .

The summer of 1909, the year of my marriage, we lived in Kingston, the capital of Jamaica. Our small cottage sat on a busy street. Dirt roads connected the houses. Chickens and feral dogs and cats roamed freely. Reminders from the earthquake two years earlier, scarred buildings and long swaths of rubble still marred the landscape. Dust covered shoes and skirts. Too far inland for sea breezes, the heat made it hard to breathe. I missed Gram's manor, the cool passageways of Walthamstow Hall where my sisters and I attended school, and accompanying Mother and Father up and down the Congo River. I missed sitting on Father's lap, listening to his stories about life on the rugged hills of his birthplace in Cornwall. His white skin burned reddish brown and covered with a thick, blonde beard. Blue eyes, one made of glass, smiling at me from behind rimless spectacles.

I longed for my big sisters as well. Both lived and taught in Birmingham. I gobbled up every letter Carrie and Nora wrote. They kept their news breezy, so I couldn't tell if they were happy, but I decided they were. Neither found a husband, which Mother made sound like a sad happenstance. Still, they shared a home, and I was sure they enjoyed adventures they chose not to tell.

My life consisted of school, church, and piano lessons. During weekday afternoons, I played outside with neighborhood children, mostly stinky boys, but didn't have any special friends. Although I liked my Jamaican school, it lacked a library. I re-read *The Little Princess* and other stories Gram gave me for birthdays and Christmases but longed for new ones to carry me away.

Three years passed since Father died in the Congo of malaria, since the missionary leadership summoned Mother, Carrie, and Nora to London, since our banishment to Jamaica. I celebrated birthdays eleven, twelve, and a few days ago, thirteen. I found my way and only complained on days Mother looked less sad.

"We're to journey to St. Catherine," she told me, her usually tight expression softening a bit. Her heart-shaped face and dewy black skin looked drawn from fatigue or perhaps worry.

I put down my family of dolls and stopped the story I was writing in my head. "What shall we do there?"

Mother's eyes looked moist, and perspiration glistened on her forehead and cheeks. "Do you remember the Herbert family? We visited them last year."

My mood brightened. They lived in a large house near Spanish Town, in St. Catherine Parish, and owned an electric fan that cooled you when standing in front of it. A wide river ran near their property, and groves of banana trees lined one side. We ate slices of pineapple and fragrant fish cakes for lunch on their veranda. Dribbles of condensation covered a pitcher of an icy strawberry drink. A maid served us, and Henry's father told stories about his Jewish forefathers sailing from Portugal to the Caribbean islands, buying and selling wares. He spoke about dancing with the native people while drums beat

African and Portuguese rhythms. Once there was a terrible storm and the ship had to outrun gigantic waves.

"No steam engines then," he'd said. "Sails carried them when the wind blew and stranded them on breezeless days. Pirates—"

"What's a pirate?" I asked, interrupting, which was rude, but I wanted to understand every tiny detail.

"Thieves who sail the open seas in swift ships. My great grandfather's boat held heavy cargo that slowed its travel. The men tried to catch them and steal their wares."

"Did they succeed?" I asked.

"Sometimes. Once, pirates boarded our family ship and there was a fierce fight. Although only merchants, my forefathers and the crew fought and defeated the scoundrels. With the cargo saved, my family sailed into Kingston Harbour and celebrated."

"What did they do? Was there a party like this one?"

Mr. Herbert laughed. He threw back his head and roared. "You ask a lot of questions, young miss. Enough stories for now." He rose, chucked me under my chin, and said as if speaking to himself, "This one will be a wonderful wife. I can tell." Still laughing under his breath, he went inside.

Later, his words echoed in my head, but at the time, they meant nothing to me.

CHAPTER FOURTEEN

Stuffed from the meal with the Herberts, I fell asleep next to Mother on a wicker sofa, my dreams filled with drumbeats, dancing, storms, pirates, and harrowing escapes.

The pleasant memory made the pending trip inviting. "For how long shall we stay?" I didn't mind missing school, but I wanted to do well on my upcoming exams.

Mother took my hands in hers. They used to be rough from thrashing through dense Congo bush, building cooking fires, and ministering to women in childbirth. Since coming to Jamaica, they'd softened, and the callouses disappeared.

"Do you remember their eldest son, Henry?" she asked. "He was there during our first stay and then visited me in December when business brought him to Kingston."

I tried to picture him. I remembered he laughed a lot like his father. "Yes, a little." Right before Christmas, he and Mother drank tea in our parlor. "He seemed nice."

"Very much so," she said, her voice low. "He wants to get to know you." She paused. "And for you to learn more about him." Her voice cracked like a walnut shell under foot.

Wariness crept through me. "Why?"

Mother's shoulders sagged, and her mouth turned down. She wore the same expression as when we sailed from England after Father's burial. "I have no choice, my sweet Gigi." I'd not heard my childhood nickname since we came to Jamaica–Gi for Grace Isabel and the next G for Graham.

When she didn't respond, I asked again, "Why?" A foreboding without a name or meaning clung to me.

"No choice at all," she said in a faint voice. "Now, no more questions."

The Herberts sent a carriage to fetch us. I wore a favorite dress Mother made. Its eyelet cotton, edged in embroidered roses, swirled when I walked and climbed in. Two muscled horses pulled us along. Mother reminded me to cover my mouth and nose with my handkerchief to protect my lungs from the thick dust kicked up by the hooves and carriage wheels.

Just like last year's visit, the people-packed house looked and sounded like a holiday celebration. We sat at a long table covered with a bright green tablecloth. Henry's brothers and sisters, aunts, uncles, and cousins talked, laughed, ate, and drank. Some elders spoke in a language I didn't understand. Henry's mother told me it was Jamaican-Patois dotted with Portuguese.

A maid carried in servings of whole fish, fried fritters, brown rice and peas, green beans, and snap peas. Zesty spices teased my nose. Cook, who appeared not to have a regular name, poked her head in and grinned when Mrs. Herbert told her how much everyone enjoyed the meal. At home, Mother portioned our food on small plates. Here, even the children helped themselves to seconds. Fragrant butter-soaked rolls, hot from the oven, were the best part.

Mother barely touched her food. She sat several seats from me so I couldn't inquire. When I looked up, I found Henry staring at me. The only men I knew at the time were old men who ushered and served at our local church. Although twenty-three-years old, Henry didn't appear as elderly as the churchmen, but I understood he was much older than I was.

Henry said, "Leave room for mincemeat tarts. Everyone speaks of my mother's exceptional pastry."

"My tummy is stuffed," I said. The earlier dread was now less intense and laughter warmed the atmosphere. "Perhaps just one."

He rose, walked to the sideboard, and snatched up two—one he kept and passed the other to me. He took a big bite. I did the same. The flaky crust melted on my tongue.

After the meal, we washed up and went outside. Henry and I sat next to each other on soft cushions. Mother chaperoned from a few feet away. I stretched and swiveled my neck. "Where is everyone?"

"Napping or resting," Henry said. "Easy to do on a hot afternoon following a big meal." An amused expression played across his face. "Do you like it here?"

I did, but some of my worry returned. "I enjoyed the tart."

"Nothing else?" he asked, cocking his head to one side.

"The veranda and especially the fan. I wish we had one." I wanted to take my words back. Envy, Mother taught, is unbecoming. "I didn't mean to say that."

He laughed the Herbert laugh, head thrown back, mouth wide open.

"I wasn't making a joke."

"No, no. Sorry. I will send you a fan."

We couldn't afford such a luxury, so I started to protest. "It's too much—"

"A gift, from me to you."

Unsure if Mother would let me keep it, I cautiously thanked him.

"You're quite welcome." He paused. "So clever and beautiful." With his index finger, he traced my cheek.

I jerked my head back.

"Your skin is the color of ivory blushed by the sun." Ignoring my reticence, he reached over and stroked my hair. "Your waves as smooth."

Before we left home, Mother had gathered up my hair, wove ribbons through and pinned it all in place. I thought my tresses looked lovely, but now I felt self-conscious. "Please don't touch me." I glanced at Mother to check her reaction to my forwardness, but she didn't speak.

"Most women like men to admire them," he said.

"Perhaps so. But I'm only a girl."

We rode home in silence. Mother stared out the window as we rumbled and swayed past sugar cane plantations and more banana groves. Although not visible from the carriage, the salty scent of the ocean reached us. I rested my head on Mother's lap, the folds of her long skirt pillowing my cheek, and soon fell asleep.

Henry and I married four months later.

Only three memory pictures of my wedding day remain. The first is a collage of white: the August sun a white blaze, my dress and the lining of the carriage as white as the clotted cream Mrs. Herbert served with her tarts, the white carriage drawn by white horses, their bridles festooned with white roses, and a long white veil covering my face.

The second memory is more sound than images: mother's stifled weeping, the minister's deep voice, and Herbert-guests telling me how beautiful I looked, like a porcelain doll.

My third mind-photo remains fuzzy since I experienced the entire wedding through a blur of tears.

CHAPTER FIFTEEN

Henry and I honeymooned at The Rio Cobre Hotel on the Cobre River, close to the sea. Frightened, I begged Mother to accompany us. She and Henry quarreled, and he relented. Mother and I shared a room and Henry slept in another.

A carriage took us to the sea at least once a week, a treat I looked forward to. The three of us walked along the water's edge, carrying our shoes, searching for conch shells. I dashed in and out, avoiding the waves. Here, the sun didn't bake you the way it did in Kingston. When I breathed in through my mouth, the air tasted salty on my tongue.

The warm, unhurried days ran into each other. For the first few weeks, a young couple, their two children and dog, vacationed in rooms next to us on the second floor of the two-story hotel. From his spot on the veranda, Henry watched Mother and me play with the children. I taught the ten-year-old how to make a simple dress for her doll. Henry joined us for meals, daily walks, and trips to the sea, but otherwise left us alone. Mother couldn't swim, which was silly since for most of her life she lived on the Congo River. But Father taught me how. I loved splashing and diving to the sandy bottom to watch a school of rainbow-colored fish swim by. There was nothing like them in the Congo or in the icy English waters. Shades of pink, blue, and yellow glittered.

I'm not sure why we stayed so long or how Henry managed an extended vacation from work, but I loved the hotel, river, and beach. On month three of our holiday, Henry and Mother's raised voices woke me. From the bed Mother and I shared, I crept to the open window to hear. They stood between our room and his, Henry's back against the gilded railing. I couldn't see Mother's face.

"I've been patient, Rose," he said.

"She needs more time." Mother's tone was just like the one she used when I misbehaved.

"You baby her."

Father used to tell Mother that, but when he said it, he smiled and squeezed her hand. Henry accused.

"Because she *is* my baby." Mother no longer sounded like herself. There was sadness now.

"No. She is *my* wife." His voice swelled. "We are going home. You to yours, and Grace and I to ours."

I scurried back and pulled the covers over my head. Unsure what the argument meant, it still frightened me. Were Henry and I returning to the Herbert family home alone? When Mother climbed into bed, she cuddled me close.

"Are you asleep, Gigi?" she asked.

I stayed quiet, too afraid to pose my questions.

The next day, Henry and I returned to St. Catherine. Mother tried to hide her tears when she said goodbye, so I hid mine.

I sat on one end of the carriage seat and stared out the window. Henry sat on the other side. Every few minutes, I sensed his eyes roving over me, but I didn't shift my gaze to meet his. We rode in silence.

That night, for the first time, we shared a bedroom. I undressed in the bathroom, slipped on a long-cotton nightgown, and climbed into the narrow bed, staying as far to the edge as possible.

"Take off your gown," he said, standing in front of me.

I'd never seen a naked man before. Even the native men and boys who lived in the bush along the Congo River wore cloth that covered their privates. I turned my head and squished my eyes shut, clutching my garment closer. Rough hands grabbed my arm and tugged the nightdress off. He pushed me down on the bed and climbed on top of me.

I didn't understand what he was doing or what he expected. He shoved himself inside of me, thrusting and grunting. Heat like flame on flesh burned my insides. I tried not to make any noise, biting my lip so hard, I tasted blood. Then he stopped and rolled off me.

"You are truly my wife now," he said, lying on his back. "This is what wives do."

. . .

I'd not thought about my wedding or honeymoon in years, but now it returned in wisps and fragments, flashing at random moments.

Mother's response to my letter and question arrived on Wednesday, the 14th of May.

"My dearest daughter,

My heart aches for you and your girls. I hoped America would bring you comforts and happiness, make up for your past sorrows.

You asked me why. It is hard to convey in a letter the worries and hopes that swirled inside me. With your dear father gone, I had no one to protect us. The Baptist Council slashed my pension. I found no opportunity to earn money on my own. I didn't want to worry you, but our situation was dire. We lived in a foreign country, away from everyone we knew and loved. Your sisters were settled with positions in England, but you and I were on our own. My partner for so many years, I missed consulting your father, his keen mind and steadfast love, sure to find a different, better answer. I wrote to your Gram and to your father's brother, but the Grahams remained uninterested in our troubles.

My concern wasn't for myself, but I was desperate for your future.

The Herberts were prosperous merchants. Henry, handsome and young, only twenty-three, promised a luxurious life. He wrote me the previous fall, asking for your hand, but I said no. At Christmas time, he visited and asked again, but still I declined. You were only twelve, I explained. Your thirteenth birthday not until April.

He said he understood. Seemed earnest, kind, and caring. Persistent, but also patient. My mother was sixteen when she married my father in Cameroon. They shared a long and happy marriage.

When he asked again that spring, I did what I thought best but came to realize I made a terrible mistake. I pray you can forgive your loving mother."

With trembling fingers, I folded Mother's letter and placed it in a satin box that contained earlier ones. Our situations, hers then and mine now, felt similarly precarious. Would I make better choices?

I placed the letter box into a drawer and closed it.

CHAPTER SIXTEEN

A month passed since Henry's arrest, and he was still in jail. Once again, Lawyer Booth summoned me.

The streets between my home and the courthouse teemed with families heading to an all-female parade of the Universal Negro Improvement Association, known as the UNIA. Some women wore long dresses, and others, the newer flapper fashion of narrow chemises that landed just below the knee. Most walked in low-heeled shoes with hats pinned to their hair. The crowd carried picnic baskets and blankets. Fried chicken and curry goat, aromas of the American south and the Caribbean, mingled as they passed.

The men, dressed in a mix of overalls and suits, all wore hats, most sporting fedoras rakishly slanted over one eye. The brilliant orator and Black separatist, Marcus Garvey, was in jail for mail fraud, but the women's brigade continued to espouse his back-to-Africa beliefs. I wondered if they realized how vast the continent was. Did Americans even know from which country the slavers captured, stole, sold them?

I didn't agree with Garvey's approach. He scorned Jewish and mixed-race people and supported the Ku Klux Klan since both the UNIA, and the Klan desired racial purity. Henry's family members were of Jewish descent, and our mixed heritage left us out of Garvey's plans. On the other hand, he preached pride and financial independence, opened businesses, and employed coloreds. I understood his appeal.

Angling my way around the clumps of moving people, I passed striped awnings and shop signs. *Patsy's Lunch. Fish meals for ten and fifteen cents.* Optimum Cigars and Root Beer sold at the corner store. The courthouse loomed ahead.

Lawyer Booth met me in the lobby.

"How is he?" I asked.

"Despondent." He took my elbow as we descended the stairs to the basement of cells. "His sister came by."

I almost stumbled. "When?" My stomach clenched and my right hand dropped to my abdomen.

"Yesterday."

"To what end?" I asked in a whisper of anticipation.

"He didn't say."

Did Mae persuade him to plead guilty? I smoothed my skirt and braced my shoulders. "I require your assistance."

The long, dank hall stretched out in front of us, cells on each side. No sunlight reached the corridor. Nor was there a place to sit, except in the visitor's rooms to our right.

I turned to Lawyer Booth. "Our daughter refuses to leave my bedroom. She barely eats or speaks. Our older daughter drags herself around, bereft. She knows what her sister suffers." I waited, letting the import of my words sink in.

Thin eyebrows furrowed into a deep vee.

"We have a younger daughter who is five." Again, I paused, hoping he'd grasp the enormity of Henry's guilt and the danger to the family if he returned.

The solicitor made a low guttural sound that turned into a cough. He turned away and covered his mouth. Was he gaining understanding? Did he see the horror? Pinpricks of possibility traveled along my arms.

"If Patricia had to testify, if I did, the devastation of my family, *his* family… there will be no healing after such an event. You described the horror of it to me, how pointed and cruel your interrogation would be while you defended him. This cannot happen."

"I'm hired to defend him rigorously."

"I understand, but do you understand the danger our daughters are in?"

He heaved his shoulders. "What do you want?"

The fraternal organization was no longer paying the lawyer. Whatever their goodwill, we'd used it up. "There is money in our savings account, money to help cover your additional expenses and that of a psychiatrist." The money I failed to collect from the bank, too concerned about the inferior quality of my forgery attempts. And thank God, because now I needed it for another urgent purpose. "You must help me persuade him that pleading guilty is in his and his family's best interests." Giving up on our savings felt reckless, but unavoidable. How much would Booth require? "You told me they will release him once cured? That is his incentive to do what is right."

"Yes and no," the attorney said.

"How so?" Lawyer Booth's unequivocal support was pivotal to my plan.

"As I explained to you, he will have to plead guilty to an unfathomable crime. His jailers won't declare him sane one year later."

Good, I thought, but I tried to sound sympathetic. "But eventually…"

"Yes, perhaps in time."

"Will you help me? I've already explained this option to him, just as you enlightened me. Surely, together, we can help him see reason."

"Prison is a dangerous place. Corruption. Brutality."

"Surely, the hospital is safer."

The lawyer stood there for at least a full minute. His starched white shirt and wool tie neat against this throat. "I will help you, for the sake of your daughters," he said, at last. "But it is up to Henry. I can share the offer made by the district attorney's office and avoid a costly and lengthy trial. I possess no power to force him, and it would be unethical for me to try."

"I understand." Hope surged through me.

"I think it is best I approach him alone."

"Thank you."

I waited in the hall for over an hour, the smell of stale cigars and cigarettes enveloping me, sitting on the stained and dusty steps. Too worn out to speculate, I'd placed the future of my family in the hands of a stranger, bribing him with money we needed to live, and counting on decency I had no right to assume. Police officers walked by. A white man, dressed like Lawyer Booth, paced in front of the doors of the two visitors' rooms. No one looked at me, no one spoke to me. Invisible, scared, I prayed to a God I'd believed in all my life, but lately questioned. What had Patricia and Sylvie done to deserve this terrible thing? Or was their sin mine? Or Mother's?

The door to one of the visitor's rooms swung open and Lawyer Booth came out. The pacing man scowled, made a comment under his breath, and pushed past him, trying to get inside.

"We're not finished, good sir," the counselor said with an ingratiating smile.

I didn't hear the white man's reply as he stalked past us, nor did I ask. Since I'd endured enough ugliness for a lifetime, there was no need to take on insults meant for someone else.

CHAPTER SEVENTEEN

Lawyer Booth's face looked grave. I braced myself for more unsettling news. "He wants to speak with you."

Despite my preparation, a shudder shook my body. "For what purpose?"

"He insists. Won't sign the withdrawal slip or accept the plea-deal without conversing with you."

"Did he appear amenable?"

"I'm unsure."

Squaring my shoulders, I nodded my agreement and followed the solicitor inside.

Henry's eyes, rimmed red, gleamed wet with unshed tears. The smell in the room reeked stronger than my last visit. I steeled myself, but a piece of me felt sad for him. We lived as husband and wife for fifteen years, buried three children together, made a life in a new country.

"Thank you for speaking with me," he said. With his left hand, the wrist shackled, he gestured for me to sit.

"How are you?" I asked before perching on the edge of the wooden chair.

"I'm unwell. The food is uneatable, and there's violence every day."

It was then that I noticed a gash over his eye and bruise on his cheek, partially hidden by his newly grown beard. Clean shaven all the years I knew him, his facial hair now looked unkempt. "Are people hurting you? Were you in a fight?"

"*Criminals* populate this place. Not men like me."

But wasn't Henry a criminal? I changed the subject by seeking a more relevant conversation. "Mae came to see you. Was it a good visit?"

"Clearly, you persuaded her to turn against me." Each word came out hard and accusatory. The chains clanged as he shifted in his seat.

"No. To help you get better." I didn't believe a cure for such an ungodly urge existed, but if so, what would I do then? I told everyone he died.

He shook his head. "The guards here, the men in charge, have no interest in my future." Puffy eyes, almost slits, shifted from side to side, skimming past my face. "You understand what the prosecutor wants me to do?"

"Yes." It was not just the prosecutor. I wanted this, but I pressed my lips together and waited.

"Prison is a horrible place. This jail is disgusting, and as you can see..." He pointed to his bruised face... "dangerous. Prison will be horrendous."

"You'll be in a hospital."

He growled. "It's a *prison* hospital. A place they put crazy, dangerous men who've murdered."

I dropped my hand to my abdomen and pressed to quiet it. "What did you want to tell me?" I asked in a whisper.

"Reconsider. Help me get out of here. I'm going to *die* in prison if you don't." Tears rolled down his cheeks. "Please, Grace. I'm begging you."

My eyes filled up as well. Blood thudded through my veins and arteries at an alarming rate. The pain in my stomach sharpened. He'd provided for us. Hugged and played with his children. We danced, enjoyed live jazz, attended salons to listen to poetry read by celebrated writers. Over shared meals, we discussed the news of the day and we worshipped together every Sunday. He worked hard and paid our bills. Henry and I expected our children–educated, church-going believers–to achieve a good life, one even better than the one Henry provided. Wasn't that our responsibility?

Henry leaned forward as far as the chains let him. "I love you. Let's be a family again. Tell them you've erred. Save me."

He'd never told me he loved me before. Jamaicans, like the British, tended to keep emotions bottled up and used words of praise sparingly. Did I believe him and if so, what difference did it make now? The memory of him on top of Patricia rose before me, her dress hiked around waist. Sylvie's sad countenance. Irene's innocence. "No." I stood.

Henry groaned, a wounded animal sound, that almost shook my resolve.

"No," I repeated.

From behind me Lawyer Booth cleared his throat. He stepped next to me and pulled out the bank document, placed it on the table, and handed Henry a handkerchief and one of the newer solid-ink fountain pens.

Henry wiped his eyes, nose, and beard. He signed the form.

"Thank you," I said.

"You will pay a dear price for this," Henry said, repeating his earlier warnings.

Not as dear as you, I thought.

Once in the hall, Lawyer Booth faced me., "It's done." He looked grim. "I will need the savings book."

My face must have showed all I'd just been through and now this latest catastrophe. Yes, I'd offered more money, but hoped somehow one or both men would not deny five children the resources they needed.

"This is what you wanted."

"How much do you require?" I dug out from my purse the book of deposits–money saved over our ten years in America. The last of our resources.

He took it, turned the pages to the final entry, and then snapped it shut. "I've a doctor in mind who will testify to Mr. Herbert's mental state. He's well respected by the judiciary here and…" The attorney dipped his head toward me. "Quite expensive." He flapped the savings book as he spoke. "This will barely cover all we must do."

Still too overwrought to speak, I nodded my understanding.

He touched my arm. "It will be over soon."

"Thank you." I knew, however, that we were not anywhere near the end.

CHAPTER EIGHTEEN

The worst happened. Well, not the worst, but frightening and terrible. Lawyer Booth told me the sentencing judge insisted I testify at Henry's hearing. He demanded Patricia do so as well, but that was impossible. "You must dissuade him," I said.

It had been hard enough being quizzed by the assistant district attorney–the questions intrusive and insulting. The man, about thirty, was over six-feet tall and his collar bone protruded on either side of his narrow neck.

Lawyer Booth impressed me. A colored man successfully navigating the halls of justice or, as he liked to say, the halls of injustice, unfairness, and luck of the draw. I found it bewildering, but my confusion did not deter me.

I answered every question and protected Patricia from the same interrogation. I explained she no longer spoke, couldn't, wouldn't. They arraigned Henry and sent him to another jail in lower Manhattan. Lawyer Booth called it The Tombs, but its real name was City Prison.

Through it all, I didn't falter. Henry must be committed. He was already dead and bringing him back to life would damn us all.

Nothing in my experience or reading prepared me for my time before the judge. I'd spent hours reading Agatha Christie mysteries for myself and children's books to George and Irene. Andy listened, but often fell asleep before the story concluded. In none of the literature I devoured was a woman like me sitting before a judge, testifying to her husband's horrible acts and character.

On the morning of May 26, I returned to the courthouse. Patricia, bathed and dressed, joined the family for breakfast, but she still refused to attend classes. Leaving Andy with her felt safer these last few weeks. The glazed look appeared more focused, and she spoke on occasion-polite answers to questions. Yesterday, she joined Sylvie in reading books to Irene and George and helped Sylvie bathe Andy and dress him for bed.

Irene stopped asking about her father, but George persisted. "Why did he die?" "Where is heaven?" "When will he return?" Sylvie perked up a little, her normally dour expression a bit brighter.

This was the ultimate step of my ruse.

The judge's chambers, a cramped space clouded with cigar and pipe tobacco, looked the opposite of what I'd imagined, as did the magistrate. A middle-aged man, clean shaven, and a bit rumpled, sat behind an enormous oak desk, his robes hanging from a coat rack to his right. A name plate declared His Honor, Judge James Wisdom. If I wasn't tense and frightened, that coincidence might have elicited a laugh. For a few seconds, I closed my eyes and prayed. God knew my heart.

I thought Henry would be there and braced myself. But it was only six of us, including Judge Wisdom. The prosecutor, a different man from the one who previously questioned me, was also middle-aged, but with wispy hair and a round belly. The psychiatrist, Dr. Field, sat at the far end of the semi-circle of people facing the judge. Lawyer Booth and I centered the arc of chairs. A petite woman taking notes on a machine anchored the other end. Before the judge arrived, Lawyer Booth explained the Stenotype machine to me, along with its legal purpose. I'd seen typewriters, but this was different in its shape and size, both narrower and smaller.

"Where is Henry?" I asked.

"This isn't the actual sentencing hearing. A preliminary step," explained Lawyer Booth. "The judge requires assurances."

Judge Wisdom began by stating the purpose of our gathering-to determine if the plea deal between the district attorney's office and the defendant was just. He then named each person in attendance. The stenographer's fingers flew across her machine, capturing every word.

"Dr. Field," the judge intoned in a deep baritone, "your findings."

"The heinousness of the crime, your honor," the doctor said, an educated southern accent coloring his words, "tells us that Henriques Herbert was not in his right mind during the time of his crime." Sharp blue eyes shifted in my direction. "I spoke with the boy for over an hour. I'm here to stipulate that it's my medical opinion he's criminally insane."

The word "boy" struck me hard. Henry was a man, but I held my tongue. We'd paid this doctor and the lawyer all our savings. I was in no position to protest his ignorance and poor manners.

"Let's hear from the wife," the judge said without looking at me or using my name. "I understand you witnessed this crime?"

Lawyer Booth touched my forearm. "Please tell the judge what happened."

As we'd discussed and I'd practiced the day before, I told the story of that horrific afternoon in as few sentences as possible. In conclusion, I said, "We all want Henry to pay for his crime and to get well so he can return home."

The judge puffed on his cigar, tilted his head back, and blew a plume of smoke towards the ceiling. "Mr. Dowd?"

The prosecutor leaned forward and looked at the other men, his eyes sliding past me. "The people concur."

Perspiration trickled from my armpits down my sides.

"We're all agreed?"

The men murmured their assent.

"So be it," the judge said.

And it was over. At no time during the fifteen minutes of the hearing did anyone look at me or, except during the introductions, call me by my name.

CHAPTER NINETEEN

June 1924, Harlem, New York

Two months have passed since the incident. That's what I called it in my mind. When you name terrible things, say them aloud, they become real. When you keep them tucked inside, secrets as hard as the marbles Mae gave the children, you can pretend.

The sentencing hearing brought back images, feelings, and night terrors. I had to find a way to keep the pictures at bay. By calling it the incident, Henry's actions became smaller, fainter, a wavy memory with no sharp edges or clarity.

Patricia missed her second monthly menstruation. I prayed the delay resulted from the trauma and not pregnancy. Sylvie and I bled on the first, but nothing from Patricia. Every morning, I found her in the bathroom heaving. She could *not* be the mother of her sister. I required assistance beyond my scope, so I sought the only person I thought might help us.

Miss Denise sat next to me on the park bench. I handed her the red and black dress I'd finished. "Your sister's birthday bash is coming up. Are you excited?"

She held up the garment. "This is great. You make me ladylike."

Warm May breezes reminded me of our home in St. Catherine. "Has your sister shared any of her plans?"

"For her soiree?"

"Yes." I tried to keep my tone light and my expression unfazed. Denise and I weren't friends. She owed me nothing. She attended the same church as Mrs. Thompson and what I required was against God's plan and the law of the land. Asking her for advice, for a name and address, might insult or outrage her, and then I'd have no place to turn and possibly lose my best patron to boot.

"Yeah. Her man hired *two* bands for dancing and the liquor will *secretly* flow."

She looked better. The bruises from earlier had faded. Blood red polish decorated nicely clipped nails. Glad for her happiness, my small laugh was authentic.

"I'm wearing this one on a date." She held the garment at eye level and tilted her head from side to side. "A real one, not a John."

"You met someone?" For a few minutes, I could enjoy someone else's happiness. "What's he like?"

"Well, *met* is a funny word in this case." She shrugged and then let both shoulders fall back into place. "He *was* a customer, but now he's my man." Her bright red lips grinned. "A gentleman. Comes to get me at my place, holds the door open, pulls out my chair so I can sit, and shit like that." She shook her head. "Sorry."

"It's fine." I was used to Denise's colorful language.

"He doesn't talk as nice as you, but he finished high school. Has a trade."

"This is wonderful news."

Her entire face glowed. "I'm damn well over the moon." She looked at me, her expression slid into a frown. "Something on your mind?"

I thought I'd composed my face exactly right and kept my tone neutral, but clearly not. At least she provided an opening. "I have no right to ask you for a favor—"

"What kind?" she asked before I finished.

"My daughter is pregnant." This was the first time I said it aloud, the first time I named it making the pregnancy real.

"Oh, I'm sorry." She twisted her mouth but said nothing more.

I plunged in. "She's only thirteen and…"

Denise raised her drawn eyebrows.

"Raped."

"Fuck."

Despite the vulgarity, I agreed with her sentiment. "Yes. I hoped you might know someone who could help us."

Denise stared at me.

"We're quite desperate," I added, my eyes filling up. "I've heard stories about the butchers out there–mutilated fetuses, women never able to have children afterwards, or worse, they die on the kitchen table." I sucked in a quick breath and hurried on. "I thought you might know someone trustworthy and safe."

"How far gone is she?"

"Two months."

Denise blinked and chewed the fat of her thumb. I waited.

"I see," she said, her eyebrows drawn together, and lips tucked under. "It'll cost ya."

I closed my eyes. I had no money. We lived off the dresses I made for Denise and her friends. The fees barely covered the rent. There was little to eat. I'd already told Sylvie the family would go to a different school in September because we had no way to pay for Catholic school. Lots of tears and anger. "Is this someone, a doctor?" I asked.

Denise made a face.

"A nurse?"

"She's good," Denise said, patting my hand. "A midwife."

I paused, afraid to ask my next questions.

As if reading my mind, Denise said, "She's good. Honest. Clean. Not a butcher, like you said. There's enough of them out there, for sure."

Air whooshed out. "Have you...?

"No. But friends have. They're fine."

"How much do you think I'll have to pay?"

"Maybe thirty or forty dollars," Denise whispered and then glanced over her shoulder as if searching for a citizen, minister, or police officer who might overhear. "She could go to jail if she's caught."

"My daughter cannot have this baby."

"There are places you could send her."

I'd considered that. Ask Mother to care for her and help find a family for the baby. When we lived in Jamaica, Mother saw both Sylvie and Patricia every month and loved her granddaughters. I was sure she'd say yes. But how could I let Henry's child, a baby created from rape, spend nine months in Patricia's womb, reminding her every day about what her father did to her? May God forgive me, but I could not let this happen. "Does the midwife have a telephone?"

Using a scrap of paper and a stub of a pencil I handed her, Denise wrote the woman's name and number.

"Thank you." I rose and put out my hand, but Denise pulled me in and hugged me. "It'll be okay, Miz Grace."

For a second, I sank into her arms. I let the strain of the last weeks show and ooze out. Then I straightened up, recalled my mantra, and smiled at Denise. "Yes, it will all work out."

But not unless I figured out a way to secure the required funds. In my head, I added up what was left from the sale of our belongings and paying off Mr. Cohen. Not enough. I needed help.

CHAPTER TWENTY

Henry's sister, Mae, lived on 141street in a Bronx lodging house within walking distance of the silk factory where she worked. She lived thriftily and, except for her fellow boarders, alone. No husband, no children.

Dried rose petals and cinnamon sticks scented her tidy room. A bed, dresser, wardrobe, floor mirror, small table, and one chair filled the space. Pictures of the Herbert family sat on top of the dresser covered with lace I made her one Christmas. Easter's framed family photo held a prominent spot.

Although she invited me to meet in the downstairs parlor over a cup of tea, I insisted we speak in private.

We both wore our Sunday church clothes. My best dress, the mauve one that hung to my ankles, was better suited for a cool spring day. I'd taken it in around the waist and bodice. Two months of eating little took its toll. Mae wore a jacket over a white blouse and chestnut brown skirt. It, too, covered her legs and appeared overly heavy for a bright June day.

I'd left Sylvie in charge of the children, promising to return in a few hours, early enough to prepare and serve Sunday dinner. We had no meat, but vegetables and flour biscuits would augment the rice and peas. The butcher gave me a sack of bones for ten cents, so beef broth would start the meal and provide some protein. I splurged on two bottles of milk and didn't dilute them. A treat for our Sunday meal.

"Thank you for seeing me," I said. Mae sat on the edge of her bed, and I perched on the only chair in the room. "How are you?" We'd not seen each other since her previous visit to my home.

"I fear you have more unwelcome news to share," she said in her usual blunt manner. "Are the children well?" Her Jamaican accent was soft and lyrical.

"Patricia continues to fade."

"She'll find her way back," Mae said. "You pamper her too much, so she wallows. Get her up and out."

My back stiffened. How can a mother pamper a wounded child too much? Besides, love and tenderness weren't the same as pampering. Mae spoke from ignorance. People accused my parents of the same. Because my sisters were so much older, I lived as an only child. Both Mother and Father fussed over me. I spent my first four years of life believing I was special.

"Do you deny it?" she asked, as if reading my mind.

I was here on a mission of great import, not to argue about child rearing. After a conscious effort to relax all the muscles of my neck and shoulders, I said, "Thank you for the bag of candies you left for the children. They love them." Mrs. Thompson gave the gift to me when I arrived home from a fitting. A note from Mae accompanied the goodies. Mae was kind and generous, just reserved. The thought gave me pause, since many would say that about me.

"A small thing," she said, but her smile showed her pleasure.

"Lawyer Booth told me you visited Henry."

"Of course, I did. Twice. It broke my heart." She glared at me.

"Did you know he pled guilty–criminally insane?"

"Yes." Her tone remained aggrieved. "Told me you pressed him." Her mouth twitched into a shrug-like expression. "That he begged you to recant."

Since this was all true, I stayed quiet.

In a sad or resigned tone, Mae added, "I said you made sense and encouraged him to relent instead."

My heart swelled. "Thank you. I am beyond grateful."

"For Sylvie and Patience," she said. "And Irene." She lowered her head and plucked at the fabric of her skirt. "Broke my heart, though. He told me about the horrors of jail, and that it was worse for colored men. Beatings, and… ungodly behaviors."

"He'll get better, and they'll let him out."

Mae shook her head. "He told me he'd die in there." She covered her mouth and hiked her shoulders. "Well, it's done. What brings you to me today?"

"The last time we spoke, you offered to help us."

The thick aroma of roasted meat found its way to her room from the kitchen. My stomach rumbled in response. The tea and toast I had before church deserted me long ago. "I don't want to keep you from your dinner," I blurted, hoping she didn't hear the impolite noise. "We need your assistance." I paused. "Urgently."

Her sharp tone returned. "I told you. I have little."

"Yes, of course. I understand… a loan."

She stayed quiet; her Henry-like eyes watched me.

I plunged ahead. "Fifty dollars. I will pay you back as soon as I'm able." Swallowing hard, trying to stave off questions or a refusal, I kept going. "It will take me at least two years, but I will send you two dollars every month. Most months," I amended. "I'm working as a seamstress, but my—"

"Stop." She held up her hand. "Fifty dollars. Why do you need such an incredible sum?"

Curry and other spices I couldn't differentiate mingled with the meat aromas. My stomach growled loud enough this time for Mae to notice. "I'm sorry. It's dinnertime and I must get home and let you eat yours." I rose. "This money is not for me. It's for Patricia. I wouldn't ask idly."

Mae stood as well.

"*Time* is of the essence." I begged her in my mind not to ask me more questions.

She stared at me for a long time. Was she working out the weeks and months, the message in my words? Did she suspect the truth? If so, good. I held my ground and her gaze. Patricia could not have this baby, no matter what it took.

The night after Denise named the extraordinary sum required, I considered returning to the tailor shop. Although the thought gagged me, my dignity meant nothing compared to the further destruction of Patricia. Perhaps meeting Denise let the possibility emerge. But even if I did go back, how many five-dollar nights would add up to the required sum? How long would it take? Henry was my only experience with men's needs, but every day seemed unlikely. I would do anything to save her, but this repugnant idea wasn't viable. Beryl couldn't help me—she'd see it as a grievous sin, never feel the same about me, and wouldn't give me the money. Or, if she did, or if I lied to her about its purpose, our friendship would never be the same. So, I didn't ask her. Mother told me Gram was still alive, but we'd not corresponded in years. Besides, if she wouldn't take us in at our lowest point, why would she help us now? Then I thought of Mae, and a wisp of hope took shape.

Mae turned and opened the top dresser draw. She pulled out her well-worn Bible, and wetting the tip of finger with each turn, flipped through the paper-thin sheets, sighing more than once.

"Here," she said, handing me six pressed-flat, five-dollar bills. "It's everything I have saved."

Tears flooded my eyes. "God bless you, Mae. This will—"

With both hands, she covered her ears like a small child, and cut me off. "Don't tell me what you're going to do."

I swallowed hard and said nothing in response.

She sniffed several times. "During trying times, the devil shows up to test us."

"You don't have to worry," I lied. "I promise to use the money only for good." Not really an untruth. The good would be for Patricia, for her future.

"I'll expect your payment the first of each month," Mae said. Her head dipped. "You can start in September... or later."

I wasn't a teary sort for most of my life. But lately, I cried all the time. My eyes brimmed over. "I promise I will pay you back every dime." I reached for Mae and hugged her.

"Go on now," she said, breaking away. "Like you said. It's dinnertime."

"Yes, it is."

"We can stop in the kitchen on your way out. I'll put up some food for you."

"I couldn't—"

"For the children. Like you said."

The trip home left me breathless. I took the bus and then walked the long distance. A sack of warm food in my hand and thirty dollars in my purse. I still had to find another ten or twenty. Denise might require another dress quickly. I sped up my gait. My children were hungry and so was I. I'd find a way.

CHAPTER TWENTY-ONE

I opened our apartment door to the sounds of laughter. Three little children ran and hid while Sylvie chased after them. Months had passed without these joyful sounds. They swelled my heart.

Andy said, "I'm here," followed by a shower of giggles. The voice came from behind the cotton curtains in the parlor.

"Where is Andy, Mama?" Sylvie said when she saw me standing in the doorway, "Have you seen him?"

"Here I am," a little voice called again, the bulge of his body clearly visible.

"Where?" Sylvie spun around in a circle. "I can't find him?"

Andy thrashed his way out of his hiding spot. "Ta Da."

"Oh, there you are." Sylvie grabbed and tickled him. Her sweet face seemed young again.

George said, "I'm hungry. I don't want to play anymore." His long, narrow countenance, thinner than ever, enlarged his brown eyes. Permanent teeth had yet to replace several missing ones, leaving gaps throughout his mouth. He flopped on the couch. "What smells so good in the bag?"

I asked, "Where is Irene?"

A small head popped up. "I'm good at hiding. Andy makes too much noise."

"She wouldn't let me hide with her," Andy said, giving his sister his best scowl.

"Aunt Mae sent home dinner." I opened the bag, filling the parlor with aromas of curried meat and stewed vegetables.

"Hurray," Andy squealed.

"Let's wash up for supper." Sylvie herded the children into the water closet. Over her shoulder, she said, "I cooked a pot of rice and peas."

"Perfect." I unpinned my hat and pulled off my white Sunday gloves. "Thank you, my darling." The money Mae gave me weighed heavily on my mind. This afternoon's meal would be satisfying, but what about tomorrow? If I didn't give the money to the midwife, Mae's gift could carry us for several months. Then what? Six children to feed and clothe instead of five. A baby to explain to others and Patricia shattered beyond endurance.

I walked into my bedroom after putting the meat and vegetables on the counter. Patricia sat propped up on the bed, two pillows at her back and neck. A glass of lemon-water sat on the tiny table next to the bed, provided no doubt by Sylvie. Patricia's hair looked washed and brushed, the waves and curls smoothed out. Her round face scrubbed and pale.

"How are you today?" I asked, moving toward her.

Sad eyes shifted in my direction.

"Your hair looks pretty."

"Sylvie did it," Patricia said. "I told her not to, but she fixed it anyway." Patricia had begun speaking again. Not a lot and never about the incident.

"Oh. Well, it looks nice." I sat on the edge of the bed, pulled up my legs, and tucked them under me. "We're all going to eat Sunday supper together. Aunt Mae sent home a treat. You love curried chicken and there's broccoli and carrots." I waited for a reaction. The last time we ate meat was when Mrs. Thompson gave us a pot of soup last week, claiming she'd made too much. Despite my embarrassment, I gratefully accepted the food. "Let's get you dressed so you can join us."

"Sylvie says Papa isn't coming home. That he got sick and died." Her big eyes widened. "Is that true?"

I felt at a loss. Lie to her just as I lied to the little ones, to the neighbors? Or tell the truth and reassure her. Let her know I will protect her no matter what. "I'm sorry he hurt you."

She curled up against me, as if trying to fit onto my lap. "Me too."

Flashes from my past, pregnant and scared, reverberated in my head. "You can eat in your pajamas and robe if you like."

She nestled closer. "I'm not hungry."

"Of course, you are." You're eating for two.

"No. I'm tired, and I threw up while you were all at church. Everything makes me vomit."

Each morning, I listened to the heaves, coughs, and flushing of the toilet. I promised myself I wouldn't leave her in the dark the way Mother left me, but here I was, pretending ignorance. A constant diet of secrets, lies, grief, and shame hollowed me out.

CHAPTER TWENTY-TWO

Images of me hanging over the toilet and vomiting pushed forward. Cold bathroom tiles pressed into my knees. Weeks after our honeymoon ended and Mother returned home, I'd been sick every morning.

Henry appeared annoyed. "What's wrong? Are you with child?"

"Please send for Mother."

He scowled at me. "I don't remember my mother vomiting all over the bed when she was pregnant."

Embarrassment colored my face.

Dawn peeked through the white curtains covering windows that faced our vegetable garden, a large plot that I joyfully worked with the cook.

Queasiness sloshed inside my stomach. My head spun, but I stayed still and quiet, not wanting to disturb Henry's sleep. He'd been so angry with me. Another wave of nausea hit me. Bile churned. I ran to the bathroom.

Henry followed me, growling under his breath.

"I want my mother." Vomit splattered on the toilet seat, and some got into my hair and on my nightdress.

"You're disgusting." He slammed out of the room.

Mother arrived the next day. The whites of her eyes looked yellow, like Father's did from malaria. Could she be ill? I studied her. She'd parted her tight hair down the middle and brushed each side against her scalp. Tiny silver earrings, a long ago present from Father, hung from her lobes. I'd not seen her since we returned from our honeymoon.

"How are you?" I asked.

"How *am I*? How are you?" She dropped her satchel on the floor and reached for me. "Let's get you washed up."

I'd vomited again. My waist-length hair hung tangled and dirty, and I smelled. Henry made me move into the extra room. I gladly vacated my marriage bed. Miserable, stinky, sick, scared, I cried myself to sleep the night before. But now Mother would rescue me, take me home, and nurse me back to health.

"I've caught something," I explained. "I don't know what's wrong. Henry says I'm pregnant." I collapsed in her arms.

She cradled and rocked me. "You're going to have a baby in about seven months," she said.

"How did that happen?" I'd seen chickens lay eggs that hatched into babies and witnessed the yard dogs give birth to litters. "How many babies?"

"Just one."

"Why?"

"When a man and woman lay together, after a while, she becomes pregnant. That's what happened to me. That's how Father and I became blessed with you and your sisters." Mother's wide-set eyes looked directly into mine. "I should have explained this to you sooner. I'm sorry."

A baby? I loved playing with dolls. Painted bisque-porcelain faces with rouged cheeks and lipstick. I made them clothes, cared for the wigs that sat on top of their heads and created stories about their adventures. Games involving my two favorites–one I named Carrie and another Nora–revolved around conversations I pretended to have with my big sisters. Baby dolls were uncommon, and I didn't own one.

I sat up. "I don't know how to take care of a baby." This news frightened me. When Henry said it, I thought he was cruel and scaring me. "Please take me home."

"You're a wife now, about to be a mother. This is your home."

"I don't want to be either."

She stood. "Let's get you bathed and wash that hair."

"If I can't go with you, stay here, and take care of me. I hate living here."

"I'm going to ask the maid... what's her name?"

My head dropped to my chest. "Leslie."

"Wait here. I'll ask her to heat water for us."

I sat on a small, cushioned stool, my head still hanging low. Surely, Mother wouldn't leave me again. I knew from family stories that three of her infants, all boys, died, the ones between my older sister Patience and me. "I buried my sons along the Congo River," she said, her voice filled with sadness. What if mine died? I rested my head on the edge of the cast iron, clawfoot tub, its porcelain finish gleaming in the sunlight streaming in from the small window above. I used to have a third doll, but I dropped her on the tiled floor and her face cracked. What if I dropped my baby?

I saw mothers walking to market, a cloth sling holding their babies against their breasts. Once, I witnessed a child sucking his mother's nipple. She saw me watching. "He's a hungry one," she said. Would my breasts be enough to feed a baby? I looked down on them. A month ago, they were small and unremarkable. Now they were plump, with tender nipples. Would sucking them hurt?

Mother bathed me the way she did when I was a little girl. She washed, brushed, and braided my hair.

Clean and dressed, I asked, "What else will happen to me? Besides throwing up all the time."

"Your belly will swell as the baby grows. You've seen many pregnant women."

I realized I had. They wobbled along, toddlers running ahead or clinging to their skirts. I patted my flat stomach and tried to imagine it large and round.

We walked into the kitchen. Mother said, "I will make you a pot of soup."

"Will I be sick until the baby comes?"

"No. Probably not." She washed and then chopped vegetables picked fresh from the garden nearest the kitchen. In the backyard, ackee, mango, and avocado trees shaded a sitting area. The sharp knife sliced through tomatoes and carrots. The onions stung our eyes and caused tears. Next, she opened and sliced two ripe avocados and put them aside. "When your child is ready to come out, you'll know."

"Will I have a boy or a girl? A girl is better."

"Only God knows." Her smile looked strained. "I will come and help you." She slid the vegetables into a large pot, sprinkled herbs, salt, and pepper, in the water, and placed the pot on the stove. "There's plenty of time."

After I told her about the woman and the baby at her breast, Mother explained that I'd make nutritious milk and it would just happen, naturally. It was all quite scary, mystifying, and miraculous.

Henry, Mother, and I sat at the wooden table. They ate an avocado salad, curried meat, and roasted sweet potatoes. The soup Mother made me looked, and I was sure, tasted, just as delicious.

"I will come see you every month," Mother promised. "And perhaps you can visit me as well."

Deep furrows creased Henry's brow.

She smiled. "Grace seems better *now*."

Henry stared at her as if trying to decipher her meaning. I was too. Feeling better because Mother arrived, and sick and disgusting when she was not with me?

Finally, he said, "Yes, monthly visits here and occasional visits there." He bent his head and tucked into his meal.

"You will hire a baby nurse," Mother said in the same pointed tone.

"*Of course*," he said, sounding aggrieved.

Patricia's voice brought me back. "Sylvie told me I'm having a baby."

I tried to keep my face from showing how startled I was. "What else did she say?"

"That's why I throw up all the time." Patricia lifted her head from my bosom and searched my face with her eyes.

Why was I surprised Sylvie figured it out? My smart girl. She saw everything and said little. After several deep breaths, I felt able to respond. "Yes," I said, memories of Mother's explanations and conversations still lingering. "We're going to a doctor soon who will see how you're doing and assist you."

CHAPTER TWENTY-THREE

I made the trip to the Bronx, just north of Harlem, alone. Patricia was too weak and frightened. After walking for over an hour by foot, I caught the IRT subway, and then hiked again to the address Miss Denise gave me. Like sharp slaps across my face, each step slammed me. Wickedness–the word bounced around in my head. Henry's evil, for sure, but mine too.

Mrs. Kline lived in a substantial brick home. Concrete steps led to a vestibule, a large wooden door, and a knocker.

A short, round woman with a toothy smile welcomed me. "You must be Mrs. Herbert," she said, extending her hand and pulling me inside. I'd assumed incorrectly the midwife would be a Negro tending to people in Miss Denise's line of work. Instead, a white woman sporting curly red hair faced me.

"Oh, aren't you a beauty?" Her accent, something I didn't recognize, was as soft as a purr. "No wonder men can't keep their hands off you."

I bristled. "You misunderstand."

"Come in. Have a seat." She ushered me into a charming, light-filled room. Curtains swayed from the breeze floating in and a four-blade ceiling fan whirred above. A glass vase of lilies and irises sat on top of an ornate fireplace mantel. Two old-fashioned Queen Anne chairs faced a modern art déco sofa.

I perched on a tufted chair.

"Tell me what I don't understand."

"I'm seeking your…" I paused, searching for just the right word, "expertise for my thirteen-year-old daughter, not for myself."

"Oh?"

"Molested and pregnant."

I expected a reaction of shock, horror, or worse, judgement, but she clucked her tongue. "Shall we have a cup of tea?" A China tea service and sweet biscuits sat on the walnut table next to the flowers. It reminded me of the porcelain set I'd sold for milk and bread money.

Not waiting for my answer, she poured. "Now, tell me about your daughter. What's her name?"

"Patience." I'm not sure why I used her given name. Like Andy, she was born with chubby cheeks and a full head of straight hair that grew wavy by age two. I loved making her gurgle from tickles and peek-a-boo. Sylvie just started to walk when Patience came. Two infants in nappies. Henry's house painting and repairing business was still making money enough to afford a maid, cook, and baby nurse. Mother came every month and stayed for several days. If Patricia gave birth, she wouldn't even have me, since I'd have to work to feed everyone.

"She's two months gone," I said. Each time I told someone, sharing became easier. Sylvie and Miss Denise knew about the pregnancy, and now Mrs. Kline. I found it much more difficult to tell a friend like Beryl. "Is there something you can…?" I paused, not wanting to offend or get myself in trouble. What if Miss Denise was wrong? I finished my question. "Anything you can do?"

"Yes." She popped a biscuit into her mouth and slurped her tea.

My fears and worries swamped my mind. I was unsure what to say next.

As if reading my thoughts, she said in a soothing tone, "My husband is a physician. He taught me, and our procedure is quite safe."

Women died having abortions. The police arrested abortionists and threw them into prison. "Miss Denise assured me of your reputation," I said.

She tipped her head toward me. "Denise is a good person. I'm hoping her new gentleman will provide her with a better life."

This surprised me. In my experience, white women didn't socialize with Negroes, and educated women shunned prostitutes.

Mrs. Kline poured herself another cup of tea. "Don't you like it?" she asked, eyeing my still full cup. "Do you want sugar?"

"No, thank you." I sipped, longing for a splash of milk.

"Cookie?" She used the American word for a sweet biscuit. "They're quite delicious." Crumbs made patterns on her chest and lap.

I reached across the table and took one but didn't eat it. "Can you describe what will happen?"

Sun rays from the large windows at the front of the house slanted across her face, making her skin and hair glow. "First, we'll try an herbal approach. Then, if the herbal tea doesn't work, we can discuss other options."

Women in Jamaica whispered about herbal brews that made pregnancies disappear, but from what I remembered, they failed more times than not. Still, what a gift that would be. I wouldn't have to bring Patricia here. She'd drink and, as Andy said, "Ta Da."

"What herbs?"

"Parsley root, ginger, chamomile, a recipe passed down from my grandmother to my mom and then to me."

"You've had satisfactory results?"

"Many times." She rose and pulled down the roller blind. "But not always."

When she returned, she sat next to me and reached for my clasped hands. "How did this happen? An aggressive boyfriend?"

Her eyes penetrated mine, looked inside beyond the physical.

I shook my head.

"A stranger?" Her voice rose in indignation.

"Worse," I said. "And I witnessed it."

Plump arms wrapped around me and pulled me closer. "It's going to be okay," she whispered several times in my ear. I sank deeper into this stranger's embrace and rested my head by the crook of her neck. Jasmine perfumed the surrounding air.

We sat together for several minutes. My racing heart slowed. A calmness enveloped me.

I raised my head. "What do I do?"

"Love her. Reassure her. We're going to make this right." She stood. "Give her a cup in the morning, at lunchtime, and again when she goes to bed. It can take a day or work quickly. Everyone is different." She smiled reassuringly. "Your daughter is so young. Her body might not be ready for a pregnancy carried to term and the herbs might give it just the nudge it craves."

It was hard to hope. "If it doesn't work?"

"You get right back here. No time to lose."

Once again, her piercing eyes made me believe she read my every thought, understood my ache and fears.

"How much do I owe you?" Surely, herbs wouldn't cost thirty dollars, which was all I had, Mae's loan.

"No charge," she said. "If we have to take further steps, it will cost, but this is free."

Oh, my. Free. I could use Mae's money to feed my family.

"I'll make a batch now." She hurried out of the room.

Relief and quiet settled around me. Before, I heard children laughing, a robin's call, the rumble of the knife sharpener's wagon on the street, but now all was quiet except for the fan's clunk and whirr. What if I'd chosen not to have one of my children? What if I visited one of the Jamaican women and asked for herbs? How different might my life be today? Shame cramped my gut. I dropped my hand and pressed against my tummy. This was different. Rape. By her father.

"Please, Lord, let this potion work," I whispered aloud. "And please forgive me for wanting it to."

CHAPTER TWENTY-FOUR

I brewed the tea as soon as I arrived home. The midwife instructed to let it steep for at least five minutes and add no milk or sugar. But a splash of honey wouldn't do harm.

Patricia looked and sounded better. She smiled occasionally and ate more at each meal. Her hollowed-out cheeks rounded to their normal shape and size. She'd moved back into her and Sylvie's room.

Miss Denise brought me business from her many friends, and they kept the landlord at bay. We lived on two meatless meals a day. Mr. Cohen's unpaid bill kept me away from his store, but the fresh produce pushcart came by. I dipped into a few of Mae's dollars to purchase vegetables and milk that I continued to water down.

Perhaps survival was possible.

I poured the boiling water over the herbs and looked at the clock, counting the minutes and seconds. The tea steeped for ten minutes, just for good measure. A teaspoon of honey might make it more palatable. I brought it to Patricia's bedside.

"Drink this," I said, handing her the cup and saucer, its painted pink roses and vines muted from years of use. The scent of ginger filled my nostrils. "It will help…" My tongue tripped over the words. "The morning sickness." What might happen if I told her the truth? It was her baby, not mine. Her life.

She took the cup and placed it on the night table. Even though it was only dinner time, she sat braiding her hair for bed.

"What are you reading?" I asked, eyeing the books piled nearby.

"They're Sylvie's." Her fingers moved swiftly through her hair. First one braid, now two. "I like this one." She lifted a volume. *The Book of American Negro Poetry*, edited by Marc Alexander. "The others are boring, but Sylvie said they'd help me pass the time."

Sylvie was my scholar, my reader. She excelled at all her subjects. The nuns encouraged us to apply to Hunter College, the free women's university on Park Avenue between 68th and 69th streets. Academics were the only criteria at Hunter. The school welcomed all religions and races. "Sylvie will make an excellent teacher," Sister Margaret Mary said. I believed Sylvie could do anything she set her mind to do. Her future depended on me doing my part.

Unlike her sister, Patricia was a less inclined student. She wasn't interested in books, music, or sewing, although I taught her how to hem dresses and make simple curtains. Henry often said a husband was the best course for her future. I kept my thoughts about that to myself.

What was certain, however, was a child out of wedlock, giving birth to her sister, would end any future Patricia might have.

"Drink your tea before it gets cold," I said. "You will feel better."

Please let it be true.

· · ·

I lay in bed waiting for the tea to work. It had to. Weariness overcame me. So much anxiety every day. Fear, worry. Was I doing the right thing, asking the best questions, and making sound decisions for the good of my family? Heavy lids. I closed my eyes and my mind drifted back to my first pregnancy and the birth of Sylvie–the same age as Patricia and equally ill-equipped.

My morning sickness subsided, and my belly and breasts swelled. Henry stayed out of my bed and Mother came often. I was happy, happier than I'd been since we returned from the honeymoon.

Sharp pains gripped my stomach like acute indigestion. Liquid slid down my legs. Mother and Henry helped me to bed. Henry sent a maid to fetch the doctor, but Sylvie wasn't waiting. She squeezed out into

Mother's hands. It was over within an hour. The doctor never came, but a baby nurse did. The nurse and Mother took over. They cared for the baby and me. My only role was to feed her. Just as Mother said they would, my plump breasts filled with milk, and Sylvie, barely the size of one of my dolls, ate greedily.

The sound of cries and moans broke into my reverie.

"Mama." Sylvie's voice pierced my sleep fog.

"I'm coming."

I scrambled from my bed, grabbed my robe, and followed the shrieks. Sylvie stood just outside the bathroom. Her gold-flecked eyes filled with what? Misery? Accusation?

Patricia lay on the floor, her white, blood-stained nightdress caught between her legs. Jumbled together, fear, relief, and grief formed a knot in my belly. I'd seen enough miscarriages, experienced them myself. Either the tea worked, or because of her tender age, Patricia's body rejected the pregnancy. Whatever the case, an answer to my prayers and I was thankful.

CHAPTER TWENTY-FIVE

The morning after the miscarriage, I scoured the classified advertisements in *The Herald Tribune* and *The Amsterdam News.* Under "Help Wanted–Female" there were requests for stenographers, a skill I did not possess. A lot more were for domestic help. "Young white girl for general housework at the shore. Immediate." "Middle-aged Irish woman wanted for plain cooking and cleaning." "Wanted for housework in the country. Young. Italian or French."

I had to find a job. Mae's money would keep us through the summer, but then what? The children had to be in school, even if it was not an excellent one. If I found work, Sylvie could take George and Irene to school before she and Patricia walked to theirs. St. Luke's had a Bible school for children Andy's age once a week. The other days… Perhaps Beryl would keep him for me.

I decided to go in person and pass as white, since all the advertisements were for white women. The only solution to the closed doors was passing. I looked white enough and sounded more so. And, as Henry said, "I'll take my white half" to the hiring agencies.

June 11 was a sunny Wednesday, the air warm on its way to hot. After polishing my black shoes, I donned a silver and black short-sleeved cotton dress I re-fashioned, stuffed my purse with white gloves, and headed out to find work.

I walked the mile to the IRT Subway and took it to 42nd Street and the *Avery Employment Agency.*

The man behind the desk reminded me of the banker who insisted Henry sign the withdrawal document. Fiftyish, balding, and potbellied, black ink stained his fingertips.

"I'm seeking a position," I said.

"You're a bit old. Why aren't you married?"

Inside, I bristled, but outwardly I showed no emotion. I kept a slight smile on my face. "Recently widowed."

He clucked his tongue. "The Manhattan and Westchester housewives seek young girls."

My white hair and widowhood made me older than my twenty-seven years, which suited me. But now, it was a problem. "I'm young, strong, and educated."

"Yeah? You sound like a foreigner."

The newspapers featured stories about the clamp down on immigration to America. The government banned Chinese for years and now they limited Japanese and pushed Caribbean people into Harlem. Ellis Island, where my family landed, was closing. I'd not read anything about the desirability, or lack, of people from England.

"British," I said, keeping my tone light and unruffled.

"Well, I need someone younger, and they prefer the French to the English. Less trouble."

The Manhattan Agency was a storefront and the *Prime Agency* operated on the third floor of a dreary office building. "Can you take shorthand?" "Use a typewriter?" "Why not try the restaurants along the avenue looking for waitresses?"

I trudged from establishment to establishment. They offered nothing that would allow me to care for my family. Low salaries and long hours. Henry warned me. Everyone did.

I returned by subway, discouraged, and exhausted. There had to be a way for the children to stay in school, eat wholesome food, and have some joy in their lives. Perhaps if I dyed my hair back to its natural black, the agencies with the better jobs would believe I was young enough. Flappers, the women in too-short dresses, paid salons to color their hair. Besides costing money, people would label me "loose" and unseemly. No one I knew, not even Miss Denise, dyed their hair.

Perspiration bathed my face and seeped from my armpits and down my back. I looked low as I felt. I found a seat in the park and sat.

"You're looking mighty sad."

I looked up into Miss Denise's almond-shaped eyes. "Good afternoon." I'd just thought about her. She sat down next to me. "Poor job seeking results."

She wore a dress I'd made for her, sky-blue with lace at the collar.

"How'd things turn out with your daughter?"

"Good and bad. Thank you again for introducing me to Mrs. Kline. She was kind, and an herbal tea remedy solved our problem."

"And the bad part?"

"She languishes since the molestation."

"She'll heal… eventually."

I nodded. Not in agreement, but in understanding.

"My guy and I are moving."

"Oh… I'm happy for you." Would it be too far for me to sew for her?

"Downtown. In Greenwich Village. His brother is opening a restaurant and we're going to help him."

"That's wonderful."

She shifted the conversation back to me. "What kinda work?"

"I've tried all the agencies with no luck."

"Working for yourself is how to go. Like you do. Why can't you grow your business?"

"I've run out of time." I rose. "Good luck."

"You could do live-in work if you didn't have kids. People hire colored folks for that," she said, standing as well.

I hugged her goodbye. Although she'd been a source for food and rent, I truly wished her well.

I walked home, reflecting on our conversation. Take a live-in position, have a home until things improved, save, and grow my business.

. . .

Beryl arrived, bearing gifts of chicken, eggs, and cheese. "Don't say no," she said, placing the grocery bags on the dining table. "Just until you find work."

"Thank you." What good friends I had. My heart swelled with gratitude. But one can't live on the kindness of others for long. The conversation with Miss Denise stayed with me. Could I make a living with my sewing if I had different customers–affluent housewives, like the ones on the society pages? How would I meet them?

"Is Patricia doing better?"

"Recovering... slowly."

Beryl broke eye contact and ducked her head.

Was I so transparent? Were my secrets and lies so obvious? "With school out for the summer, at least she has her siblings around." But for how long? For a brief time, the plan I formed in my mind would mean separation and heartache.

Beryl unpacked the groceries, and I placed the items in the icebox and pantry. "Did I tell you I was four years old when my parents sent me away?" I asked.

"You never said."

"Andy will be four next March." I whispered this more to myself than to Beryl.

"What are you suggesting?"

"I'm not sure. I haven't thought it through yet."

"Send Andy away?"

Thinking aloud, I said, "My mother knew it was time for me to attend school in England. If I send the little ones away, for a few months, and Patricia, Sylvie, and I found live-in work, we'd save enough to start over." I looked up at Beryl. "Does that make sense?"

Her faced crumbled. "Where would they go? No. You're not thinking clearly." She shook her head. "We'll figure something else out."

Which is what I wanted my parents to do, but they didn't.

CHAPTER TWENTY-SIX

The memory bubbled up with all the feelings intact. Because I was so young and the memories sharp, someone must have told me the story. But whenever I think of it, I remember every detail, sound, and scent.

The day was hot, and the sun burned our skin–Mother's and mine. Sweat glistened on our faces with no breeze to dry it. We were traveling by ship on the Congo River, a small steamer built by Father. Although I wasn't afraid because I was with Father and Mother, I knew danger was near. Not everyone was ready for civilization–the British Baptist Society's idea of it.

The river smelled earthy, like a marsh. The Congo was a life-source for the people who lived along its banks, like we did in Bolobo. People used it for bathing, washing meats and vegetables, and drinking water.

On this day, Mother and I sat on a narrow bench along the interior side of the steamer, the hem of her dress trimmed in grime from walking miles to the river and sloshing up and down muddy banks at each stop. We faced the open port side, protected by wire fencing that edged the ship all the way around. Lifebuoys dotted the wires, ready to save anyone who fell overboard. I sat on her lap, the swaying of the boat the perfect rhythm for rest.

Father stood at the wheel with the captain, both dressed in white pants, shirt, and hat. Sweat dripped under Mother's high collar dress and she said her skin itched from the heavy stockings and sturdy boots– clothes she hated wearing. She often asked Father, "Why can't I dress like a man? I accomplish the work of three." "What would people think, Rose?" he responded, laughing.

Father, Mother, and I steamed along a quiet stretch of the great river. Lush tropical rainforests edged both banks. Monkeys darted from tree to tree. Guinness, one of several hired boys, watched for hippos that swam under the boat and tried to tip it over and for the crocodiles that stayed close, waiting for us, a tasty meal, to tumble into the water. Not that the Graham family would make much of a supper.

Mother and Father were lean, all wiry muscles, bones, and gristle, their physiques the result of working from sunup until darkness. I was barely a morsel worth eating. To this day, I can feel her fingers stroking my hair and then see her touch her own crinkly crown as the ship huffed through the waters. I thought she was beautiful, but she shrugged off compliments. I don't think she believed them.

The Baptist Council charged my parents with establishing and helping maintain schools in the small villages that lined the river and to bring medicines and letters from relatives in neighboring communities. An aunty dictated her message to Mother, who wrote it down and then read it to a niece (and all relatives and friends gathered) in a village fifteen kilometers away. Both Father and Mother knew many native words, and the villagers were learning English.

But then trouble hit.

"Hippos," Guinness shouted from his post.

Father ran from the bridge. His narrow, beard-covered face, all but hiding sapphire eyes under bushy brows, lifted his gaze toward Mother, who waved him away. "We're fine."

"Heave-to," Father shouted into the wind. The skipper swung the wheel hard. Mother clutched me tight. Black steam coughed and screeched from the single smokestack.

"Hang on, Rose," Father said. He joined the helmsman. Together, they pulled the wheel. The ship lurched to the right. Mother stumbled backwards, and I flew out of her arms. Tumbling, my head banged against the deck.

"Gigi," Mother screamed.

Ship-caused waves slapped the sides and spray drenched my face. Mother crawled toward me.

"Rose, is she alright?" Father yelled from the wheel as he and the helmsman steadied the ship.

"Yes, I have her."

The boat righted itself. Years ago, before I was born, the family owned shakier vessels. Father travelled to England and commissioned a new steamer. The ship builders sent the unassembled parts to the continent in eighty crates. It took one-thousand men to carry the crates to the river. The shipbuilder who accompanied the crates died during the crossing. Father taught himself and instructed the men on how to construct the ship. "As sturdy a vessel as they come," he said, and yet the danger was still real.

Drenched from the spray, Mother lifted and carried me to the tiny cabin that sheltered us from the rain. Blood dripped from a gash on my head and Mother staunched it with her handkerchief, all the while cooing to soothe me.

That's the day Mother decided it was time. Time to send me to England. She'd lost four children by then, and she would not lose another. Besides, she knew this day would come. Education was essential, according to both my parents, and England was the best place for me to receive it, just as my big sisters did before me.

Her decision changed my life. I had so many questions. Still do. Why did Mother and Father remain on the river instead of letting Father sail while Mother stayed home with me? Why didn't they both figure out a way to keep me?

Will my children have comparable questions, fears, and hurts?

. . .

On the day of my crossing to England, I remember Mother's face scrunched tight as a fist–the look she had when she held back potent emotions. I can feel the comfort of her bosom, my face nestled between two small mounds, breathing in her scent of sweat on clean skin washed in the barrel outside our home, the river grasses that clung to her long skirts, and the earthy fragrance of Father's pipe tobacco that perfumed us all.

I never saw Father cry. His white skin, tanned from the African sun, covered with a thick blond beard, his one good eye that saw everything. He never told me how he lost his left one. He kept two rows of fake eyes in a wooden chest.

I remembered seeing tears for the first time in his live right eye. The glass one never changed.

Carrie and Nora made this trip to the Walthamstow Hall Girls School in Seven Oaks, outside of London, several times before. For each crossing, Mother accompanied them. This time, she stayed behind.

"We can't afford for me to go, plus our work is at a critical stage." They'd built many schools but needed more trained teachers, so Mother filled in. An outbreak of Yellow Fever killed too many, and a shipment of medicines was due. "I must stay and help. Children are dying." Tears seeped. "It will be an adventure with your sister, and Nora will meet you upon arrival."

None of these explanations and reassurances sounded right, or enough, to my young ears.

At the harbor, Mother crushed me to her. "Say your prayers every night, my sweet Gigi, and I will say a prayer for you." Her body shook against mine.

Eighteen-year-old Carrie kissed Mother and Father on their cheeks and took my hand. Together, we walked towards the ship, a giant steamer with upper and lower decks and chimney stacks already puffing white-grey smoke. Two servants, young men as black as Mother, struggled behind us, lugging filled-to-the brim trunks.

Later, I recalled, or Carrie described the harbor. Shouts from merchants and dock workers loading ships for England, America, and other ports along the African coast. The stench of unwashed, sweating people, animal waste, and the fishy brine of the sea.

But, at the time, I didn't recollect smelling or hearing anything. I barely felt the people pressing against us as we made our way to the German-owned steamer.

"When will I see Mother again?" I asked, terrified the answer was never. "Will Mother forget me?"

"Of course not. And Nora and I will be there too. Now stop tugging." Nora had stayed behind at school to save money.

"No." I twisted away from Carrie's hand. "Mother." My curls, tied in white ribbons, flew behind me and bounced on my shoulders and back. The cotton dress, sent from England by Gram for the voyage, swished around my ankles as I ran.

Mother hurried toward me, and Carrie scurried after me. The three of us met among a swirl of people–black, brown, ivory, and every shade in between. The stink of people bumping into us and the burning coal from the ship collided with Mother's sweet scent.

She grabbed me. I buried my face in her bosom. "Goodbye my Gigi. Please go with Carrie." Her voice was wet and heavy.

Carrie waited until Mother released me, then she hefted me into her arms. "Hush, stop wailing like a wild beast."

Father, at the same spot Mother left him, neither moved nor spoke, but I saw the slump in his shoulders and how low his head hung.

Carrie carried me back to where she left the servants. I clung to her neck, stared over her shoulder at our parents, and wondered why they didn't love me enough to keep me.

The first night at sea, I vomited. The ship rocked and creaked. Carrie, pale and drawn, used a dirty rag one of the crew members gave to mop up my vomit.

"Swallow this peppermint. It will quiet your tummy."

I still do that, suck on a bit of candy or sip peppermint tea when my stomach rebels from a meal, or from stress and worry. It comforts me the way it did during those roiling days at sea.

I grasped her thin frame, wrapped my arms around her legs. "Please take me home. I'll be a good girl. I promise."

"Be a brave girl instead." Her voice scolded, but I saw sadness and pain in her eyes. Or did they smart from the smoke-filled air as the crew prepared a paltry meal of salted fish and vegetable broth?

Did I remember all this, or imagine the scene, or was I piecing the experience together from shared family stories, seen through my little-girl prism?

It didn't matter.

Whether conjured or blurred memories, the remaining ache in the marrow of my bones and depths of my gut was real.

And yet, here I was contemplating–no, deciding to send my babies away just as my parents banished me.

CHAPTER TWENTY-SEVEN

August 1924, Harlem, New York

June breezes gave way to July heat and humidity, reminding me of Kingston. Miss Denise and her gentleman moved away in August. The police crack-down on streetwalkers dried up my business and left unpaid bills. We lived on two meals a day of mostly broth and vegetables, unless Mrs. Thompson, Beryl, or Mae sent home food. My children grew thinner. Just as Mother knew it was time to send me away, I was equally sure. Not forever. Not the seven years of my separation. But I had to settle everyone before the school year began in September, earn enough money for an affordable apartment, and build up enough business sewing for wealthy white women to support my family. That was my new plan. Then I'd get the children back.

At the school in England, I had my big sisters, and Gram lived close enough to visit. Andy, George, and Irene would have each other, and I'd make sure they were close enough for me to see them often.

What might I say to my children that would make them understand, not be afraid, nor as angry with me as I was with my parents, not doubt my love?

I had no way to feed and clothe them. Mother's words repeated themselves in my head. "I had no choice."

• • •

The weight of my decision pressed down on me. Sylvie, Patricia, and I sat around the kitchen table. My mother explained nothing, or at least her explanations felt paltry. I had to do better. Honesty, however, often extracted a high price.

"We're running out of money." I watched their faces and body movements, trying to gauge their reactions. Two fans stirred the stuffy air but did little to cool us. Sweat bathed my face. "My work has dwindled to almost nothing, and I'm late paying the rent and utility bills." Memories of the ride to the Herbert's home in Jamaica, the smell of the dust in my nostrils, caused me to pause. To wait. The girls remained silent. Neither moved. "Aunt Mae lent me thirty dollars, a most generous gift, but there is little left, and beginning in September, I must pay her two dollars a month."

"What are we going to do?" Sylvie asked, clumps of her paisley dress clutched in two fists at her sides, its blue, green, and gold swirls complementing her striking eyes.

"Become domestic workers."

Following the advice of Miss Denise, I approached dear Mrs. Thompson, who offered this lifeline. Several members of her church worked six days a week in Jewish homes in Westchester, the county just north of the Bronx, but a long way from Harlem. The Irish girls refused to work for Jewish families, so they hired Negros. The agency man said I was too old, but Mrs. Thompson assured me the Jewish women would be less picky. I bristled at this remark, an insult to both the Jewish ladies and me, but I thanked her.

"Each of us will seek a position in a respectable home." The words turned my saliva sour.

Patricia, her eyes already moist, asked, "What does a domestic worker do?"

"How will we go to school if we're working all day?" Sylvie asked.

After my wedding and honeymoon and Mother left me with Henry, I still hoped to attend school. In fact, because Henry enjoyed a steady income, I believed I might enroll in a private academy with the other children of Black and mixed-race gentry. I knew how important an education was. Mother urged him and mentioned two of the best private schools in St. Catherine. Pregnancy and motherhood put an end to that dream.

"You're ahead by a year, so dropping out won't be terrible," I explained to Sylvie. "Once we're together again, you can enroll and finish high school, apply to Hunter College, just as we planned." The urgency and pleading in my voice betrayed my lack of confidence. "It will only be for a few months until we can each save enough." The possibility of selling fine dresses and lingerie to the wealthy women of Westchester and others in Manhattan sounded far-fetched at times and an achievable dream at others. "We'd start our own business, like the businesswomen Madame Walker and her daughter."

Sylvie's silent stare cut.

"It will work. You'll see. We'll make it so."

Patricia said, "This is my fault." Tears dribbled out the corners of her eyes.

"No. That's not true. It's my responsibility to take care of you, to protect you."

"Papa made me promise not to tell you. He said you'd leave all of us if you found out."

"Your father is the villain, not you." I rose and walked to her, squatted down. "We'll be together again soon."

Damp, molten-chocolate eyes blinked and searched my face.

"What happens to the little ones while we're living in someone else's house, scrubbing toilets?" Sylvie demanded.

I prayed about this every day. "They'll be with a loving family who will take care of them until—"

Sylvie cut me off. "What home? Auntie Beryl? Auntie Mae?"

"A few months. I promise. I'll reunite us."

She pushed back from her chair, stood, and placed her hands on her narrow hips. "What home?" she repeated.

"I don't know yet."

"Why can't you work harder, make more money?"

The echoes of my childhood confusion and hurt bounced in my head. *Why did you remain on the river instead of letting Father sail while you stayed home? Why didn't you both figure out a way to keep me?*

"I tried, called, showed up at the agency placing female workers, asked every friend and acquaintance."

"You sent Pappa away. This is your fault." Sylvie pointed her finger at me. "And yours." She swung her accusing digit toward her sister. "He told us never to tell. Ever." With sagging shoulders, she swung back to me, wiping her dripping nose and wet cheeks. "He said you'd leave us, and you are. *You* are sending us away, not Pappa."

And there it was. "He told us never to tell." Confirmation of what I'd known was true from the day I found Henry on top of Patricia. "He hurt you both."

Sylvie sucked in a breath.

"What if he hurt Irene?"

Now Sylvie was shaking. In a tortured whisper, she said, "I hate you both. I hate all of you." She spun around and stomped toward her bedroom.

For a long time, I sat, holding Patricia. "It's not your fault. Sylvie doesn't hate you. She's upset." When Patricia stopped sobbing, I helped her to my room and tucked her in. And then I went to comfort Sylvie.

CHAPTER TWENTY-EIGHT

The Foster Home Department and New York Children's Aid Society placed orphans and street children in homes. Police officers swept them up, and the department shipped many, via train, to states out west–Kentucky, Illinois, Nebraska, and Kansas. Children worked on farms for room and board. The department was new, poorly staffed, and didn't require licensing or monitoring foster families. With little screening and almost no follow up, terrible things happened to some, but others became beloved members of a family.

None of these options were acceptable. Only a safe, temporary home in New York City made sense. We belonged together, and I had to get my babies back as quickly as possible.

Reverend Copes, an elderly man with a full head of hair as white as mine, accompanied me to the Foster Home offices. He'd been the Episcopal priest at St. Luke's for over thirty years. This August day, the stifling air made breathing difficult. Reverend Copes and I sat side by side in front of Mrs. Barker's desk. Sweat dripped down my sides. A small electric fan faced the administrator. The Reverend and I received no benefit from its whooshing blades. For a few seconds, the purr of the fan sent me spiraling back to the fan Henry sent us after the visit that doomed me.

"This is a temporary situation," the reverend explained. "Just until Mrs. Herbert can save enough money and bring her children home."

Unlike my circumstance, most of the children placed by the department arrived abandoned or orphaned.

Mrs. Barker sniffed. "I understand," she said, sounding quite the opposite. "However, there is a significant difficulty. We may not be able to... *accommodate* your family."

I wanted to run. This was all wrong. Beryl and Sylvie were right. I shouldn't do this. It took Mother and Father seven years to get me. Andy would be eight if, like a glass of spoiled milk, my history continued to repeat. Before coming here, I felt resolute, confident I was making the right decision for our future. But now...

Mrs. Barker said, "We have very few Negro families able to take children." Her voice reflected the stern, disapproving look on her lined face.

Reverend Copes cleared his throat. "We'd like someone in Manhattan, the Bronx, or Queens," he said. "Places the trains, trollies, or buses reach."

I wasn't sure how I'd get from Westchester, north of the Bronx, where most of the live-in domestic jobs were, to the Bronx or Queens, miles away, but there weren't placements for colored children in the affluent suburbs.

Mrs. Barker sorted through a stack of index cards. Swollen fingers stopped on one and pulled it out. "The Wilson family lives in Flushing, Queens." She read the front and then flipped the card over. "They're Negros, older, in their fifties. They asked about another child."

I rubbed my palms against my dress, leaving damp streaks on the fabric.

The Reverend, whose deep-set eyes searched my face, reached over, and grasped the top of my right hand. "Tell us about the Wilson family," he said. I understood his grip was to keep me from bolting or sliding to the floor in a faint.

Like Judge Wisdom, Mrs. Barker's eyes slid past me. She spoke to the Reverend. "They are fostering a ten-year-old male. Perfect company for the older boy," she said, referring to George. "He's a railroad porter, and she's a homemaker."

"Would they all be in one bedroom?" I was unsure which answer I wanted. Being together might be a comfort. George and the boy having their own room may make my son happy.

Mrs. Barker finally looked at me. "There are three bedrooms," she explained without warmth or empathy. "How they divide them is up to the Wilsons."

"What's the house like? Is there a yard?" When we lived in the Bronx, my babies had grass under their feet. Perhaps Queens was similar.

"The house is spacious enough for another child."

"But we're three."

"Yes, yes. I understand."

Reverend Copes asked, "Are they a church-going family?"

"Methodists." She stayed quiet. Perhaps waiting for an objection. When neither the Reverend nor I spoke, she continued. "I can't insist on Episcopalians. Besides, I'm not sure this is going to work since there'd be three rather than the one, they requested."

"If they agree, may I meet the family first before deciding?"

Mother and Father had a long-standing relationship with the headmistress of Walthamstow Hall. Nora and Carrie attended many years before I arrived.

Mrs. Barker pursed her lips. Wrinkle-slivers framed her mouth. Her eyes shifted back to Reverend Copes.

"This is an unusual case," the Reverend said. "One that suggests special accommodations."

Mrs. Barker's hard stare and damning words pierced my remaining composure. "It's not my place to make it *easier* for her," she said, once again ignoring me. "She's abandoning her children and asking the state to pay for their upkeep."

A sob escaped. Then another. I lifted my head as high as I could and sucked in stale air. "I'm not—"

With a confusing shake of her head, Mrs. Barker interrupted me. "First, there's paperwork to fill out. Once you've completed all the forms to my satisfaction, then we'll see if the Wilsons will take three siblings. If everything is acceptable, you can visit and leave the children. If not, you return home."

She pushed a sheaf of papers toward me and an ink pen. "Start here." She pointed to the first line on the form.

With the papers in my hand, I said, "Surely, they will want to meet the children first."

"Most irregular," Mrs. Barker said. "Not the way we do things." She shook her head again and her glasses slid down her nose. "Fill out the forms. I'll submit them. If approved, I will notify the Wilsons you are coming. The children and you travel to Flushing, visit, decide, and then contact me."

Her tone of voice reminded me of Henry's–so confident they were right. I rarely spoke that way. I nodded my assent, feeling both humiliated and indebted, despite her disapproval and condemnation. But something else brewed and swept through me. Patricia's eyes, Sylvie screaming her pain at me, fanned an anger. It boiled and hissed; its steam clouded my vision. From the terrifying first night, my pregnancies and losses, during all the years of marriage, raising our family together, I'd made peace with my situation. Henry provided for us. The children were happy and healthy, attending good schools. I had friends, my volunteer work at the church, and occasionally evenings at jazz clubs, salons hosting writers of poetry and the newest fiction. A life most would call good, privileged even.

Since the incident, I suffered bouts of sadness, terror-filled dreams, and constant belly-pain. Fear colored each day as I tried to protect my girls and feed my family. Gratitude balanced it to a degree. Beryl, Mae,

Miss Denise, Mrs. Thompson, Mrs. Kline, the members of my church, and Reverend Copes. Even grateful for Lawyer Booth.

But something ripped inside me the morning I found Patricia on the cold tiles of the bathroom floor with her nightgown high on her legs dotted with blood-splatter blooms. Sharp as a penknife's tip, it sliced at the guilt and anguish. And now, on the day I made plans to give my babies away, that wound transformed into a white-hot hate. I understood I had to forgive, but…

I'd told everyone Henry died. Today, sitting in front of this heartless woman, I wished, and may God forgive me, I prayed it would come true.

CHAPTER TWENTY-NINE

Beryl's spotless apartment spoke to her sense of duty and Mac's success. He'd graduated from the prestigious Howard University's school of dentistry and then traveled to Jamaica to marry his childhood sweetheart. He returned to New York with Beryl five months pregnant and joined the practice of a prominent Negro dentist in Harlem. Within a few years, he struck out on his own.

I glanced around with admiration. Large windows, two bedrooms, a spacious kitchen and dining room, and plenty of light streaming in from un-smudged glass. Sepia family photos sat on a piano and potted flowers and herbs graced the windowsills. Although many of his patients bartered for his services, enough paid him and his partner, another Howard graduate, in cash.

Screeches and laughter filled the home. Josh and Nick, twin boys George's age, played a game battling an imaginary villain with toy swords. Saturday afternoons, after Bible Study, I found Beryl and the boys at home without Mac, who worked six days a week.

Beryl said, "Play in your room. Auntie Grace needs a bit of quiet."

With under-their-breath grumbles, they moved their game.

"Thank you," Beryl said with a touch of sarcasm to their retreating backs. She turned to me and spoke in a voice filled with concern. "How are you? How are... have you decided?"

My errand urged me on. "I've come to ask for two favors."

Beryl's eyes widened. She was aware of my dire situation. Of course, not fully. Secrets are for few to know, otherwise it isn't a secret.

"I've made two decisions of great import about the family's immediate future, now that Henry..." I swallowed, gripped the paper-wrapped package on my lap. "Now that Henry can no longer provide for us."

"What do you need? I have a little money stashed away—"

"No," I interrupted. "Thank you, but no." Her response didn't surprise me. A stalwart Jamaican woman, she was always generous. With effort, I settled myself. "I'm placing the little ones in a temporary home in Queens."

Beryl gasped. "What?"

"For as short a time as possible."

"A home? In Queens? I don't understand."

I explained about Mrs. Barker and the Wilsons. My voice cracked several times, the way a teenaged boy might, but I got through my sorrowful tale.

"What about Patricia and Sylvie?"

"We'll each work as domestics."

Beryl's brow and eyes collapsed downward, and her lips compressed.

I waited. With the decision made, my misery subsided. The envisioned end made the burden easier.

She opened her eyes. "Patricia isn't well."

"Yes, it's true." Although Patricia no longer spent hours in bed, she appeared to sleep-walk through the day. A haze hung over her and followed her everywhere. "But I must push ahead. I will find a suitable placement for each of them and one for me."

"How will Patricia manage? She's—"

"There are no other options. I'm doing my best." Again, I swallowed–the effort scratching my dry throat. "It's for a short time."

"How long? I could keep them for weeks. Even a month. The boys can sleep with Mac and me and yours in the boys' room."

Beryl's kindness tested my resolve. "Thank you, but it will be several months." My shoulders slumped. I thought I'd worked through all the sorrow. "Not more than a year." I didn't want to believe a year of separation was possible, but…

Beryl heaved a loud breath. "What did you want to ask me?"

Relief swept through me, flooding all my senses. From our first meeting Beryl and I bolstered each other–through her twins' whooping cough, Mac's early struggles to get his practice under way, and the death of Olive. We celebrated birthdays, piano recitals, and New Year's Eve together. I felt less shaky asking Beryl for a favor than I did going to Mae.

I pulled my handkerchief from my purse and dabbed at my eyes and nose. "Might you and Mac drive us to Queens? It's a long and complicated journey and with three children and their belongings…" My voice trailed off.

"You said two favors. What's the other?" She asked this in a resigned tone tinged with sadness. I couldn't tell if she was agreeing to the first request.

"I'm selling everything and moving before the next month's rent is due." Heat infused my cheeks.

"Selling?"

"Yes, I've found a family who purchases belongings… mostly after someone has died."

"Oh."

I lifted the package on my lap. "This is for you."

Beryl eyed the gift wrapped in brown paper and tied with string.

"I couldn't bear a stranger owning them." I held the parcel in my outstretched arms.

She accepted it, pulled the string, and unwrapped the soft bundle. "Your lace tablecloth and serviettes." Now she looked like she'd cry. There wasn't a time when she visited, she didn't admire the set.

The package rested between us on the table. For several moments we both sat, looking at the lace. I was giving up everything. I lost everything, including my children, just as Henry said I would, as Lawyer Booth predicted, as the white police officers foreshadowed. My head sagged to the right, slowly, as if pulled by an unseen force.

"Grace?"

With difficulty, I lifted my head.

"What did he *do* that's worth all this loss? You said he had an affair. Surely, there are ways to forgive that sort of thing."

I stared at her for several seconds. Her eyes never left mine. "He molested Sylvie and Patricia," I said in a whisper. Beryl was the second person aware of the whole truth. I shared some of it with Miss Denise and the midwife, but until now, only Mae knew Henry raped his daughters.

Beryl's hand covered her mouth and eyes brimmed over. Finally, she said, "I see."

But she couldn't. It is one thing to hear what happened and another to witness it. "I found him on top of Patricia." Saying it aloud once again made it real. "Inside of her."

Beryl came around, crouched down, and hugged me the way Miss Denise did. We stayed like that for a minute. She pulled back. "I'm so sorry to learn this. A girlfriend is one thing. Even money spent on her and not on his children." Her voice shook as she spoke. "But nothing as disgusting as this."

Beryl returned to her seat opposite me.

"Now you understand. The price is high, and I require your help."

"Of course."

"As for the second favor…" After her offer to take the young ones, my confidence increased. "Once we drive the children to Queens, the girls and I will require a place to stay while we seek employment…" I didn't finish. Waited, concentrating on keeping my head upright, its heaviness growing with each second and my eyes–they fluttered about.

Muted squeals from the boys' bedroom seeped in. The tall grandfather clock clicked the passing minutes.

"My in-laws can take the twins. You stay with us. And, of course, we'll drive you. I must check with Mac. But yes, you're my dearest friend."

"And you are mine."

CHAPTER THIRTY

Another portion of my plan required selling our belongings, both for the money and because we must empty the apartment. Mrs. Thompson, who seemed to know everyone in Harlem, gave me the name and address of the Spooner Brothers shop on 127th street, just off Lenox Avenue. They specialized in estate sales after the death of a loved one, but she assured me they also bought from people who were moving or in need of cash.

The August sun beat down on pedestrian-crowded sidewalks. Women wore cool cotton dresses with short sleeves, front pockets, sashes at their waists and wide collars. Men strolled by in suits and overalls.

I scanned the names of the various shops lettered across the glass fronts. Spooner Brothers Goods and Gifts stood in the middle of the block. The detritus of lives ended or gone wrong filled the storefront window. An Upton electric wringer-washing machine stood next to a jewelry display and an Underwood typewriter. I stared in awe. Would my plain items be of interest?

A giant man stepped out before I opened the door. Muscular arms and shoulders, he was as dark as Mother, with a wide nose like Beryl's.

"Afternoon," he said, and then grinned at me. When he smiled, his eyes brightened. "Are you looking for something special today?"

"Yes. Well, not exactly." I stammered rather than spoke like the articulate woman I was.

"Please, come in." He swung the door open and extended his thick arm, gesturing for me to enter. "We have lots of 'not exactly' items."

"Thank you." I looked around the stuffed store, every corner packed with material goods, including beds, sofas, and a sewing machine much older than mine.

"Why are you sad?"

His impertinent question caused me to recoil.

"Sorry, it's just that such a beautiful young woman should laugh and smile. Allow me to introduce myself." He made a little bow. "Jonathan Spooner, at your service."

I dressed up, not wanting to look desperate for money and therefore taken advantage of. If Henry were alive... here... he'd handle the transactions. Of course, it wouldn't be necessary if he were still with us. The cream-colored dress with pearl buttons from the collar to the hem ended just above my low-heeled shoes. Henry told me I looked too pretty to wear it anywhere but at home. The smoke-gray cloche complemented my silver hair and Mother's silver earrings–a wedding gift. I even rouged my lips with the faintest of color.

"Grace Herbert," I said.

"Well, Miss Herbert, what's brought you to our establishment?"

I was about to correct him, but the words didn't come out. "The same reason everyone comes here. To sell belongings."

He laughed. Big teeth crowded his mouth. "If everyone came to sell, we'd be out of business in a month."

A flush warmed my cheeks. "Yes, Of course." I scanned the room again. "All these items must make you sad. Lives ended or forever changed."

"Not true. At least not all." He waved me over to a corner offering baby clothes, a bassinet, and sets of booties. "The family's children outgrew this bounty, and they're happy to move onto the next stage of their lives." He pointed to a stack of books. "Ran out of space, so they cleared out to make room for more. You don't see that every day."

"I see your point."

"Ah, and I get a smile for my trouble."

This man took too many liberties.

"Uh oh." He snapped his fingers. "Just like that, she's stern again."

"Sir, I'm interested in selling my household goods."

"You came to the right place." He cocked his head. "Is it a sadness that brings you?"

I turned to leave. He was rude and too personal and...

"Wait. Don't go." He reached me before I could open the front door. "Tell me what you're selling. Let me get my notebook."

I stood there, debating whether to stay or leave. What choice did I have? While I dithered, he returned.

"Please, let's sit. Tell me about your treasures."

We sat on a "For Sale" moss-green, curved sofa. "What is the procedure?" I asked. "How do you decide what you'll purchase or pay?" I'd sold some items already to neighbors and a church-friend. I took what they offered as long as they promised to tote it away.

"You tell me about your items. If I'm interested, we set an inspection day and make you an offer." His grin and bright eyes beamed at me again. "How does that sound?"

"Fine, thank you." I told him about the living room furniture, bedrooms, and Victrola. "I noticed you sell clothing." A rack of men's suits and lady's dresses and gowns lined one wall.

"I hope you're going to keep the lovely dress you have on."

Heat flushed my face again. "There are suits from my... deceased husband."

"Ah. My condolences."

"From Al & Joe's Men's Wear."

"An excellent establishment." He scribbled in his notebook. "Let's find a time my father and I can come by."

"You and your father decide together? The sign says Spooner Brothers."

"My uncle and dad. But now it's the two of us—Pop and me. He's more the numbers guy. I'm the salesman."

I fidgeted with my gloves and purse. Rose. "Please make the visit soon," I said. "We're moving, not once, but twice."

CHAPTER THIRTY-ONE

Sunday was Mac's only day off. He promised to drive us to meet the Wilsons, the family Mrs. Barker of the Foster Care department identified for us.

Sylvie's face, her eyes squinted, lips and chin thrust forward, tugged at my resolve. "Are you coming?" I asked. Nervous energy kept me moving as I smoothed the spread over my bed and re-fluffed the pillows. "Auntie Beryl and Uncle Mac are driving us in their new car."

She crossed her arms and scowled.

"I fear there are too many." I patted and shook the pillows for the third time. "Probably best if you keep Patricia company." I was prattling and not making much sense.

"Why are you doing this?" The gold flecks in her eyes darkened.

My breath caught. I choked on my words. "You know why." I stopped fussing with the bed linen and straightened up. "I can't keep having this fight with you. It's done."

Her accusing stare pierced my flesh and mirrored every mistake I'd ever made. I sank onto the bed.

"You're sending us away. *You*. No one else. You're making us pay for something we didn't cause."

I was paying too. Couldn't she see? But it wasn't her responsibility to understand.

Irene bounded into the room. "Where are we going?" Spiral curls brushed around the handle of a wooden spoon, bounced, and swayed as she spoke.

"Yes, Mama, tell Irene where you're taking her. Explain it to her so we can all *understand*."

"On a trip," I said to Irene, but my eyes searched Sylvie's.

"Will there be cake when we arrive, like when we visited Aunty Mae?"

I shrugged. "I've packed treats for each of you." With the last of Mae's money, I splurged on sugar, flour, a triangle of cheddar cheese, butter, and tomatoes. Beryl baked a loaf of bread and filled one of the new Thermos Jugs with lemonade. That was something Henry and Mac shared–wanting to possess the latest inventions before everyone else in the neighborhood. The night before, I made ginger biscuits dusted with confectioner's sugar. This morning, I packed cheese, tomato, and butter sandwiches. A fitting extravagance for this devastating day.

George wriggled as I smoothed back his hair and straightened his shirt color. "A trip to where?" he asked.

On my voyage to Walthamstow Hall, Carrie told me about the first time Mother took her to England. "You will make friends and learn."

"Is that what happened to you?" I asked.

"Yes, and no," Carrie said. "There were wonderful books to read. Pianos and violins. Poetry to memorize. But not everyone was kind."

"Why not?"

She gave me a quick hug. "Nora and I were different." The only colored girls in the entire school. "You're lucky because Nora and I will see you every Sunday."

"Only on Sundays?"

With gentle hands, she patted the top of my head. "During the week, you won't miss anyone because you'll be so busy learning new things."

The memory wisp reminded me a week was long for a child to wait.

"It will be fun, but also scary," I said to George and Irene, trying to be truthful and prepare them. "We're going to meet a family and visit their home. You'll stay there for a brief time."

"Two days?" George asked.

Like Sylvie, he was a realist. My practical boy who spoke his mind. "Longer."

"A week?"

"I'll call you every Sunday that we're apart and visit you as often as I'm able."

"How many Sundays?"

"I'm not sure." Tears welled, so I turned my head. "Let's finish getting ready. We don't want to be late."

Andy played with wooden trains on the scatter rug in the children's room. "We can take all your toys. Put them in this bin." I handed him a small crate. The blanket he snuggled for sleeping lay folded on a chair. "Irene, get your dolls and tea set and put them into this pillow sham." I turned to my Georgie. "You can put your toy soldiers on top of Andy's toys."

A knock on the front door made me jump. Everything, a sneeze or cough, sent my heart thudding.

Sylvie answered the door. "It's Auntie Beryl and Uncle Mac." The anger left her voice, but the sadness and dullness of defeat remained.

Beryl's face looked tight and drawn–her visage a mirror of Sylvie's.

"Okay, children. Kiss Sylvie goodbye," I said, keeping my tone light and a smile on my face.

Beryl asked, "Where's Patricia?"

"She's resting." She refused to leave her room. I begged her, but she curled into a ball on the bed.

Sylvie hugged each of the children. "We'll come see you soon." She looked me in the eye. "Isn't that so, Mama?"

"Yes." A few months. Three or four.

. . .

Despite the grim cause for the trip, it felt festive. The five of us, Beryl, the children, and I, clambered down the stairs to the waiting car by the curb. Long and black, it gleamed in the morning sun. Its hood ornament reflected the sunrays, and the two round headlamps looked like watchful eyes.

Their Grandma Moore, Mac's mother, kept the twins while we drove to Queens, and in a few days, when we moved in with Beryl and Mac, Josh and Nick would stay for a week with her. I didn't know how long it would take to find placements. I prayed for a place where Patricia could be with me or, if not, with Sylvie.

Beryl sat next to Mac in the front, and the little ones and I squished into the back with George on one side, Irene in the middle and Andy on my lap, his bin of toys under our feet. Their satchels of clothes and belongings rested in the car's boot.

This was the first time the family traveled by automobile. As we rumbled south, the storefronts and crowded streets of Harlem, colored and some white folks, shoulder to shoulder, gave way to wider avenues and fewer people who looked like us. Shops, some with unfurled American flags waving in the afternoon breeze, abutted each other. Men and women moved along the sidewalks. Cars, not unlike Mac's new one, rolled in front and behind us.

"Kids, have you ever driven across a bridge?" Mac asked, his voice as excited as a child's.

"What's a bridge?" Andy asked.

Before I could respond, Mac jumped in. "A construction marvel that spans the East River and takes us from Manhattan to Queens."

"Like you build with your blocks," I added. "So, your trains can travel under them."

Mac chatted about constructing the bridge, and the five boroughs of New York–Manhattan, Queens, Brooklyn, Staten Island, and the

Bronx. His enthusiasm spread to the children. Thin necks stretched to peer out the windows. The mix of cars became far greater, and horse-pulled carriages scarcer, as we drove further south, seeking the 58th Street entrance to the Queens Borough Bridge. The car rocked each time we bumped over trolley tracks and huffed when waiting for trolleys to pass.

Earlier, Beryl begged me to reconsider. She promised to search for sewing patrons. On Sunday, she brought me ads for the Walker School, teaching young women how to style hair and open their own salons.

"The schools cost money I don't possess," I explained.

"This isn't right," she insisted.

"I agree," I said, "but this is what I must do."

CHAPTER THIRTY-TWO

We pulled in front of the address given to me by Mrs. Barker and climbed out of the car. Even though we were only miles away from Harlem, the air was cooler. Trees shaded both sides of the street.

The two-storied wood frame house sat on a small plot, its neighbors a few yards away. It reminded me of our former home in the Bronx. The pointy roof and short stoop of three steps was different, but the front yard, filled with herbs and plants, looked a lot like this one. Mac, Beryl, the children, and I walked to the front door. Two doorbells indicated an apartment number and the family name below. Number 101, Wilson. I pressed.

"Mama," Andy said. "I have to pee-pee and I'm thirsty."

I rumpled his hair and then re-smoothed it, so he'd look... lovable. A sob lodged in my throat, but I swallowed it before it escaped. "A few more minutes." I looked around at the quiet street. A neighbor watched us from her porch–young, with a baby on her hip and another grasping her skirt. I pressed the buzzer again.

The man who opened the door had mahogany skin, a smallish nose with flaring nostrils, slicked back hair, and protruding ears. "The Herbert family?"

"Yes." I put out my hand, and he shook it. "Grace Herbert." I introduced Beryl and Mac Moore. He told us he was Edward Wilson.

Andy said again, "I have to pee-pee." He clutched his crotch.

"Of course." Mr. Wilson ushered us in. "Peter, show... what's your name, young man?"

"I'm Andy, but really Henriques Andrew Herbert, and so is my papa," Andy said in his big boy voice. The words were intelligible, even though the pronunciation was off. "My father died." Andy paused, as if considering this anew. Henry came up with the nickname. He had an Uncle Andrew and liked how American the shortened version sounded.

"Nice to meet you, Andy. This is Peter. He'll take you to the bathroom."

Peter looked to be George's age, with smallish eyes and cropped hair.

"Thank you." My throat continued to hurt, making speaking difficult. "May I trouble you for a glass of water?"

Mr. Wilson led us into the parlor. A plump sofa, matching chairs, and ornate tables crammed the small room. Heavy drapes framed the windows, blocking any breeze. Perspiration popped out on my forehead and nose. A tabletop fan moved the stifling air around.

"I'll fetch the water and bring in some chairs from the kitchen." He hurried out while we stood.

Shoulders squared, head high, I said, "This is very nice." No one agreed with me. I patted my face with my handkerchief.

The boys returned, and then Peter took the other two children to the toilet. Soon, we all had water and seats, but no discussion.

A tall woman who towered over Mr. Wilson swept into the room. A full-length apron, like the one Mrs. Thompson used, covered a long brown skirt and blouse, both the exact shade of her skin. Narrow framed, a shiny coif of waves framed her heart-shaped face. A frosted cake, slicing knife, forks, small plates, and serviettes all sat on a tray she balanced on her palms. Mr. Wilson brought in a pitcher of lemonade and glasses.

"There's cake," Irene said, clapping her hands.

During the drive, the children consumed the sandwiches and drank most of the lemonade Beryl made. I'd wrapped the ginger biscuits in paper and placed two in each child's pocket.

Mrs. Wilson served everyone. The children gobbled down the sweet and Mac ate most of his, but Beryl and I barely touched ours.

"Well, now," Mrs. Wilson said. "Let's chat."

Esther was a homemaker and Edward a porter working for the railroads. Peter, their foster child for the last two years, attended public school nearby. Esther carried the conversation. She asked the children questions, gave them seconds of the cake, and queried me about their likes and dislikes, daily schedules, and proclivities. Neither the water nor the lemonade did anything to ease my dry, tight throat. Croaked answers, sometimes too short and other times too loquacious, struggled to make her like my darlings. "Irene is very smart, and George is the serious one. Andy, of course, is still a baby."

"At three years old?" Esther asked, her eyebrows as arched as her tone.

"Our baby," I said, embarrassed. "He can use the toilet, but still has occasional accidents."

"I see."

"Will they share a room?"

"Peter and George in one and Irene in a den we've fixed up for her." Her eyes rested on Andy. "He can't stay with us."

"What do you mean?" I lowered the volume of my voice. "Can't stay?"

"As I explained to Mrs. Barker, I have no interest in small children. Irene is too young, but I consented after hearing of your predicament. Managing Andy is too much to ask."

Through this, no one else spoke. George and Irene huddled together in one chair. Andy sat on my lap, his thumb in his mouth. Tears escaped and ran down Beryl's plump cheeks.

"I... I have no way to keep him," I said. My breath turned hot. Clammy sweat bathed my face. "I've not agreed to this."

CHAPTER THIRTY-THREE

I forced myself to stay upright.

Esther said, "Our neighbor, Mrs. Creamer, will take care of Andy. It's all arranged."

"Arranged by who? Is this Mrs. Barker's doing?"

"It's quite settled. You'll like Sallie."

As if on cue, a rap on the front door jolted the air.

Edward let in Mrs. Sallie Creamer–the young woman who'd watched us arrive.

"I don't know her." I shook my head. "Beg your pardon," I said to the new arrival. "But no one explained this to me." Terror swelled up. My children had to stay together. "When did Mrs. Barker discuss taking Andy?" I asked Sallie Creamer.

A wan smile moved across Sallie's youthful face. Her skin was rose brown. She looked no older than twenty. The baby on her hip was nine or ten months and the toddler clinging to her not yet two.

"I've just joined the program. Your boy will be my first."

No one was answering my question. I looked over at Beryl and Mac for support, but neither said nor asked anything.

"She's a widow," Esther said. "Like you. And this is how she's keeping *her* children."

I took several deep breaths to get a rein on my emotions. These women held my children's immediate future and wellbeing in their hands. I tried a different approach. "I'm sorry you lost your husband," I said to Sallie.

She leaned in close to my ear and whispered. "He ran off, but that's what we say to people."

"Oh." More life echoes. Should I have taken in children and kept my own? How much money would a person earn caring for others' children? Not enough?

"Police hot on his trail," she said. "But he's a good person. Just got in a spot of trouble. He'll be back."

Trouble? Police? He'll be back? Andy could not stay with this woman and my doubts grew that Mrs. Barker made this arrangement.

"Is The Foster Home Department paying you for Andy's care?"

Esther jumped in. "I'm paying her from the money they send me. You must understand. I asked for one child and received three. This is a fine arrangement. We're right next door to each other."

I wanted to grab all three children and run. But then what? It is awful to feel beholden and helpless. My only recourse was to get the children back as quickly as possible and stay in constant touch with them.

Mac, looking anxious, said, "I think we should head back." He stood and pulled up Beryl.

I clutched Andy around his middle.

Esther agreed with Mac. "We'll see you next month for a visit?"

A month? No. But I held my tongue. One disagreement at a time.

"Absolutely," Mac said. "I'll drive Mrs. Herbert myself."

"I have to see where Andy will live." My hand dropped to my belly, which grumbled and cramped.

"It's clean and orderly," Esther said.

I stared at Mac, begging him with my eyes. How could I leave without seeing Mrs. Creamer's cleanliness, Andy's bed, and bath? How could I leave under any circumstances?

"We'll wait," Mac said. His tone was grave and uncomfortable.

Beryl, the children, and I followed Sallie to her home. She opened the door and ushered us in. A replica of the Wilsons' in size and design, but it was much airier with no heavy drapes or dark oversized furniture.

"Why is Andy staying here?" asked George.

I had no words of comfort or explanation for him or me.

Sallie said, "Don't worry. I'll treat him like my own." The little girl clinging to Sallie's leg watched me with huge brown eyes. While the empathy in Sallie's voice offered a teaspoon of comfort, the solemn-eyed toddler added to my worry. Shame, guilt, and anxiety swamped me.

Two beds, one above the other, lined one wall in the bedroom, and along the opposite wall a cradle stood.

Sally said, "Andy will sleep on top because he's older." She glanced at me. My face must have shown my thoughts. "He'll be quite safe."

Beryl asked questions I didn't hear–a low buzz behind me. The room swam. Irene and George opened a toy box. They beckoned Andy, but like Sallie's toddler holding onto her mother, Andy clung to my skirt. Lightheadedness rippled in waves. I bit into my lip, breathed through my nose, and repeated my mantra in my head. "I am the daughter of courageous explorers and missionaries. African and English blood provide grit and grace. I will get my children back in weeks, a few months at the most. I will see them every week, despite what Mrs. Wilson thinks is best."

"Mama, I'm speaking to you." George's narrow face and round eyes peered up at me.

"I'm sorry, darling boy. What did you say?"

"Does this mean I won't get a puppy?"

Beryl stepped in and gripped my elbow, her faced streaked with dried tears. "What a wonderful gift to look forward to when you're all together again." She leaned down and kissed George's cheek. "Now, let's get back to the Wilsons so we can say our goodbyes." Her voice sounded thick and strained. "Come, Grace. It's time to go."

The Wilsons stood on their stoop as we trooped back.

"We'll return in a week, just to make sure all is well." When I said this, I realized I was capitulating to the terrible arrangement made behind my back. Hopelessness flooded my core.

"Not wise." Esther folded her hands. "They'll require time to adjust. Your presence will cause difficulties. A month is best."

As if he understood, had followed the conversation, and didn't approve, Andy started wailing his loud, aggrieved noise. That got Irene and Sallie's baby crying as well. Only the toddler and George stayed quiet.

"I will return next Sunday."

Esther pursed her lips but said nothing more.

With an effort honed over the years, I kept my own sobs inside. Still holding Andy now straddled on my hip, I knelt in front of George. Flashes of Carrie holding my hand on the dock, the smell of the brine, filled my mind. "Georgie, my sweet boy, take care of Irene. You're the oldest and Mama is counting on you."

His eyes went wide.

"Obey Mr. and Mrs. Wilson."

"Yes, Mama."

"And comfort Irene when she's frightened or sad."

He rubbed his nose and nodded his head.

"Visit Andy whenever Mrs. Wilson says you can. Ask her."

His lower lip wobbled. "Yes, Mama."

"Say your prayers every night."

He nodded again.

"Mrs. Wilson, may George and Irene visit Andy daily?"

Sallie Creamer jumped in. "Sure," she said. "Mrs. Esther and I are great friends. We speak every day. She gives me advice about my children and the housekeeping. She's been teaching me how to cook. I mean, more dishes than I already know."

I remembered how alone I felt in Jamaica with two babies less than a year apart. And then in the Bronx with a third.

"Plus, my mother-in-law lives upstairs and helps when she can. She works but makes time for me."

Thank goodness. Another adult. "Being able to see and play with each other every day will be a blessing. Thank you." To George, I said, "I'll see you next Sunday." I lowered Andy, and together, we approached Irene. "Be a brave girl." The words echoed from my past. I put her hand into George's. "Mama loves you both so much." I kissed each one before rising. Finally, my legs trembling, I took Andy to Sallie. "His comfort blanket and toys are in that crate inside." I pointed to the box sitting by the ajar front door. "George and Irene will remove theirs and then you can take the crate."

"Don't worry," Sallie said. "Andy will be sad at first, but then we'll have fun. You'll see."

I turned to Mac. "I'm ready." I was not. How could I continue repeating my parents' fraught decisions?

"No need to worry," Esther echoed. "They'll be fine."

"Of course, they will."

My sobs waited until we were in the car–Mac driving, and Beryl sitting in the back with me, holding my hand.

. . .

The ride home was somber. Wind whipped through the open windows, bringing in dust, hot air and noise. What had I done?

Mac said, "I can't promise to bring you here every Sunday."

"I understand." My brain was too clouded with grief to either plead or conjure a different solution.

Beryl said to Mac, "We could on many Sundays, couldn't we?"

"It's my one day off."

"It's fine, I'll find a way," I said. I didn't want my friends fighting over my plight.

Beryl said, "And on the other days, I'm sure there are buses and trains that will carry you here." She squeezed my hand. "We'll help you figure it out."

The car got quiet again and the street noise louder.

Mac asked, "How are you going to find work?"

It took a few seconds to process his question because images of my babies stayed vivid in my mind. "We're to be maids in the homes of others."

I'd answered as if we all had placements. Domestics scrubbing other people's toilets and living in tiny rooms off their kitchens. Each of us in separate houses. Patricia and Sylvie unable to go to school.

"But not for long," I added, lifting my head. "My children will return." I am the daughter of missionaries who fought the Congo River, fended off disease and famine, built schools and water-wells in the middle of the bush. I come from strong British and African stock. "We'll be a family again soon."

. . .

Sylvie, Patricia, and I ate our supper of vegetable stew and bread in silence. We cleared the table, washed, and put away the dishes, as if taking part in a wake without the benefit of friends and family members to comfort us.

"Good night, Mama," Patricia said, shuffling to her shared room.

"Can I ask you something?" Sylvie said.

We both curled up on the couch. I picked up my knitting. "Of course."

"What happens if we all can't find work?"

"We're going to think positively." My needles click-clacked. "And pray."

CHAPTER THIRTY-FOUR

On Monday morning, after leaving Patricia and Sylvie at Beryl's, she and I waited for the Spooner Brothers to appear as agreed. I still felt hungover from the trip to the Wilsons, as if I'd had too much wine at an elaborate, but unhappy, feast. When someone knocked on my door, I found it difficult to move.

Beryl said, "I'll get it."

Two men, both tall and broad-shouldered, entered. "Vincent and Jonathan Spooner," the older one said, holding his fedora in his hands.

Beryl introduced herself. "The lady of the house," she said, pointing to me.

"Grace Herbert." I stretched out my hand. "And you're Vincent?"

"Yes." He shifted his head toward the other man. "That's my son, Jonathan. I believe you two met last week."

Jonathan grinned his big-tooth smile. "Nice to see you again." He dipped his head in the same bowing gesture from our first introduction.

I shook his hand as well.

Vincent was already looking around with a notepad and pencil in his hand. The next blow to my dignity. We needed money to pay back Mae, hold us until our first paydays for jobs I'd yet to secure, start my new business, the one in my head, and put aside for when we'd come together again. How would I replace all the items I was selling? Wherever we lived, we'd need furniture, dishes, pots, and pans. The few treasures I planned to take with me included books Sylvie and I enjoyed reading. Just a few, including the latest from Miss Agatha Christie and a novel that Henry disapproved of because it spoke of colored women having dreams and forging their future–*There Is Confusion* by a woman I admired, and Henry disparaged, Jessie Redmon Fauset.

"Anything in the other rooms?" Vincent asked.

"Beds, wardrobes, and a Victrola." I kept my tone as business-like as possible–as if I were speaking with Miss Denise's friends, making a deal for new frocks.

He walked into each of the bedrooms.

"May I offer you a glass of water?" I asked Jonathan.

Beryl said, "I'll get some for everyone."

Jonathan studied me. When I caught his eye, he cleared his throat. "Sorry. Didn't mean to stare."

It was hard not to smile back. There was something infectious about him, and irritating.

Beryl returned with mismatched glasses filled with water.

"Thanks." Jonathan swallowed a mouthful.

Beryl said, "I'll bring water to your father."

The silence between us felt loud. I had to look up at him because he was so tall. "Would you like a seat?"

"Nah. I'm fine. Where're your kids?"

Another impertinent question.

"Uh oh. I did it again. Made you frown."

"What makes you believe I have children?" A foolish question since much of the furniture for sale made it obvious.

Vincent returned in time to save me from this unnerving conversation.

"You selling the silverware as well?" he asked, pointing to the set spread across newspaper pages on the parquet floor.

Beryl and I were polishing each piece when the men knocked on the door.

I nodded. Before the incident, I'd planned to pass on the flatware, a wedding gift from the Herberts, to Sylvie, and hoped she'd do the same for her firstborn. But now... I eyed the beautiful array, the handles' intricate scrolls curled around the bottom and wound up the sides of each piece–dinner and dessert forks, soup and teaspoons, and steak, fish, and butter knives, serving spoons and forks, and a pie and cake wedged shaped utensil.

Vincent squatted down and lifted a fork, examining it with slitted eyes. "We'll give you $55 for everything. Cash. Now." He made it sound like he was doing me a great favor.

I'd already sold the icebox to my neighbor, Mrs. Salmon. Crystal glasses, stemware and the ivory music box were gone. I took whatever amount the purchasers offered, not understanding what our belongings were worth. But Henry bragged he'd paid $100 for the Victrola, an exorbitant sum. "That seems less than their true value," I said.

Vincent scratched his scruffy beard. "Takes time to sell everything. Have to transport and store it until who knows when someone will want any of it."

Jonathan said, "The Victrola will sell quickly. Luxury item like that in the store window will bring people into the shop."

Vincent gave him a hard stare.

"She's a widow."

My hands ached from squeezing them together. I was not past utter humiliation.

Vincent said, "Okay. $75 for the lot." He turned to his son. "*Best* we can do."

Jonathan flashed his smile. Was this all a show they'd practiced?

Vincent asked, "That Singer work?" He pointed his finger toward my sewing machine.

"No," I said too loudly. "I mean, yes, but it's not for sale." The machine was our lifeline, the means to earning enough money to live on our own. And, in the meantime, I could make extra wages sewing for the unknown family who'd hire me.

"I thought you were selling it." He scribbled on his pad and looked up. "$65."

"One hundred," I said, startling myself. "And you can have our entire record collection as well. Some of the most popular jazz artists." I turned. "Let me show you."

Vincent grunted and shook his head as if saying no, but he and Jonathan followed me. I opened the crate of records I'd planned to give Mac and Beryl as another thank you. Vincent flipped through the stack, rose.

Jonathan said, "It's a good deal, Pop. I'll sell the Victrola and records within a week. You'll see."

Watching Vincent stare at his notebook, I was about to take the $75 offered before he deducted the money for my Singer, but he stuck out his hand before I spoke. "Deal. $100. When do you vacate? Can we take some of the load now?"

One hundred dollars in my pocket. I sold my children's inheritance, almost every item I held dear. Beautiful belongings, but they lacked value since they couldn't keep my family safe, fed, or sheltered.

Two other men joined the Spooners and, together, they shouldered, tugged, hefted, and dragged everything I owned except my sewing machine out the front door and down the steps. They even wrapped and packed the water glasses we'd just used. When the apartment was empty, Jonathan returned. His face shone with sweat and ropy veins bulged along his neck and arms.

"Thank you for your help," I said. Because of him, I had one hundred dollars in my pocket instead of seventy-five. "You stood up for me."

"My absolute pleasure." He did his bow thing again. "If you need any more assistance… moving from where you're going, or to a place you're going to next…" He pulled out a card from his breast pocket and handed it to me. "Just call me, no charge. Happy to help."

I thanked him again and walked him to the door.

"Or," he said. "If you just want me to irritate you, I'd come right over." He laughed, turned, and bounded down the steps.

"Hmph," Beryl said. "That man was flirting with you."

"I noticed."

"Doesn't he understand Henry just died? I mean, that's what everyone believes. He knows no different. Shame on him."

I looked down at his card in my hand. "He offered to help us if we needed it. For free."

"You are a young and beautiful woman. Trust me. It won't be free."

I regarded his business card again. "You're right, I'm sure." And just as I did with Henry's knife, I tucked it into my skirt pocket.

CHAPTER THIRTY-FIVE

Fordham Road in the Bronx ran west-east from the Harlem River to Bronx Park. Trolleys, autos, and bicycle riders trundled by. A horse pulled a street-cleaning wagon overflowing with garbage. Wending along the busy thoroughfare, heading east past dozens of small shops, Patricia, Sylvie, and I trudged, heads down. The August sun beat down on us, and the heaviness of purpose slowed our steps even more.

At the gathering spot, clumps of colored women stood or sat, each clutching satchels or stuffed paper bags. Cars approached, and the occupants inspected each woman before selecting one or two, mostly for day work. The scrutiny seemed invasive, degrading, as if the women were animals or on the slave-block for sale. Rarely were women chosen for live-in work.

I couldn't accept a position without the girls having one too, so I stood by them, examined the drivers and passengers, and made an assessment, just as they judged us. Except I had nothing to go by, and no leverage or alternatives.

As soon as we moved in with Beryl and Mac, I'd scouted the location, taking the train and bus, and then walking. The dark-skinned women, the fewest in numbers, stood together on one street corner. Women with lighter coloring stood alone, scattered about. Miss Denise warned me that some were looking for "my type of work." But I didn't see anyone soliciting for paid sexual favors.

I approached one of the waiting women, who smiled at me. The unsteady, tar-stained crate she sat on wobbled whenever she shifted her weight.

"Hello."

Her head dipped in a quick nod.

"My daughters and I are seeking live-in work, and I was told this is a good place to find it." I forced a smile and kept my hands steady by gripping them.

"Don't know about good," the squat woman said.

"What type of work are *you* interested in?"

"Whatever. I got kids and no man, so…" She shrugged. "That fancy accent will land you a place. The Jews hire us. The white women want French and English but settle for Irish and find them through agencies and Help Wanted ads."

"Why do Jewish families hire coloreds?"

"Because the Irish won't work for them, and the white women don't want us."

The bigotry of people confused me. Weren't Jewish women white? In Jamaica, there were prejudices, but Henry's Jewish clan did well. Shades of black and brown mattered. The darker you were, the more difficult your journey. It all made little sense to me. Looking around, I said, "So many are here already."

"It's best to come by 8:00 a.m. for day work."

"We require places to live." I flushed with embarrassment.

"Then the afternoon, like now, is smart. The men leave their offices and drive their women over. I arrive early to get a suitable spot. Have nowhere else to be." She made a shooing gesture. "Here they come. Git. Don't stand next to me."

I stepped back and watched. Cars drove up. Men in the driver's seat and women next to them. Many with children in the back. The adults leaned out the sides as the automobiles cruised by. Some hopeful workers spoke to the people in the cars. The "shoppers" scrutinized the ones leaning in. Would they check teeth, squeeze breasts?

I fled.

Yet here I was, back. We dressed carefully and, just in case, each carried laundered clothes and toiletries, a butter sandwich, and an apple tucked into a cloth bag.

A green car rolled by, roomier than Mac's. The driver appeared to be my age, in his late twenties. A grey fedora, less battered than the one Vincent Spooner wore, slouched over one eye. His wife seemed younger, a girl Sallie Creamer's age. An expensive wig framed a narrow face. When the sun hit the grey silk of her dress, the fabric shimmered. They stopped, and the woman beckoned me.

"You don't look Irish," she said without even a proper introduction. Long thick lashes fringed wide-set eyes. A tiny scar above her right brow added interest to a comely face.

I realized she thought I was white. "I'm not."

"Oh." Her previously bored tone became animated. "You're British?"

"Yes."

"Why are you here? Agencies would place you in a few minutes."

The woman said this with some bitterness, which I understood. All the hierarchies of race were hard to both fathom and keep up with. So much hate based on such ridiculous criteria kept one off balance.

"I had no luck with the agencies," I said. Of course, I should have explained I'm colored. Not sure why I didn't.

"Are you seeking day work or live-in?"

"Live-in."

The woman swiveled toward her husband. "I've truly wanted a lady's maid since forever." The statement sounded like a toddler's request, an excited plea to a parent. "She's a wonderful find."

Her husband looked at me from the corners of his eyes. "If she's so great, why didn't the agencies want her?"

"Please."

Without making eye contact with me, he said, "Okay," in the way one might concede to a child asking for a scoop of ice cream before dinner. "If someone reputable can vouch for her."

Although he didn't ask me directly, I said, "My Episcopal priest. He's known us for many years."

The wife turned back to me. "We're Jewish." She waited a beat and so did I. "Is that a problem?"

"Not for me," I said.

"Can you start at once? We live north of here in Pelham. It's a big house. Everyone tells me how beautiful it is. You'd have your own room and bath."

She knew nothing about me, but appeared to judge me by my accent, skin color, or my clothes, and carriage. "Lovely," I said.

A lady's maid sounded better than a charwoman. Better, but still awful. In Jamaica, others cared for us. In America, when Henry was… alive, I did all the housework, but for my family, not strangers. I stopped these selfish and indulgent thoughts. The girls' situation could easily be worse with children to tend and teach, along with cooking and cleaning. Nor did I have any idea about the duties of a lady's maid. Nevertheless, I swallowed to moisten my throat, and replied, "I can't leave until my daughters secure satisfactory placements."

"Daughters?" She pulled back as if slapped.

"Two–ages thirteen and fourteen. They seek live-in work as well." The disapproval on the woman's face caused me to speak faster. "Both are smart, educated, and hardworking." Each word scraped my throat and stung my tongue.

The woman slumped against her car seat. "I don't need *all* of you."

I rushed on. "They're both good with children. Perhaps positions as governesses," I said, pointing to my girls, standing side by side, holding hands. "The oldest speaks a bit of French, and they both play the piano." Sylvie had the strength to manage being away from me. But Patricia…? "Might you employ two of us?"

"They're colored," she said, sounding incredulous.

"Yes."

"You're colored?"

"Yes," I said again and then repeated her question to me. "Is that a problem?"

"I just thought you were British."

Her husband wanted to know why I was standing on a street corner seeking employment, well now they both understood. I wanted to run.

"Where in Britain are you from?" I heard a hopefulness in her question.

"My father's family lived in Cornwall and then moved to Birmingham."

She frowned at me.

"I attended school at Walthamstow Hall in Sevenoaks, Kent, just outside of London."

"London." Her face brightened. "Were your daughters born there as well?" The anticipatory tone returned.

This intimate conversation happening on the sidewalk between two strangers astounded me. She was shopping, and I was for purchase. Each step on this journey was a tumble from respectability.

"What about your husband?" she asked without waiting for me to speak. "Are you married?" Now I heard judgement.

"He died."

"A widow." She turned to her husband as if this was a desirable happenstance. "We *must* hire her. No one need know she's a Negro."

The husband heaved his shoulders. This time he looked me up and down before patting his wife's arm and speaking across her. "I can *try* to find something for your daughters among our friends and acquaintances. Can't promise. You say they can read?"

"And write and play several instruments." I hoped the sarcasm I tried to hide didn't come out.

With a bit of impatience and long suffering in his voice, he said, "Give me a few days. Do you have a phone?"

His wife clapped her hands the way Irene did.

Time was a luxury. And our stay with Mac and Beryl grew more uncomfortable each day. The twins would soon return from their grandmother's home. "Let me write it down." I printed my name and Beryl's number.

The woman spoke again. "We're the Jacobs…" She glanced at the paper in her hand. "Grace."

"I look forward to hearing from you." Hopeful, but also more frightened than I'd ever been.

CHAPTER THIRTY-SIX

On the Monday after I left my children with strangers, I called Mrs. Wilson from Beryl's home. Beryl's living room had two comfortable sofas and several chairs arranged for conversation. Too nervous to sit, I held the candlestick portion of the phone close to my mouth, and the other to my right ear, and waited for the operator to connect us.

Mrs. Wilson answered. "Afternoon. With whom am I speaking?"

"It's Grace. I hope you're enjoying this beautiful day," I said, keeping my tone light.

"You've caught me scrubbing the clothes of three children."

Ignoring her annoyed and rude attitude, I plunged ahead. "I won't keep you. Please let me speak with George first."

"The children are outside playing." Her tone continued to hold a sharp edge.

I sat and tried to quiet the anxiety surging up. "Please call them in. I'm sure they'll be happy to speak with their mama."

"I'm hanging up. You're going to upset them. I told you. Give us a month."

The operator informed me my party hung up but there was no need. I heard. With shaky hands holding the phone, I asked the operator to reconnect us. "Your party is not picking up," the operator explained. "Please try again later."

Surely, the officials would not approve of a foster mother keeping an actual one from speaking with her children. Should I visit Mrs.

Barker again? Demand she chastise Mrs. Wilson and force her to let me speak with and visit my children.

Beryl popped her head in. "Everything all right?"

I shook my head. Everything was the opposite of fine. Beryl sat next to me as I tried Mrs. Creamer. My voice shook with emotion. "How are you and your family?"

"Very well, thank you. You sound upset." Babies cried in the background. "Oh, they're having a fit. Hungry and wet. What do you want?"

"How is Andy? I'd like to speak with him." The cries grew louder and more demanding. "A quick hello."

"Mrs. Wilson won't like that. She said no contact for a month. But he's okay. So well mannered. I wish my kids…" The cries turned into screeches. "Bye." The call disconnected.

Beryl asked, "What did she say?"

"Andy's fine, but Mrs. Wilson rules. No contact." Fury welled up. "If Mac is able, even if he isn't, I'm going there on Sunday."

Although I telephoned several more times, neither Esther nor Sallie allowed me to speak with my children. Numb most of the week, I helped Beryl with her chores and kept the girls busy. We knitted, read, and played Dominos. We hadn't heard from the Jacobs, and our week was almost up. Saturday evening, I asked Mac how we could travel by train, bus, or trolley to Queens. Before he could answer, the telephone rang.

True to his word, it was Samuel Jacobs. He found placements for both girls. One in the Bronx, and one in Yonkers, only a few miles from the Jacobs' home in Pelham.

This was exciting and sad news. The final scattering of my family, but also the first step in earning enough money to come together again.

"Yonkers is perfect for Patricia and I'm sure Sylvie will do well in the Bronx," I said. Pelham and Yonkers abutted each other, making getting to Patricia easier. Did public transportation exist in the suburbs? If yes, I could visit Patricia during the week after we'd both finished our chores.

"No. It's all set," Samuel said. "The Fishers believe thirteen is too young. They were hoping for someone at least sixteen, but I convinced them..." he paused. "Based on *your* description, that Sylvie is quite mature and educated for her age."

"But Patricia—"

"I've gone out of my way for you. For my wife. If you don't want to work for us, fine." He sounded angry.

"Thank you. The arrangement is fine. I appreciate all you're doing for us."

"Okay then." He cleared his throat and then did it again. "The Fishers are away. They return in a few weeks."

"What happens to Sylvie until then?" Alarm must have come back into my voice.

"Calm down. She can stay with you in the meantime."

This was what I wanted for Patricia–extra time together to ease her into the new arrangement.

When he didn't ring off, I asked, "Is there something else?"

"There is." Another nervous cough. "Mrs. Jacobs would like you to send the girl up by herself. Without you or your other child."

"What? I must see where she's working and help settle her."

"Mrs. Jacobs would rather you didn't. I don't care that you're colored, but my wife... She wants her friends to think..."

Sweet Jesus. He wanted me to dump my girl so his wife could lie about my race. "I'm not sending my daughter upstairs alone."

The silence that followed was loud enough for me to hear him thinking and weighing my words. If we lost these placements, I didn't know what I'd do next. "Surely, as a father, you understand?"

Still no response. My heart rate sped up and my gut clenched. "She's thirteen. A child."

"Okay." He hung up.

I'd lost control of my circumstances–Sallie Creamer took Andy, Mrs. Wilson not letting me speak with my children and denying me visitation, and Patricia working the farthest away. Alone. And now my employer wanted me to pass.

Beryl asked, "You're ashen. Is everything okay?"

"No." I sat down and tried to manage all the angst swirling inside of me. "Yes. I'm fine." My lips moved into a tight smile. "We're to start first thing in the morning." Which meant I couldn't keep my promise to visit the children on Sunday.

.   .   .

Sunday morning, August 24, was a bright day with scudding clouds. The humidity was as high as the temperature. Fans kept the apartment cool, and Mac graciously offered to drive us to the Bronx. Not to Flushing as I'd hoped, but to Patricia's place of employment.

Mac grabbed our belongings. "I'll load the car while you have your goodbyes." He lugged them all out the front door.

"I'll ride with you." Beryl patted my back.

"No need but thank you." I thought staying positive with Mac was doable, but more difficult with Beryl, who understood me so well.

Beryl nodded her head, but her eyes appeared moist. "Call me. Let me know how things are going." She paused. "Will they let you make phone calls?"

An excellent question. How else would I speak with the small ones during the week?

As if reading my mind, Beryl said, "You'll need to give Mrs. Wilson and Creamer your new address and phone number and let them know you're not coming today."

"She won't care." I know I sounded angry. "Sorry. It's just so much."

Beryl leaned into me. "It's temporary."

What was the definition of temporary? Months? A year? Longer? Another detail popped into my mind. "I must tell Mother how to reach me. May I give her your address? I don't want her to fret." How would I explain all of us in different homes? Better to say we're staying with a dear friend. "And we'll visit the children next Sunday, no matter what that awful woman demands."

Beryl cast her eyes down before raising them to meet mine. "I'm unsure if Mac can drive you."

He'd said as much. "Really, don't worry about us. We'll find our way there."

"I'll try not to, but it won't be easy."

Beryl hugged each of us goodbye. Patricia's eyes appeared dull and the slump to her shoulders added to her ill appearance. Sylvie's lips made a grim, straight line.

Mac returned. "Ready?" He eyed the sewing machine tucked in a corner of their parlor.

"I'll come back for it." How or when, I didn't know.

The front seat of Mac's auto was comfortable. Patricia and Sylvie sat in the back. The car rolled forward and quickly blended in with other vehicles, pushcarts, buggies, and pedestrians that crowded Harlem's streets.

Patricia asked, "What are they like?"

"I've not met them, but I'm sure they're nice." How could I be certain? What if we didn't like them? Once again, my alternatives seemed nonexistent.

"You'll visit me on Sunday? Even if Uncle Mac can't drive you?"

"Yes, absolutely." There must be a way to get from Pelham to the Bronx and then to Flushing. I'd figure it out.

CHAPTER THIRTY-SEVEN

The Grand Concourse in the Bronx was a wide, tree-lined boulevard that stretched over five miles north, from Bronx Borough Hall at 161st Street to Van Cortlandt Park. Apartment buildings, six stories high with broad terraced entrance ways, stood on each side of the roadway. Finished in 1907, the French architect modeled the concourse after the Avenue des Champs-Élysées in Paris. Upwardly mobile Jewish and Italian families escaping the congestion of Manhattan moved into the art déco buildings.

The drive from Harlem gave me a chance to imagine how I might visit Patricia. The IRT Jerome Avenue Line stood a few blocks away, and a double-decker bus caused us to wait for it to rumble by before proceeding. All signs of hope for transportation.

Cora and Noah Perlman's building stood on the corner of McClellan and the Concourse. The family lived on the second floor in a three-bedroom unit. Patricia would sleep in the nursery with the two youngest–six months and two. The older children–Jamie, age eight, Ezra age, seven, and Florence, shared a room.

Mac dropped us off. "You're sure you'll be, okay? Don't need me to get you to your next stop?"

We had all our belongings with us. "Mrs. Jacobs assured me we'll be in her capable hands." I surprised myself by leaning over and kissing his shaved cheek. Mac was not a demonstrative man, and, except for my recent and constant crying, neither was I. "We so appreciate you and Beryl. Thank you for everything."

Mac squirmed a bit in his seat. "I wish it were more."

Satchels in hand, we scrambled out of his car, waited, waving, until Mac drove off. We walked through the front doors. Everything about the building was modern. Geometric shapes in browns and golds decorated the tile floor. A huge circular fixture hung from the ceiling, providing light. Everything gleamed and shouted, new and tasteful. The three of us eyed the self-service Otis elevator.

"Do we want to try it?" I asked the girls. Patricia shook her head, but Sylvie slid the iron cascading gate open, and we stepped inside, closed the gate, and selected the second floor. With groans and clicks, it took us up.

We rang the Perlman's bell and Dahlia Jacobs answered as if this were her home.

"Oh. Didn't my husband tell you to send the girl up alone?" She darted a glance over her shoulder.

A woman's voice called from inside the apartment. "Come in. Right on time."

Dahlia's flawless skin, eggshell white, glowed with youth and health. Her cotton dress hung modestly. With her face scrunched with annoyance, she ushered us in and made introductions. "This is my lady's maid, Grace. The one I told you about," she said to Cora. Dahlia lowered her voice to a whisper, as if saying the next words would curse all who heard them. "A recent widow."

Cora held a baby wrapped in a blanket. Nearby, a toddler banged a wooden spoon against an empty bowl. "Nice to meet you."

"She's the girl's... guardian." Dahlia shot a look at me. I chose not to correct her.

"Joseph, stop that." Cora said from her spot on the gold and brown sofa, the colors matching the tiles in the hallway and lobby.

The toddler banged louder.

I tugged Patricia's hand, pulling her next to me. "This is Patricia. She's kind, and smart."

"Is she a hard worker?" Cora shifted the baby. "Gabe is hungry. I'll need to feed him in a few minutes before he cries." She turned toward the little boy on the floor. "Joseph, I said stop it."

Did making her bed and helping with the dishes count as industry? "Yes," I said, answering Cora's earlier question.

"Good, because I can't keep up with all I have to do." Cora didn't offer us a seat. "During the day, there is washing and ironing, dusting, and cleaning. When the children come home from school, they need to washup, eat, and do their French and piano lessons."

Alarmed, I said, "Patricia doesn't speak French. Her sister does." I pointed to Sylvie, who dipped her head in acknowledgement.

"Oh."

Dahlia jumped in. "Sylvie has a position with the Fishers. They were quite insistent." She turned to me. "Didn't you tell me Patricia plays the piano beautifully?"

"Indeed." A stretch of the truth just like the question about working hard, but good enough to help three young ones.

Cora's lips pursed and brow crinkled. Joseph banged on the wood floors before returning to his bowl.

Dahlia pressed. "Housework and helping Jamie, Ezra, and Florence with their lessons while you tend to your youngest will be an immense help, don't you think? And Patricia will be with the babies at night so you can sleep."

Patricia reached for my hand and took it, the way she did when she was Andy's age.

"Yes, you're right." The infant, Gabe, fussed. Cora bounced him in her arms. "I'm exhausted all the time." Dark smudges circled pale blue eyes.

"This is an *excellent* arrangement," Dahlia said.

I wanted to ask, *May I inspect Patricia's room? Which days will she have off? What happens if she's ill?*

Dahlia spoke before I could. "I'll give the girl a quick tour and then we must go."

Sylvie leaned close to my ear. "Did you notice all the books?"

Filled bookshelves lined every wall. In fact, there were books piled on top of others, stacked on the floor in corners and on tabletops. One more reason the Perlman household was a better fit for Sylvie. I prayed the Jacobs and Fishers were also scholarly. "Who is the reader in the house?" I asked Cora as we all trooped through the apartment.

"Why, everyone, of course," Cora said, rocking Gabe, whose fuss turned into a cry.

Toys scattered across the floors made an obstacle course. We peeked into each room and found rumpled beds, the covers lumpy and askew, and cereal bowls still on the kitchen table, all underscoring Cora's declaration she required help.

"I'd like to look at the nursery, please," I said when the tour appeared over. Did they have a bed for her and a wardrobe for her clothes? And where was the loo?

The nursery was spacious, with two iron cribs painted white, and a narrow bed against the opposite wall.

"So, we're all set." Dahlia said as she steered us toward the entranceway. "I must get Grace settled. Ivan is waiting for us downstairs."

Ivan?

Joseph, the toddler, took his spoon and slammed it into his mother's knee. "Stop." She snatched the utensil from his fist. Joseph screamed, threw himself down on the floor face first, kicked his chubby legs, and howled. As if the surrounding drama didn't exist, Cora smiled. "Thank you, Dahlia. You and Samuel are so good to us."

"My pleasure," Dahlia said.

Joseph yelled louder.

Cora lifted a glass of water from a table within reach and poured it over the back of the child's head, flattening his reddish-brown curls.

I gasped.

Sylvie made a sound on the edge of a laugh.

Not moving, the boy fell silent, a pool of water around him.

Hand covering the pearls at her neck, Dahlia said in a strangled tone, "We're all set, then." She turned to Patricia. "Welcome to your new home."

Patricia's fingers dug into my palms.

"May we step into the hall for a private goodbye?" I asked.

Both Cora and Dahlia appeared confused.

"She's thirteen," I explained.

They still looked quizzical. "This is the first time we've been apart." And she's healing from trauma, scared, hurt and angry, and she just witnessed… what? I glanced back at Joseph, who now sat next to his mother sucking his thumb, as she dried his hair with a cloth. Even the baby stopped crying.

In the hallway, I took Patricia's face in my hands. "I will get us out of this, but for now, I need you to try your best. Please, darling girl, it won't be long. Months." I'd said this so many times and with each saying, I doubted more. How would I ever fix this?

"I don't like it here. She's not a nice person."

"She is. She just needs your help. Then everything will be better. You're so good with Andy."

"Andy never behaved like *that* boy. Don't make me stay."

"I must." I pulled Patricia close, hugged and kissed her.

Dahlia and Sylvie stepped into the hall. "Time to go." Dahlia said. "Ivan is waiting, and Samuel will be home soon."

Patricia stared at me, her molten brown eyes digging into my soul. We left her dazed and oh, so sad, which is how I felt.

CHAPTER THIRTY-EIGHT

Pelham, NY August 1924

Ivan, the portly Negro chauffer and handyman, drove Dahlia, Sylvie, and me north, leaving trains, trolleys, and noise behind. Pelham, where the Jacobs lived, was a grassy haven of single-family homes with wide lawns and trees older than the town.

The car stopped in front of a grand house–far grander than any home I'd known except for Gram's in England. And that was a long-time-ago memory. Perhaps the Pelham house was more palatial.

The Long Island Sound, a tributary of the Atlantic Ocean, served as Dahlia and Samuel's backyard. Three stories high, with an attic and basement, the house was wide enough for the first floor to contain the kitchen, pantry, dining room, sunroom, parlor, library, and music room. A governess's bedroom, nursery, children's bedrooms, and a playroom, for babies yet to be born, spread across the second floor and a suite of adult bedrooms occupied the third.

A chauffeur and a mansion–it left me in awe.

Dahlia showed me to my room, a space just big enough for a bed, vanity, and wardrobe, off the bright kitchen. A small water closet with a toilet and bath abutted my room. Until the Fishers returned, Sylvie and I were to share the narrow bed, much like the one Patricia would sleep in.

That night, I slept fitfully, bumping into Sylvie when I turned and turned again. I dreamt about my first night in Walthamstow. Now, like then, too afraid to sleep, too sad, and exhausted. Near daybreak, I dropped into a deep sleep.

. . .

Monday morning, Ivan, his wife Lotus, the cook, Sylvie, and I sat, sharing breakfast in the kitchen. What a magnificent space. A collage of windows at one end of the room–panels, arches, and ovals–filled the space with light. Cabinets lined each wall with the stove and icebox crammed against them. The Jacobs even had a modern Kitchen Aid Food Preparer for making cakes.

We tucked into our food. Fresh fruit, scrambled eggs, crispy potatoes, and toast with jam crowded our plates. It had been months since we feasted this well.

"I must call my children today to make sure everything is going well." I glanced around the room. "Where is the telephone?"

"In the parlor," Ivan said. "You need permission to use it and then only at supper time because Mrs. Jacobs likes to keep the line free in case Mr. Jacobs or some of her church… not church…, the place where she worships. In case one of them rings her up."

This was new information. I expected free use. Why didn't I ask more questions before agreeing to work for them? "Must I ask each time?"

"Sure. It's theirs."

"Besides phoning everyone, I must visit them. How might we get back to the Grand Concourse? The building where we left my daughter, Patricia."

"Walking and then the train. I can show you the way."

"And Flushing from there?"

"Dunno."

Lotus, however, was full of advice. She stood five feet tall with a round face and rail thin body. Unlike most cooks, she ate little of what she prepared. Cinnamon-brown skin glowed with youth, but I suspected she was older than she appeared, with grey hairs hidden under the colorful scarf wrapped around her head. I don't remember ever seeing her tresses.

"Ivan can drive you to 241st street," Lotus said. "That's in the north Bronx where the IRT train line begins."

"Can't be taking their car without their say so," Ivan said, referring to the Jacobs. He appeared less educated than Lotus and a quiet presence to her exuberant one. Married with grown children, she and Ivan lived in the converted carriage house behind the main building. While Ivan had many responsibilities, including driving, caring for the car, handyman, and occasional gardener, Lotus only cooked.

"If you go early Sunday morning, they'll be asleep, and you'll be back before breakfast," Lotus said, her face and voice charged with animation. "Plenty of time to eat and get ready for church."

"I don't want anyone getting in trouble because of me," I said.

"Phish." Lotus swirled a folded corner of her toast in the eggs before popping the morsel into her mouth. "You catch the IRT. Transfer to the 3rd Ave El at 125th street in Harlem."

"We lived in Harlem."

"Before your husband died?" Ivan asked.

I nodded.

Lotus swallowed and shushed Ivan. "Let me finish. Walk to Second Avenue and take that line to Gun Hill Road. Transfer again until you ride over the east river to Queens."

"That's how Uncle Mac drove us," Sylvie said. "Do trains travel over their own bridges?"

"Of course, they do," Lotus said.

"And once I'm on the other side?" I asked.

"You walk from there."

The trip sounded daunting, complicated, and long. "Could we get to the Grand Concourse first and then to Flushing?"

"One or the other, if you're gonna get back here by bedtime." She dabbed her mouth with a serviette.

"We have to do both," Sylvie said with an edge to her voice, echoing my thoughts, but not my choice of tone. Before the incident, in normal times, stories, strong opinions, and questions spilled out, but always politely. Now Sylvie either said little or made angry demands.

A girl Sylvie's age, who didn't live in the house or on the grounds, joined us. "Any food left for me?" Tall and curvy, she wore a maid's uniform and cap ready for work.

Lotus introduced Cecily and then dished food onto the newcomer's plate.

"Why are you trying to get to the Bronx and Flushing?" Cecily asked, her mouth full of eggs and potatoes. "I overheard you."

"To visit my children."

She eyed Sylvie, but didn't ask the obvious question, nor did I inquire where she lived or how she got around. Did someone drive her to Pelham? Were there buses? I'd find a moment to investigate.

When the Jacobs finished breakfast in the dining room, Ivan drove Samuel to the railroad station that took him to work in Manhattan. Sylvie and Cecily cleared both tables and washed the dishes, while I helped Dahlia choose her clothes for the day and styled her hair. She had several women's meetings to attend once Ivan returned.

Dahlia had yet to explain my duties. With my mind fixed on speaking with, and visiting, my children, I chose not to ask just yet.

"We must visit my daughter in the Bronx," I said to Lotus when I returned to the kitchen. She and Sylvie were preparing the evening meal. Sylvie sliced vegetables and Lotus seasoned a large slab of beef. "And my babies in Queens."

"Why are you all living in different places?" Ivan asked. He sat akimbo, blackening Samuel's shoes.

Lotus said, "Mind your manners."

"You don't have this coming Sunday free," Ivan said, his buffing brush moving at a blurring rate.

"It's our day off." This was central to the arrangement I made with the Jacobs. One day off every week.

"Yeah, but you just got here. Ya gotta earn it."

Lotus agreed. "Be two or three weeks before you get a Sunday."

Three weeks. Patricia would be desperate for us to come… the small ones too, but my darling girl was in so much pain. "Surely, I'm allowed to use the phone during supper time."

The couple looked at each other and shook their heads. "Gotta earn stuff 'round here," Ivan said. "The Jacobs call 'em privileges."

"They're good people. Fair. Respectful, but with rules," Lotus explained.

Ivan agreed. "Not too many, though. Just do your job without a fuss."

"I assured my children. I haven't spoken with them in over a week."

Ivan admired the shine on the leather. "They'll survive."

Sylvie let out a groan.

Later, settled in our room, Sylvie put down the book she was reading. I sat braiding my hair into long plaits.

"The little ones must be wondering where we are." Sylvie turned her cat-like eyes on me.

I had no answer for Sylvie. Yet.

CHAPTER THIRTY-NINE

Tuesday morning bloomed sunny and hot. Sylvie and I washed up and joined the household staff for a sumptuous breakfast before starting our daily chores.

I joined Dahlia in the Jacobs' overly warm parlor, filled with sofas, tufted chairs, a grand piano, and a sideboard. Unlike the airy kitchen, this room was dark like the Wilsons, with heavy drapes on the windows.

I liked Dahlia. Although she lived a cloistered life, she played the piano, sang, and enjoyed learning about my love of jazz, dancing, and listening to poetry. I found her easy to speak with. So far, my lady's maid duties comprised of keeping Dahlia company, discussing her various committees, styling her hair, and helping her choose her outfits.

But Sunday promises loomed. I searched for an opening.

Dressed in a dark, modest housedress, long and loose, Dahlia flopped on the nearest sofa. I brought her a glass of cold water and tiny sandwiches Lotus sent on a tray and rested them on a table next to her.

"May I speak with you about a pressing matter?" I began. Dahlia cut me off.

"I have one too," she said before scooping up a sandwich and taking a nibble. "You must take me to a salon in Harlem." She took another bite. "And a speakeasy."

I stood in front of her, mystified by her request.

"Come sit." She patted a spot on the sofa. "We've only just met, but I trust I can tell you anything."

I sensed her loneliness. Samuel's commute to work, his long hours, and then the return trip, left her alone for eleven to twelve hours a day. Neighbors waved, but so far, none visited. She had friends from her synagogue, but they didn't appear close. They all had children, like her friend, Cora. The empty nursery upstairs was a sad reminder of what Dahlia lacked.

"My husband escorted me," I said. "You must ask yours to accompany you."

"Respectable Jewish housewives from Pelham don't ask their husbands to do any such thing." She offered me a sandwich. "What's a speakeasy like? Smokey? Dark? Dangerous? Did you worry the police might raid the place?"

Although we were close in age, I felt years older. I took one of the offered crustless squares filled with a tasty white fish and bits of tomato grown in Lotus' vegetable garden.

"Come on. You must know a gentleman who'd take us. A brother or cousin?"

What I required was use of the telephone, the fast-approaching Sunday off, and assistance visiting my children. As Ivan explained, after two or three weeks with the household, Dahlia allowed calls during the evening meal hour, and not earlier. Mr. Jacobs sometimes called home, which lifted Dahlia's spirits. It was obvious she loved him. And she expected to hear from fellow committee women, planning future meetings and good works. The line, therefore, had to remain free during the day. After supper, Samuel and Dahlia retired to the parlor, where Samuel sipped a brandy, and Dahlia played the piano for him. Since the telephone was in the parlor, there were no calls allowed after the supper hour.

Could I say yes to the trip to Harlem in exchange for using the phone each day and having this Sunday free? Jonathan Spooner popped into my mind.

"You've just thought of the right person. I can tell from your expression. Do you have a beau?" She clapped her hands in that little girl gesture I witnessed the first time I met her. "You do."

"Perhaps we could strike a bargain," I said, surprised by my boldness.

"A bargain?"

"Yes. You help me and I arrange for a trip to a club in exchange."

"You're in my employ."

"A trip to Harlem is not a responsibility of a lady's maid." Although unsure of the full extent of my tasks, I was sure about this.

She appeared to ponder my remark before deciding. Then she scooted back and turned her body towards mine. "Tell me what you want in exchange."

"I must see Patricia and my youngest children. They're temporarily living in Flushing, Queens."

"More children?" She dropped her eyes and plucked at a loose button on her dress. "How many do you have?"

"Five. The youngest is three, and Sylvie is the oldest."

"That's the exact number I'm going to have."

I stayed quiet and waited. When someone wants to discuss a painful topic, silence can provide the courage.

"Miscarriages." Still looking down, her tone was sad, but tinged with wonder, as if unsure why. "Too many."

"I lost three children," I said, surprising myself again. Sharing intimacies with a stranger, my employer, was not appropriate. In fact, ever since the incident, I've surprised myself regularly. "It's no one's fault."

"But you kept trying?"

Trying was a strange verb for my relationship with Henry, but there was no reason to say more. "Yes."

"Samuel believes it makes me too sad. He doesn't want to go through it all again."

"I'm sorry."

"Me too." She tilted her head. "I'm not giving up." We sat for a few moments, neither speaking. Then Dahlia brightened. "I accept your bargain. Let's get you to your children this Sunday and plan a perfect day to visit a speakeasy. Samuel must be out of town when we go."

"May I call my *acquaintance*?" I wanted to correct the impression that I had a beau.

"Of course."

"And perhaps Ivan could drive Sylvie and me to visit my children."

"Oh." She shook her head. "Ask your beau to do both."

"He's a friend."

"I don't want to explain to Samuel." Her lips curved up for a second. "You understand?"

Jonathan might think poorly of me–asking for two enormous favors and we'd only met. Plus, request he take a white woman to Harlem, to an illegal establishment, putting himself in danger for not one, but two strangers. Mac promised to drive me to Queens in a month. He was the more sensible person to prevail upon. Of course, he would never agree to a speakeasy.

"I understand," I said. "So, I shall phone my children today and let them know we will visit them on Sunday."

Dahlia nodded her consent.

"And then I'll give my gentleman friend a call."

CHAPTER FORTY

Jonathan Spooner said yes. He agreed to take us to the Bronx and then to Queens on Sunday, the last day of August. He sounded happy I called him. However, I didn't mention the speakeasy. Yet.

"I get to meet your children. I like that."

At a loss for words, I didn't respond.

"I can hear you frowning." His warm laugh came over the line. "You don't want me to know them? I can wait in the truck and not look, but I gotta watch the road while I'm driving."

This was a mistake. I was a married woman, even if Jonathan didn't know. Plus, he drove a truck. Dirty, noisy, coal and delivery trucks were common enough. Could the four of us fit in one of them and would we arrive covered with black dust?

"And you don't find me funny, either. Most folks do."

"I believe you are kind," I said, realizing I missed his joke.

"I'll take that while I work on the rest."

With conflicting emotions, I gave him the address, and we agreed on 9:00 a.m. Sunday morning.

The calls to Patricia, George, and Irene were more difficult than I anticipated. I expected Mrs. Wilson to continue to block me, but I was unprepared for the actual conversations.

We called Patricia first, but she barely spoke three sentences. "I'm fine," she said, sounding the opposite. Cora assured me Patricia was a tremendous help.

"On Sunday morning, we're coming to take her for a day."

Cora said, "Dahlia told me that wouldn't happen for several weeks." She sounded panicked.

"She's changed her mind. We'll be by on Sunday."

Mrs. Wilson picked up.

"You will let me speak to my children. Mrs. Barker agrees with me," I lied, ashamed, but determined.

"Humph."

"Please put George on first," I said, repeating my request from last week.

Solemn Georgie assured me he and Irene were having fun. "Mr. Wilson plays soldier with me, and I let Irene feed them pretend tea and biscuits. They hate it, but I don't let her know."

Oh my. "You're such a sweet boy. Thank you for taking care of your sister. Does Peter play too?"

"His mother came and got him. Are you taking us home?"

My heart and stomach clutched.

"His mama told Mrs. Wilson she'd been trying for a long time."

Did that mean, like me, it took a while to gather her funds, or were there rules preventing Peter from going with his mother? I assumed my children were mine to reclaim as soon as I was ready. Was that true? "Sylvie, Patricia, and I are coming on Sunday. How many days is that from today?"

George stayed quiet for a moment. I pictured him counting the days on his fingers.

"Three."

"Exactly. Now tell me about Andy. Do you play with him every day?"

"We play outside. But Mrs. Creamer's babies are always crying, so she doesn't let Andy stay in the yard so much."

"Does he seem happy?" What an unfair question. "Does he laugh a lot?"

"Not a lot." I heard sounds of a slight commotion. "Irene is pulling on my shirt to speak to you."

Irene was full of tales about her dolls and tea parties. She stopped mid-story. "When are you coming to get us?"

"Mama loves you so much. Please don't cry. Do you have your cuddle dolly? She might be sad too and need you to comfort her. Let her know how much you love her, just like I love you."

I assured her we'd see her on Sunday and sent kisses over the line.

Mrs. Wilson came on. "They're still bawling. I told you these calls would upset them. They were fine all day and now this."

"Nevertheless, I shall be there Sunday morning to take the children for the day."

She broke off the conversation.

Agitated, I phoned Sallie Creamer. The operator told me there was no answer and to try again later. Unable to phone after supper and disturb Samuel and Dahlia in the parlor, I vowed to call the next day.

After I hung up, and Sylvie and I completed our chores, including me hand-sewing all of Dahlia's dangling buttons, we returned to our room. Sylvie appeared sullen. I expected excitement and a bit of gratitude. The calls were sad, but the upcoming visit was soon. We were both told no use of the phone or days off for several weeks and yet she spoke with her siblings, and we're diving to the Bronx and Flushing in a few days. I felt accomplished, negotiating the bargain with Dahlia. Of course, just as I didn't mention the speakeasy visit to Jonathan, I didn't share it with Sylvie either.

We sat on the edge of our shared bed while Sylvie brushed my hair, untangling waves that hung down my back.

"How are we going to get to everyone? Mr. Ivan and Miss Lotus made the trip sound impossible."

"A friend of mine will drive us. We'll travel to Patricia first and then the little ones and be back in plenty of time." Excitement surged. Saying the words served as an antidote to Irene's tears and not speaking with Andy.

"What friend? Uncle Mac?" She stopped brushing and turned to face me.

I recognized my error. "Not actually a friend. A kind person who has agreed to assist us."

"Uncle Mac said he'd bring us."

"Yes, in a month. But we can't wait until then. Sunday is his only day—

Sylvie interrupted me, her face in a frown. "Who?"

"His name is Jonathan Spooner. We sold our—"

"The man who has all of our belongings and is going to sell them to strangers?"

I miscalculated. She was in terrible pain, and once again, I failed to notice. "I have a plan for leaving here. Shall I tell you about it?"

The gold flecks in her eyes darkened to brown and gleamed with unshed tears.

With both my arms, I grabbed her stiff body into a hug. Her arms hung at her sides. "I know your father hurt you and all of this…" I swung my arms up and out to capture every evil and sad thing that happened. "Is so painful. Too awful to bear."

I grabbed her again, and she lowered her face to my shoulder and sobbed.

"I'm so sorry, my sweet girl."

Henry broke Sylvie and Patricia. Was there any way for them to heal? For four months, I focused on our physical survival. But the girls' hearts required repair as well. Soon, the Fisher family would return to Yonkers and take Sylvie away. How could either of my daughters get better if they were apart and working for strangers?

CHAPTER FORTY-ONE

Dahlia sat in front of the mirror in her dressing room while I brushed her hair, just as Sylvie brushed mine. Silver gleamed on the back of brushes' stiff bristles. Whenever Dahlia left the house, she hid her tresses under a wig. She explained that covering one's hair was part of her religion. But at home, she let it hang to her shoulders. Glossy and soft, her mane cascaded in waves not unlike mine.

"What does one wear to a speakeasy?" she asked. "I've seen pictures of 'flappers' in straight, short dresses with lots of beading and shimmer."

"And long strands of pearls hanging from their necks and feathers in their hair."

"Samuel likes me in modest clothes." Dahlia giggled. "My friend Gladys told me the flappers have tossed their corsets, and I noticed they don't have bosoms." She laughed again, a nervous sound and looked down on her chest, reminding me of the first time I met Miss Denise.

Heat suffused my cheeks. Dare I say it? I cleared my throat. "I can make you a dress and appropriate lingerie."

"You know how to make flapper dresses?" She sounded both excited and skeptical.

"Yes. Day dresses, and gowns, too." Women wore simple house dresses at home, day dresses when running errands or going to a job in the city, and evening clothes for events.

Until now, we were speaking to our reflections in the vanity mirror. Now, Dahlia turned to face me. "Really?"

"I sewed for a living after my husband passed."

"By hand?"

"My Singer Sewing machine and basket are at my friend's home." I swallowed. Tried for a more confident tone. "If Ivan picked them up, by the time my gentleman acquaintance is ready to take us to a Harlem club, you'd have the perfect dress and undergarments."

"And you can do this in the latest style?" Dahlia changed her voice to a snobbier pitch and tone. "Because today's women, according to the 'Ladies Home Journal,' are striking out for comfort and freedom." She shifted back to her New York accent. "But that's not the case in Pelham."

"I've been sewing since I was a girl. We could find a picture of a dress you like, and I'll make it for you."

Dahlia clapped her hands and then frowned. "The bobs they wear are quite short. Samuel would not approve of a haircut."

"Buy a wig that's bobbed." I lifted her hair and pulled it back. "You'd look lovely."

"I doubt Mrs. Schwimmer sells wigs like that."

"We could tie your hair up and wind a band with feathers on the side. Have you seen pictures like that?"

Dahlia grinned and then frowned–the excitement gone in a flash. "Yes, but I must cover my hair. It's the law."

The Jewish women I knew in Jamaica covered their hair with scarfs, and so did Christian women, like Lotus. "One problem at a time. Let me get my sketchbook. We can talk through the design. Have you photographs of dresses you've admired?"

"Not a word to Samuel."

"Of course."

My first customer for the new business–the work that would reunite my family and sustain us into the future. I had to stitch the best dress I'd ever made.

. . .

Inspired by ready-made clothing ads in the newspapers and fashion pages of 'The Ladies Home Journal,' I sketched two original dresses that might suit Dahlia. One had a dropped waist and hung just below the knee. The fringe began above the knee, so when one walked, flashes of thigh peeked through. The other followed the curvature of the woman's body, with rhinestones decorating the bodice and, like the first, fringe hanging below the knee. We discussed colors, beading, faux jewels and, of course, length. For the first time in… when did I last experience so much hope and pleasure? We settled on a design, but covering her hair remained an unsolved problem.

The fabric and dry goods store in Pelham added to my good mood. Bolts of silks, imitation silk, rayon, every type of cotton, and woolens, lay stacked on counters. I was as excited as Dahlia, who chose seven yards of a black, silk-cotton blend. She ordered silver beads and black fringe.

This would be a daunting task. I'd never made a dress like this one, but I felt this was the first step of my journey home. If Dahlia liked the dress, and then asked me to make one closer to what she and her friends wore to meetings and the Synagogue, and at evening affairs, additional orders might materialize. There were a lot of "ifs." Even so, I was on my way.

"My, that's an extravagant order," the lady behind the counter said. "Where is Mr. Jacobs taking you?"

Dahlia blanched. We'd discussed her answers to sharp questions before embarking on our fabric search, but now she looked caught.

"A friend of Mrs. Jacobs is attending a costume ball," I said. "We're surprising her with a dress."

"Oh," the saleswoman said. She pursed her lips. "Your order will be ready on Monday."

We left, both of us giggling.

"Thanks for rescuing me," Dahlia said. "How long will it take to make the dress?"

I didn't know, but I responded, "Several weeks." And prayed I could pull it off.

.   .   .

At supper time, I called Sallie Creamer again. The operator let the phone ring for over a minute.

"I'm sorry, madam. You'll have to try the number later. No one is answering."

I tried Mrs. Wilson again. When the operator connected us, I heard spoons and forks clinking against dishes and the low babble of my children's voices and Mr. Wilson's baritone. My knees almost gave out.

"Do you know where Mrs. Creamer is? Is she all right? There's no answer when I call." Panic colored my voice. "How is Andy?"

"They're fine. Andy continues to adjust well."

"Really? Why doesn't she answer her phone?" Relief edged in, but the worry held on.

"Not everyone enjoys being interrupted during their supper." She sounded like she was speaking of herself.

"I apologize for disturbing your meal. Please tell Mrs. Creamer, I'll be there on Sunday."

Esther made a noisy sigh, as if I were inconveniencing her and Sallie. "I'm sure I will," she said.

"Thank you. I won't disturb you again. We'll see you after church on Sunday morning."

I let the relief blossom and shoved the worry aside.

CHAPTER FORTY-TWO

Beryl pressed her palms together as if in prayer. "I'm glad to see you." She ushered Ivan and me inside.

The apartment was cool, quiet, and smelled like cinnamon and lemons. Mac was working and Josh and Nick playing with friends in front of the building. I made introductions.

Ivan eyed the Singer still in the parlor's corner. "Looks heavy."

"I'll help," I said. "But might we have a cup of tea with my friend before we leave?"

"Yes, do come in and sit." Beryl showed us to the kitchen table. "How are you really?"

"Well. Hopeful." Mindful of Ivan, I shared some of what transpired since we said goodbye five days earlier, but not everything. He appeared too interested in our conversation, plus I didn't want to be rude. "I've written Mother. Explained we were in transit and asked her to send letters to your address."

"I promise to alert you when one arrives. Please phone or write. I miss you all."

In a grumpy tone, Ivan said, "Most unusual to get your first Sunday off. Not earning your privileges."

Lotus was happy for us and Cecily indifferent, but Ivan appeared resentful. I made sure my smile and tone were warm. "Mrs. Jacobs was most considerate to make an exception for the sake of my children."

"She's a good sort," Ivan agreed.

Beryl said to Ivan, "And you're kind to drive them."

"Not me. Wife and I are heading to church and staying for fellowship."

"Oh." Beryl's face contracted into her frown, the one that unpleasantness caused, and turned to me. "Did you tell Mac you'll need his help on Sunday? Because he's not said anything, and we've promised the children a family outing. With summer ending and school starting…"

I took a deep breath. "Mr. Spooner is driving us. I didn't want to—"

"Mr. Spooner?" She sounded outraged, even more so than Sylvie.

Ivan's eyebrows shot up.

"Yes." No more excuses. "We need help, and he offered. A generous act."

"Indeed." Beryl's eyes flicked toward Ivan and then back to me. "Of course. Lovely."

I gulped down the last of my tea. "We must go. Thank you."

Beryl pulled me aside, out of earshot of Ivan. "I have news. Henry wrote me, asking for you."

My hand dropped to my clenched belly.

"He wanted your address. Said his sister had no information either."

"How did you respond?"

"I've not yet written back. I wanted to speak with you first. But that's not all."

I waited. What else could go wrong?

"Mae came around looking for you. Your neighbor, Mrs. Thompson, saw her knocking on your door and gave her my address."

Mae. How thoughtless of me. She loved her nieces and nephews. I kissed Beryl's cheek. "I will write to Mae straight away."

"And Henry?"

"Please ignore him. He's lost all rights to me and my children." My eyes filled up. I dabbed at them and my damp cheeks. "You are a dear friend."

Beryl's expression suggested she had more to say.

"What? Did something else happen?"

She shook her head. "I'm worried about you. Are you sure you know what you're doing?"

"About Henry?"

"No. Mr. Spooner."

"What about him?" My cheeks felt warm. I anticipated Beryl's concerns and didn't want to hear them.

"You're not experienced in the ways of... unmarried men."

I tried to reassure both of us. "He is helping, that's all."

Her face told me I'd missed the mark. "I pray for you every night," Beryl said, squeezing my hand.

"And I for you and your family."

• • •

Sunday morning at 8:50 a.m., Ivan rushed into the kitchen. Cecily just finished washing the breakfast dishes. Sylvie dried and put the plates, cups, saucers, and glasses in the designated cabinet. She moved sluggishly, her expression blank.

"He's here in a beat-up Model T truck," Ivan said, sounding both excited and judgmental. "Looks like he cleaned it up for you. It's dented, but shiny." Ivan, dressed in his pinstriped-church suit with a white shirt, sported a yellow handkerchief in the jacket pocket. A Lotus touch, no doubt.

Lotus, also dressed for church, handed me three head scarfs, and aprons. "You'll need them. Keep your hair in place and grime from your clothes."

"Thank you." To my ears, I sounded breathless and not at all dignified.

Once I understood we'd be riding in a truck, I quizzed Ivan, since I was unfamiliar with the type of vehicle a business like the Spooner Brothers might own.

"No glass covering the windows on the sides," Ivan explained. "Only the windshield. Lots of dust in your face and seats for two, not four."

My emotions bubbled and popped. Delighted, we were going to see Patricia, George, Irene, and Andy, just as I promised. Were they happy, scared, angry, healthy? My anxiety sparked. Sylvie remained devastated, and the thought of Jonathan driving us kept her upset and quiet. What might I say to comfort her or give her hope? And there was another feeling I had difficulty acknowledging. Despite everything, I was eager to spend the day with Jonathan.

With my help, Sylvie tied her hair up with one of Lotus' scarfs and slipped on the apron over her dress. Long on Lotus, the apron hit mid-thigh on Sylvie.

I, too, had a scarf and apron, but I didn't put them on. I wore a deep-burgundy dress with a bow at the neck. Unlike many of the straight-lined flapper dresses, it tucked at my waist and draped over my hips to the tops of my t-strap heels.

Embarrassed, I admitted to myself that I wanted to look nice for Jonathan. He made me fluttery inside. Married to a man whose touch I hated–this revelation frightened me. Had I ever felt like this before? I searched my memory, but no man's image emerged.

"You're all dressed up," Sylvie said in an accusing tone.

"Please bring the picnic basket." Once again, I ignored her rudeness.

Lotus packed a lavish lunch for seven, with cool drinks in Thermos Jugs, and iced cupcakes, one for each of us. Her kindness humbled me. Sunday was her only day off and still she prepared a wonderful morning tea, as my mother would call an American breakfast, and now lunch. Doing as I instructed, Sylvie thanked Lotus, and grabbed the picnic basket and blanket.

"We'll have a good time." I rubbed Sylvie's back. "Patricia and the little ones too."

Sylvie lifted her accusing eyes. "And Mr. Spooner? What will you say about him?"

"There's nothing to tell."

Clouds kept the August sun at bay, which was a blessing since both Sylvie and Patricia would travel in the uncovered flatbed. Moisture, along with hydrangea and peonies, scented the air.

"Morning," Jonathan said, with a small bow. "How're you ladies this fine day?"

I introduced Jonathan to Sylvie.

"You're as lovely as your mother."

Despite her earlier disapproval, Sylvie blushed at the compliment.

Jonathan walked us to the back carrying a wooden stool. The gate to the flatbed lay open. A clean, thick blanket covered whatever debris or rust was underneath. He placed the stool on the ground.

"Let me help you up, Miss Sylvie."

"I can manage."

But she couldn't. The ascent was steep. She placed her hand in his, stepped on the stool, and Jonathan, his large hands around her waist, lifted her the rest of the way, before nesting the picnic basket and blanket next to her.

"You comfortable?" he asked.

Sylvie nodded but offered no thanks or comment.

"Take this, my darling," I said to Sylvie, handing her a handkerchief. "You can cover your mouth and nose if there's too much dust." Flashes of my trip in Henry's carriage, the wheels and horses kicking up dirt, flashed.

She took it, and once again, with no thank you in return.

Jonathan closed the gate. "Hold on here." He patted the top of the flatbed gate. "When the ride gets bumpy." He turned toward me. "Even when you're worried, you're beautiful."

My eyes darted to Sylvie to see if she heard him. My frown eased, and I smiled at him. He knew I had five children, and one a sullen Sylvie, and was still interested. Or he flirted with every woman he met. I shook my head internally and reminded myself I was still married. Unavailable. There was no future for us, even if that was Jonathan's hope. I had no interest in marrying again. I almost laughed aloud. Marry? We'd just met. What was wrong with me? Why did this man fluster me so? No. An unfeasible situation. When I added Sylvie's reaction to this benign… well, this trip, it underscored the impossibility of a relationship with Jonathan.

The truck had a built-in step to climb into the driver's seat, but not one on the passenger side, so I used the wooden stool and Jonathan helped me in. He was so close that I smelled the soap he washed with, and the toothpowder he used to brush his teeth.

"Do you ever wear that lush mane of yours loose?"

Another impertinent question and yet it made me smile–a tiny, ladylike one. "At home, in the evenings."

"That would be something to see."

I caught myself. "You're not likely to have the opportunity."

He laughed. "Your moods shift like the wind." He shook his head, a smile playing at his lips, and walked around to the driver's side.

Cecily, Lotus, and Ivan stood in the doorway, watching us. I returned their waves goodbye. At the last moment, I looked up. From the second-floor window of the empty nursery, Dahlia stared down at us. When I waved to her, she pulled back from view.

CHAPTER FORTY-THREE

The closer we got to the Grand Concourse, the more anxious I felt. A week ago, we left Patricia. Cora Perlman seemed overwrought and disorganized. Had the household settled down? Was Patricia well?

"Can I ask you a question?" Jonathan said.

I was watching the activity on the streets, my nose and mouth covered with my linen handkerchief. Once we left Pelham and reached the Bronx border, cars, bicycles, pushcarts, and trolleys crowded the avenues. Unlike the rural, north-east Bronx where we used to live, commerce, houses, apartment buildings, and stores filled up this part of the borough. Loud and dusty, the stench of gasoline and trash left on the curb penetrated my face covering. With trepidation, I turned toward Jonathan and waited. He asked such blunt questions, and often made inappropriate remarks. I stayed on guard.

"My folks, younger brother, and I left Alabama and landed in Queens. All four of us got jobs at a fancy Forest Hills hotel," he said, eyes on the road. "Mom worked as a maid, and Dad as a waiter. Thomas and I toiled in the gardens, and I mean toiled." Jonathan laughed. "We were young and strong, but at the end of every day, we soaked in a tub to ease our cramping muscles."

"How old were you? Had you finished school?"

"Is that important to you?" His tone sounded defensive.

"I'm sorry. I didn't mean to pry."

The truck bumped over trolley tracks and rolled through a busy intersection. A distant train rumbled by.

"Not prying," Jonathan said. "Just a touchy subject. We had to drop out and work."

Just like me, I thought. "Were you disappointed?" I remembered my despair at my pregnancy and losing school, books, and discovering new things every day.

"Yeah. I enjoyed learning and playing baseball, but I understood. Life was hard in 'Bama.' My parents wanted us to have better lives."

"How old were you?"

"Fifteen. My brother Thomas was sixteen."

"How did you get to Harlem?"

"Well, that was my question for you. From where'd you get that fancy accent?"

"England." After pausing for a bit, I turned the conversation back to him. "It must have been hard for a colored family to start a business."

"Uncle Brad, my dad's brother, owned Spooner's Goods and Gifts in Harlem. He urged us to join him, and they renamed it Spooner Brothers."

"What happened to your uncle? Does he still work with you?"

"They killed him and Thomas."

Startled, I asked, "Who?"

"Foul play, but the police didn't investigate. Said they were drunk. We never found the murderers."

I thought about my encounter with the New York police.

He turned toward me for a second. "You were in England, and then what?"

Jonathan was clever and persistent. "My father died. We moved to the West Indies. Jamaica. That's where I met my husband."

"You loved him a lot?"

"My father? Yes. He was a kind and generous man."

"You know I meant your husband."

I weighed my answer. I didn't want to encourage him. "Yes."

A loud, "Aoogha," blasted from an auto perpendicular and to our right. The Klaxon horn was deafening and caused a startled flock of birds to fly up. Jonathan braked and let the offending car cross in front of us.

"And he treated you well?"

"Tell me about working at the store." I had no intention of discussing the state of my marriage with Jonathan. "Do you enjoy it?"

Jonathan eyed me and shook his head—not in response to my question, but to my evasion. "It beats slogging through mud and dodging bullets."

"Oh?"

"Lots of guys had it worse than me."

I realized he was talking about the war, which ended six years ago. America didn't enter World War I until 1917, three years after it began. Many soldiers returned shell-shocked or gravely wounded. The white officers, however, assigned most of the colored men support jobs rather than combat. I'd never met a Negro soldier before.

"Where did you serve? Were you injured?"

"Harlem Hellfighters, under the French. They treated us a lot better than the American officers. Racism followed Black folks into war and back. W.E.B. Dubois thought serving would change everything." Jonathan shrugged. "Yet here we still are."

Many urged Negro men to forgo Europe's war—white people fighting other white people, and still treating coloreds poorly. But, the eminent scholar, Dr. Dubois, urged Black men to fight for their country as a way for us to achieve equality and respect.

"Are you sorry you enlisted?"

"Nah. Not really."

"You fought in France?" In Walthamstow Hall, I met a French girl whose missionary father was English. She told me amazing stories about her home. "I'd always wanted to visit."

"Yeah. But being in a war is different from visiting."

Embarrassed, I blushed.

Jonathan glanced at me before returning his eyes to the road. "But I understand what you mean. Experiencing other countries is a good thing, whatever kind they are."

The truck bumped over another set of trolley tracks and stopped for a knife sharpener pushing his cart. The old man's pushcart became stuck. Jonathan hopped out and helped the man lift and right his wagon before jumping back in. The truck lurched forward.

"How many countries have you been to?" Jonathan asked. "England and Jamaica. Any others?"

"The Congo, where I was born."

"Wow. Now that's a tale I'm looking forward to."

"Hmm. Let's trade stories. You tell me more about your experience during the war and…" I saw the building up ahead. "Turn here," I said, suddenly eager and worried. Please Lord, let my Patricia be well.

CHAPTER FORTY-FOUR

Jonathan and Sylvie stayed with the truck while I entered the grand lobby and rode the Otis elevator up. One second after my knock, the Perlman's door swung open.

"Mama." Patricia flung herself into my arms. "Where's Sylvie? Didn't she come with you?" Pale with dark circles edging her eyes, she looked around me, her gaze searching up and down the long hallway.

"Downstairs, waiting for you." I smoothed her hair and kissed each cheek. "We missed you terribly."

Cora Perlman, holding the infant, Gabe, stood in the doorway behind Patricia. "Good morning. What time will Patricia return?"

"Suppertime." The scents of cooked eggs and fragrant bread competed with a diaper in need of changing.

"There's so much to do." Joseph, the toddler, hid behind his mother's skirt, peeking out every few seconds.

"It's her day *off*. She'll be back to eat and then rest in her room." My newfound boldness bubbled up without hesitation. It no longer surprised me.

Cora's face looked as drawn as Patricia's. "I don't receive days off or rest," she said.

My heart went out to her. "I remember those times. My first three babies, each only a year apart."

"Your daughter. She is your daughter, correct? You're not her guardian, as Dahlia suggested."

I hated to admit Dahlia lied, but I wouldn't compound it. "Yes."

"Like Patricia, you're colored."

I didn't respond.

"She's been a tremendous help."

"I'm glad. However, she requires time to recuperate from the six days of work."

Cora dipped her head once. "We'll see you this evening." She closed the door and the click of the lock turning reminded all of us that this wasn't Patricia's home.

Jonathan climbed out of the truck when he saw us coming, his eyes shining and a wide grin across his face. "You must be Miss Patricia. I'm glad to meet you." He stuck out his hand and Patricia shook it. "Miss Sylvie is eager to see you."

On cue, Sylvie leaned out. "Hi, sister." Her enthusiasm was a welcomed sound. "We're riding back here."

Patricia glanced at me, asking a silent question with her eyes.

"She missed you as much as I did," I said, choosing not to explain why we were riding in Jonathan Spooner's truck and not Mac's car.

After helping Patricia into the flatbed, Jonathan and I watched the sisters hug each other. The terrible accusations faded away.

In silence, we drove from the Bronx to the Macomb's Dam Bridge into Manhattan and then south to the Queens Borough Bridge over the East River to Flushing. Telephone wires stretched from one wooden pole to the other. A Queens' train line rattled overhead.

After such an intimate conversation, Jonathan and I appeared reluctant to return to the stories of our lives. He seemed pensive. Just as well. Sharing my life story wasn't something I should do.

Jonathan broke into the quiet. "Almost there. Excited? How long since you saw your kids?"

"Two weeks." And yes, my excitement and anticipation mounted with each mile. "Before this, we'd never been apart for more than a school day."

We braked in front of the Wilson's home. Jonathan pulled out his octagon-shaped pocket watch. "It's eleven," he said. "Not bad."

"I'm unsure where we can go for our picnic, but I'll ask Mrs. Wilson to recommend a park."

"I'll wait in the truck," Jonathan said. "I used to hang out close to here, back when we worked in Forest Hills. There are quite a few grassy lots where we can sit. I brought balls for the kids."

His kindness continued to throw me off balance. "Do come in and refresh yourself. Then we'll find a spot to have our lunch."

"I don't want the Wilsons to imagine anything unseemly about you." His face and voice appeared serious rather than his joking and poking.

"There's nothing to think." I regretted my miffed tone the second my words came out.

"Truth rarely stops folks from believing the worst and sharing it with others."

We walked around to the back.

"I bet you'd like to stretch your legs." With Jonathan's help, Sylvie and Patricia clambered out and down.

Before I rang the bell, the door opened. Esther stood in front of us, arms akimbo. "There's no need for upset," she said before peering around me at Jonathan. "Come in."

"Why might I be upset?" I asked, my heart rate beating faster.

George and Irene rushed toward me. I grabbed, hugged, kissed, and examined them. They both looked clean and flashed big smiles.

Irene said, "Mrs. Wilson told us we'll have the whole day together."

"Yes. I've brought a picnic lunch and there are balls to toss." I turned to George. "Do you want to bring your soldiers?"

He dashed off.

"Let's give your dolls a day outside," I said to Irene.

She hugged my legs before running to her room.

Sylvie and Patricia came in and Irene and George squealed. Hugs followed.

"Please take everyone outside, Sylvie. I'll be a moment."

The house was warm and dark. Esther's agitation made it more so. "Please tell me why I might be upset," I asked again.

"It's not my fault." Esther wrung her hands. Perspiration bathed her brown face. "I completely trusted her. Edward did too. He's at church counting the tithes and offerings. Serves as a trustee—"

"Esther, please. Tell me what's wrong."

"We both thought she was a responsible person."

I pressed my palm to my belly. "Is this about Sallie Creamer and my Andy?" Despite the terror I felt, my voice was calm.

"She disappeared. Just packed up and left. The mother won't tell me where they've gone. They're renters. We're not. Mr. Wilson and I worked and saved so we could own our—"

I cut her off again. "What happened? From the beginning."

Sylvie poked her head in. "Are you okay, Mama?"

"Yes, my sweet. Give me a few more minutes. And close the door behind you." No need to frighten the children.

With every blow since April, I dissolved into a teary mess with stomach cramps and wobbly knees. Not today. This day required me at my best. I squashed the panic. "When did you last see them?"

Esther blinked several times. "Shall we sit?"

I wanted to say no, but my knees shook. We walked into the dark parlor, she switched on a lamp, and I sank into a chair.

"Where to begin?" Esther said.

I folded my hands in my lap and took several deep breaths. "When did you last see Andy?" Squeals from the children playing outside made me more anxious rather than less. "How long ago?"

"Let's see. Friday, Sallie dropped by. Said she'd run out of butter and flour. I packaged up some and inquired how things were going." Esther's eyes kept dancing away from mine. "She sounded cheery. All was well. I asked when Andy might play with his siblings again." Esther pursed her lips. "I cannot abide lies. It's an awful habit and a sin in the eyes of the Lord."

"And?"

"She said Saturday."

Waiting out the spinning of this tale was fraying my nerves to the point of pain, but I kept myself upright and attentive, searching for any clues to Andy's whereabouts. "Did she come by the next day as promised?"

"No. I haven't seen her since."

Edward Wilson stepped into the parlor carrying a sack of groceries. "Who's the gentleman outside with the children?" He slipped off his hat and turned to me. "Howdy do. Esther tell you about Andy?"

I swallowed and steadied my breathing. If he went missing yesterday, why was I only now finding out?

Esther said, "I was explaining it to her now. And I don't know who the man is."

A thud against the side of the house sent Esther to the window. "What are those children doing out there? Our tenants upstairs will be down here complaining any minute. Elderly folks, who—"

I interrupted again. "For how long has Sallie Creamer lived next door?"

Esther twisted toward me, her mouth working. "Since March."

Another thud followed by squeals sent her back to the parlor window. She threw it open. "What are you doing?"

My patience was gone. "Esther."

She pulled back from the window. "There's no cause to yell."

Edward lowered his sack to the floor. "I can understand you're upset," he said, his tone even. "We're as worried as… well, concerned."

I searched both of their faces. "Where might Sallie take Andy? And why?"

Sadness and guilt filled Esther's eyes. She shrugged.

"That's unacceptable."

CHAPTER FORTY-FIVE

Should I call the police? I forced myself to think. "You said the mother is still next door in the upstairs apartment and they're renters. Who owns the house?" Perhaps the owner lived nearby and could provide additional information.

"We pressed Creamer's mother," Edward said. "She either has no information or is not telling."

"Have either of you met Mr. Creamer? Sallie told me he was on the run from the police, but he's innocent."

Edward tugged at the black tie knotted at his throat and stretched his neck. "They call him Cleveland, but his real name is Job, from the Bible." Rubbing his hands together as if warming them despite the perspiration bathing his face, Edward blew out a breath. "He runs with soldiers tied to the biggest King in the borough."

I covered my mouth with both hands to keep in the screams. They placed my three-year-old son with a woman whose husband was a criminal, a low-level 'soldier' working for a 'numbers-King,' like Miss Denise's brother-in-law. "What's the King's name?" Might I ask Miss Denise for help again?

"He's called Tommy-Gun around here because he uses them for other nefarious operations–bootlegging and such."

News stories about Chicago gangsters, Tommy-gunning their way through bank robberies, filled the papers. I'd not read about the like in New York. "Knowing this, why did you let Andy stay with Sallie? Never mind. When you searched for him at the house, did you find anything? Are his clothes still there, his toys?"

The two looked blankly at me. Esther made a strangled noise.

"Is the apartment locked?" Panic surged. "Who has a—"

"I do." Esther jumped up, thrashed through a drawer, and retrieved a key. "She gave it to me for emergencies."

The three of us bolted out of the house.

Jonathan called me as I dashed across the front yard, around my playing children, to the house next door, with Esther puffing a few steps behind and Edward several strides ahead.

Jonathan, running alongside me, asked, "What's going on?"

Esther, key in hand, stepped forward. With shaking hands, she stabbed the key, trying to get it into the lock.

"Let me." Jonathan took it from her and opened the door. "Grace, what's wrong?"

"Andy is missing."

"Mama?" Sylvie called from the Creamer's lawn.

"Mind the children," I called over my shoulder, and the four of us dashed into the house.

"Andy, are you here?" I moved from room to room, searched under beds, and in wardrobes. "Andy?" I spun in a circle. "Where... Oh, no." I spotted his comfort blanket in a basket of laundry. My knees gave way, and I sank to the floor.

· · ·

Still clutching Andy's blanket, Jonathan helped me up.

"We have to ask the mother again," I insisted.

"Ask her about what?" Jonathan said.

Edward responded. "Tommy-Gun Barns, Cleveland Creamer, and Andy."

"Damn." Jonathan's hands shot through his hair. "Okay. I have people around here. Folks we can check with."

"Why take Andy? I don't understand."

Jonathan peered down at me with dark eyes and a drawn mouth. Whatever the reason, he clearly believed the situation was dire.

"Tell me."

"They call it White Slavery when white women get stolen and forced to… do things with men. Government clamped down on immigration to slow the trade because lots of foreign women, including Asians, are victims. Plus, they want to preserve the 'homogeneity' of America. So, no one cares when men snatch *our* women and children. Police blame the victims."

This sounded familiar and, therefore, believable. It was my experience with how the police viewed what happened to Patricia.

"You say Cleveland Creamer's mother lives upstairs?" Jonathan asked.

Edward nodded.

"Let's have a talk with her."

We stepped back onto the front porch and rang the upstairs bell. Waited. Rang it again. Jonathan pounded on the door with his right fist.

I twisted around to see if the children were safe and playing. Patricia sat on the grass with Irene and her dolls. She giggled and pretended to feed one with blades of grass. Sylvie played catch with George. She glanced up and caught my eye. I reassured her with a wave. Jonathan pounded again.

"I'm coming. Stop all that racket." A small, fair-skinned woman with drawn eyebrows stood in the doorway. "What do you want?"

I said, "Where is your daughter?"

"Who's asking?"

"She's been caring for my little boy, Andy. And now they're gone."

The woman sucked on a sweet potato skin. "Yep. Left yesterday."

"Where? Why?"

"Didn't say." She moved to close the door.

Jonathan put his foot out.

She stopped pushing. "I don't know anything."

I asked, "Where does your son work and live when he's not home with his family?"

"I already said—"

Jonathan jumped in. "We don't believe you." He thrust out his chest and lowered his face to hers. "Tell us. Now."

The small woman pulled the peel from her mouth and leaned back, but Jonathan's face remained close to hers.

"He stays over in Jamaica, near the Negro cemetery. He's a good boy. Wouldn't hurt your kid."

With a slow, deliberate motion, Jonathan removed his foot, and the door slammed shut.

I found it difficult to swallow. The sequence of events I started in April, the chain everyone warned me about, stretched before me. It was all coming true.

CHAPTER FORTY-SIX

We left Sylvie in charge of her siblings, and the Wilsons responsible for their safety. After grabbing an apple for me and one for Jonathan, I gave Esther the picnic basket of food and drink. Edward pledged to drive everyone to a park, just as I'd promised. Irene's tears, and Patricia and George's solemn eyes, weighed on me, but I had to rescue Andy.

At first, Jonathan tried to persuade me to stay behind, but when I insisted, demanded, he relented. We set off for Jamaica Village and the cemetery, in search of Cleveland Creamer.

"We'll find Andy," Jonathan said. His hand reached across the seat but didn't touch mine.

Without responding to what he couldn't promise, I stared out the open window. The scenery outside the truck changed from residential to commerce. As it was Sunday, the streets and sidewalks were empty. Church bells rang in the distance. Hot August air blew in while my mind swirled around the past and the future. I found it difficult to focus on the current danger since the potential outcome was unthinkable.

A memory pushed forward. Initially, I was uncertain why I remembered this day. "I ran away from school," I said without preamble. "Time plays tricks on one's mind. In my memory-vision, I was five or six."

"In England?"

"Hmm. An older girl called me an ugly word and when I told our teacher, she scolded *me*. Instructed me to stop fretting about nonsense and focus on the math assignment. I hated mathematics, so perhaps the teacher... Mrs. Marston, perhaps she handled it correctly."

"Doesn't sound like it." For a moment, he turned his head and shifted his gaze toward me. "What happened? Were you gone long?"

I made a short, laughing sound. "Until I got hungry and lost." It must have been early fall, because I wasn't hot nor cold and I wore only my school uniform. Trees with brown, gold, orange, and red leaves lined the streets. "A man asked me where I was going."

"What did you do?"

"I told him about running away. My belly rumbled loud enough for him to hear. He took my hand and led me back to the Headmistress' office." The clarity of the memory surprised me. "Miss Ford was a large woman–tall, broad, and imposing. She summoned my sisters, Nora, and Carrie, and told them what I'd done."

"Were you in big trouble?" Jonathan slowed the truck and let another pass in front of us before lurching ahead. "Did she punish you?"

"They reacted to the man who helped me, and not to my sneaking away." I now had clarity about why this memory.

"I understand." Jonathan said this in as serious a tone as Nora, who told me to never go with a strange man again. Did terrible things happen to little girls back then? To little boys like Andy?

I peered at Jonathan out of the corner of my eye. He was quite handsome in a rough and tumble way. Not smooth, narrow, and symmetrical, but wide, and off-center. I liked his face and the timbre of his voice. Grateful he was helping me, I wondered what the future might hold for the two of us. These were wicked thoughts, so I pushed them away. We had no future. Nor did I want one.

Jonathan sensed my scrutiny but misinterpreted the reason.

"You're scared. I get it," he said. "But we'll find him. I promise."

We pulled in front of an immense warehouse several stories high. Rows of dirty windows marked each floor. Jonathan jumped out of the truck. "Stay here. I'll be right back."

I obeyed, my mind still on the memory. Did people steal children in every country? Back then and today? What might have happened to me? What might Andy endure? I clambered out and ran to catch Jonathan.

He whirled around. "Go back."

I shook my head.

"You are a stubborn woman." He reached out again, and this time, I let him take my hand. "Stay close and quiet. Let me do the talking."

Andy was my son, not his.

"Promise?"

Without waiting for my response or taking my acquiescence for granted, we walked to a wide side door. Tar held planks of wood together. Jonathan thumped.

The door swung open. A thick man with a scar across his cheek stood in the entranceway. "What?"

"Looking for Cleveland. Has he been around?"

"Who the hell are you?" The scar-faced man spoke to Jonathan but kept looking at me.

"Spooner."

He scratched his beard-covered chin. "Related to Vince and Harold?"

"Son and nephew."

The man pulled his attention from me and trained his glare on Jonathan. "What do ya want with Cleveland?"

"He's taken the lady's three-year-old son, and we intend to get him back."

"His kid? Family dispute?"

"No. To sell."

Hearing Jonathan say that aloud rocked me. I grabbed his arm to steady myself.

The scar-faced man growled like an angry dog. "We don't let that sort of thing happen 'round here. Against the code." He eyed me again. "Why not call the police? They'd trip over themselves to rescue a white boy."

I found my voice. "He's colored. And three. Still a baby."

Scar-face looked me up and down. "Okay. I see." He turned back to Jonathan. "Creamer hangs out by the tracks in a boarding house with a red door. Can't miss it."

We returned to the truck. Jonathan explained the Long Island Railroad carried folks from Manhattan to Queens and beyond. Colored people fled the slums of Manhattan and moved east. Houses went up and streets created with no plans or safety inspections. The humblest lived along the tracks next to warehouses and businesses dependent on the railroad to deliver their goods or bring them materials.

"How do you know these people?" I asked. Scary criminals, number-runners, and men with names like Tommy-Gun, were not part of my world.

"Doing business in Queens and Harlem requires connecting with all types." He peered at me from the corner of his eyes, much as I had done earlier, observing him. "Your husband never paid protection money? What kinda business was he in?"

I realized I didn't know if Henry encountered corrupt police or gangsters. He went to work every day. We had enough to eat, and money left over for education, music, theater, and poetry. Did criminals extort him or pay him?

When I didn't respond, Jonathan said, "My uncle started Spooners in Jamaica Village before moving it to Harlem. When my family migrated here my brother and I had to earn respect from neighborhood toughs."

"Did you?"

"Lots of brawling and not backing down, no matter the injuries... yeah. So, my family has a certain reputation in these parts."

"A good one? What did fighting and stubbornness achieve?"

He made a laughing sound, short and mirthless. "Positive is the way I'd describe it. Therefore, folks will help us find Andy."

"Because they're afraid of you, or respect you?"

"Both."

Jonathan appeared normal, like Mac, and funny and kind. But he was a tough? I thought of Henry's knife tucked away in my room at the Jacob's. Might the evening require such a tool to keep Andy safe? I had neither experience nor desire to use the knife. Even so, I wished I'd brought it with me.

"Will we find Andy in time?" I asked, knowing Jonathan didn't have an answer. The sun was low in the sky. Six o'clock. I only had an apple to eat since breakfast. My mouth felt dry. Was Andy hungry and thirsty, too? Frightened? Harmed? Sold? My hand dropped to my clenched stomach. Sold. Sweet Jesus. "He's very smart and brave." My voice cracked. "Tries hard to be like his big brother."

"I'm hopeful," Jonathan said. "Not everyone who breaks the law is evil."

"Is Cleveland Creamer?"

He shrugged, but otherwise did not respond.

. . .

Rundown apartment buildings and sagging houses competed for space with a gas company and mortuary. Exposed electrified tracks cut through the neighborhood. Unlike Flushing, no graceful trees or flower gardens adorned the landscape. Smoke from burning wood, coal, and trash smarted my eyes and set me coughing.

"You, okay?" Jonathan asked. He stopped at a railroad crossing, leaned out the window, and listened. I did as well. No train rumble or whistle followed, so he drove across the covered tracks.

My coughing spell subsided. "Which building?"

"That one." Jonathan pointed to a soot-covered frame house with a dull-red door. "Looks like the place our scar-faced friend described."

I grabbed Andy's comfort blanket and climbed out. Together, Jonathan and I walked into the boardinghouse. Music seeped from a nearby room. Raised voices clashed from another. Oil used for cooking and frying smelled sour, as if re-used for one too many meals.

A tall woman, eye to eye with Jonathan, approached us. "Who you looking for?"

Jonathan told her. She pointed out the correct door and Jonathan rapped.

I cried out when Sallie Creamer answered.

CHAPTER FORTY-SEVEN

Sallie looked defeated. Orange and black rings circled her right, swollen eye, and a bruise marred her cheek. Her oversized housedress looked in need of a wash.

"Where is Andy?" My heart rocked. "What happened to you?"

Jonathan said, "Let's step inside." He opened the door wider. Her toddler sat on a cot while his baby sister slept next to him. Neither Andy nor Cleveland Creamer were in the room.

Sallie covered her face with both hands.

Jonathan grabbed them and pulled them away. "Where's the boy?"

"Job took him," she said, using Cleveland's given name. "I'm sorry. I'm so sorry."

Jonathan stepped closer and glared down at Sallie. "Where? Tell me now."

He didn't utter "or," but I understood it. Or what? Why was I concerned about her? She stole my child and yet...

"Are your children safe?" I asked. He beat up his wife. Did he thrash his children and my Andy?

"Yes. He'd never—"

"Never what?" I demanded.

"He owes a loan shark a lot of money from gambling." Bootleggers often tied illegal alcohol and gambling to their enterprise and speakeasies offered both. "He's going to pay off his debt using Andy. The man... he buys and sells colored children." She collapsed onto the dirty floor, shaking, and wailing.

Buys and sells. I tried to catch my breath.

"Get up. Stop bawling." Jonathan tugged her to her feet. She swiped her cheeks and nose. "What's the shark's name, and where does he do business?"

"When I tried to stop him…" She pointed to her battered face. "He did this."

My hand touched her shoulder, and I kept my voice soft and calm. "Thank you for trying to save Andy." With a gentle squeeze, I tried to convey empathy. "Please tell Jonathan the loan shark's name."

"Job calls him Lucky Strike or just Lucky, because he smokes a lot."

"And where is Lucky's establishment?" I asked in the same soothing voice.

.   .   .

Dusk brought a cool breeze. My raspberry dress, spotted with soot and perspiration, added to my bedraggled look and emotions. We were eager to get going. Desperate, in fact. But I needed the restroom. Sallie gave us both drinks of water, allowed us to wash our hands and faces, and relieve ourselves in the hallway water closet. With deft fingers, I re-pinned my hair as it had fallen, and loose strands hung down my back. I took another minute to wash out the spots on my dress. Our appearance could make a difference in persuading people to return Andy. We lost ten precious minutes at Sallie's. Every second that ticked by increased the danger for Andy. I hurried to the truck and the waiting Jonathan.

Jonathan said, "The place might be dangerous."

"I'm coming with you." Damp circles dotted the skirt portion of my dress. I flapped the material to quicken the drying. "I'll be in danger sitting in the truck in this area."

Jonathan puffed out a loud whoosh of air. "True enough."

My brave front was more acting than real. Inside, my stomach ached, and my heart continued to rock. A headache lurked behind my eyes. If I was this afraid, how might Andy feel?

The Kit Kat operated in the basement of a ragged hotel. The tricky part, he explained, was getting in without the password. Because speakeasies were illegal and raided with some frequency, many set elaborate systems for letting in legitimate customers eager to drink, gamble, listen to music, and dance. At least they'd welcome us. Men and women of all races mingled in all but the poshest clubs.

"Okay," Jonathan said. "We'll go in arm-in-arm like we're together to have fun. I'll mention... Didn't you say your friend married a numbers-King?"

"Her sister." I searched my memory-bank. Shook my head.

Jonathan tugged on his mouth, raked his hair with both hands, and then chewed his lower lip. "One possibility is go-gangster. Demand speaking to Creamer. Tell him we have his wife and kids. Mother too."

"Why would the man Cleveland owes money to care about you taking the kids? Plus, isn't that outside the criminal code, like the scar-faced man said?"

"Right." He returned to tugging on his mouth.

"What if I entered as a white woman looking for my servant's child?"

He stared at me. "Why didn't you call the police?"

I tried to think. "I enjoy a glass of whiskey from time to time and don't mind such places of business."

"Who am I in this play?"

"My driver." I drew myself up and continued. "Kidnapping a child to sell, well, I shall have to speak with my woman's club of suffragettes." Many speakeasy owners found the protesting woman more difficult to handle than the police. At least coppers took payoffs, but nothing deterred the woman.

Jonathan nodded. "That's good. Might work." A grin spread across his face. "And I'm happy to drive you anywhere, any time."

We walked through the hotel lobby that housed the Kit Kat club, me in front and Jonathan a step behind, holding his hat and Andy's blanket. Nothing about the hotel entrance suggested a club operated below. Once again, I rehearsed my lines in my head. A woman stood at the check-in desk. She offered a bright smile.

"Good evening," I said, my mouth hot and dry. I licked my lips. "I'm unaware of today's password to enter your establishment, but I have urgent business with the proprietor." Was I too vague? Jonathan's presence behind me made me both comforted and agitated.

The clerk made a beckoning gesture to a dark-skinned man standing nearby. He approached me.

"What can I do for you?" He eyed Jonathan and then returned his gaze to mine.

"I'm here about an unpleasant matter," I said, making sure my British accent came across crisp and posh. "It appears a man named Job Creamer—"

"Known as Cleveland, ma'am," Jonathan said from behind me.

"Yes. Of course, Cleveland has stolen a child from a Negro woman in my employ."

The man stretched his neck, peering around us. "You got police on the way?" He sounded annoyed rather than afraid.

I explained, as Jonathan and I practiced, about enjoying drinks in establishments like this. "I have no desire to disrupt your business…" I emphasized my next point. "Unless they don't return the child."

The man's eyes darted about. "You're threatening to call the coppers, but you haven't yet, is that it?"

"I'm not threatening, good sir. Rather, I am assuring you the members of the Forest Hills Women's Suffragettes are steadfast in their quest to shut down every establishment like yours in Queens." I chose the wealthy community of Forest Hills because people there had both money and influence. "If I leave without the child, I will return with forty irate women."

His eyes penetrated mine. This had to work. If we were too late… No. I banished fear and thoughts of defeat and stiffened my back.

"What's the kid's name?"

"Andy, something. He's the child of my maid." My eyes widened. "How many children do you have down there?"

Now he looked nervous. "Okay, give me a minute."

"My driver…" I pointed to Jonathan, "Will handle the transfer." The act would fall apart if Andy saw me and yelled, "Mama." I spun on my heels and walked out the door. Either it worked or didn't. Please, please, God, let them bring my baby to me.

Ten minutes later, Jonathan approached the truck with Andy sleeping in his arms.

CHAPTER FORTY-EIGHT

Words were inadequate to describe the relief, love, guilt, and joy, washing over and through me. My actions and decisions led to this catastrophe. I cuddled and kissed Andy.

A terrible thought hit me again, one I'd tried to keep at bay. "How can I tell if he's been... violated? What might someone who likes little boys do?" Just saying those words aloud sent rivers of shudders through me.

Jonathan said in a quiet voice, "Check his backside."

"For what?" I lifted him to my shoulder and tugged down his pants. "What am I looking for?"

"Abrasions. Blood."

Oh, sweet Jesus, help me. His round bottom was clean. No visible wounds. I tugged up his pants. Andy slept on. "What else?"

"There's no way you can tell."

Tell what? But I kept my lips pressed together. Awful pictures swirled in my mind. With determination, I pushed them away.

Andy opened his eyes. "Hi, Mama." And then, in the next second, he returned to sleep. Did they give him a drug to make sure he didn't know what was happening to him? Tears spilled down my cheeks. I must have made a distressed noise.

"What's wrong?" Jonathan shifted his gaze from the street to me and back. "Did you find something?"

My voice failed me.

He moved the truck to the side of the road. "Grace, is he okay?"

"I'm terrified. Suppose we were too late."

"He's safe now."

"I should have done more…"

"You were great. Pulled it off." He drove forward and back onto the paved road. "Smart and brave."

"Not brave. Terrified."

"Bravery has nothing to do with fear. Two different things. During the war, every day was terrifying."

"Afraid to die?"

"No, scared of the fight, getting pierced and sliced with a bayonet or shot. The enemy soldiers captured and tortured our guys. Stuff like that. Yet lots of daring acts transpired despite the terror." He tipped his head toward me. "Believe me. You're brave."

Still sniffling and cuddling Andy, I said, "I have a mantra I repeat in my head." I paused. What an intimate thing to share. I found it easy speaking with Jonathan. He made me feel safe. A mental laugh zipped in and flew out. Safe was not the only emotion he elicited. I had no words to describe them, having never experienced them before. "Whenever I face something daunting, I remind myself I'm the daughter of courageous British and African parents, who together fought the Congo River, rhinos, and crocodiles. Thrashed through the bush to dig wells and build schools and hospitals. Bring the Word of God."

"They were missionaries?"

"Yes. They worked together for decades."

"Like my parents." He made a half-laugh, half-grunting sound. "Fighting thugs who were seeking protection money, and thieves trying to take from us."

I looked down on Andy's sweet face, still asleep, and wondered if he'd speak with the reverence and understanding Jonathan shared for what I had to do for his safety? Might anger and hurt prevail?

For the rest of the trip, we drove in silence, wrapped in our thoughts.

We approached the Wilson's house at 8:00 p.m.

"Wait. Please stop." A new panic welled up. "How can I leave my children here?"

The truck idled on the street corner with the Wilson's home just ahead. It was long after the time we promised Cora and Dahlia we'd return, and we were still hours away.

Jonathan said, "Where else could you go?"

I thought of Mac and Beryl. Grab my babies and the five of us move back in with them until I found a different, safer place. But then what? Might Mrs. Barker offer another foster home? Could we find three more live-in positions? How many months would that add to our separation?

"What if Cleveland Creamer returns? His mother is still next door. Might he try to take Andy again, beat up the Wilsons the way he hurt his wife, or harm Irene and George?" My sodden handkerchief did a poor job of stopping the flow. "I can't put my children in danger again."

Jonathan rested his forehead on the steering wheel as if in prayer and then lifted his head. He said in a quiet voice, "One option is to work at our store while the kids return to school."

"I can't afford another apartment." I looked down at Andy's sweet face and watched his easy breathing. "And who'd take care of Andy while I worked?"

Jonathan didn't respond at once. When he did, he rested his hand on my arm. "We'd figure it out together."

Together? "I don't understand."

"You do."

"Are you asking me to *live* with you?" The thought filled me with trepidation. Henry raped me on our marriage bed when I was thirteen. I knew no other experience. What would Jonathan expect of me?

His voice took on an urgency. "Sorry. I meant no disrespect. We'd get married first."

I sensed his intense stare but didn't turn toward him.

"We have a spacious apartment above the store. Used to house both my parents, my brother, uncle, and me. Now, it's just my pop and me living there. Plenty of room."

Careful not to disturb Andy, I twisted away and looked out the window. Jonathan and I met only months before. Just as I married Henry with no understanding of who he really was, married-off for money, wouldn't this be the same? Besides, marrying again was impossible because I was still married to Henry. Mother and Father's images working side by side swam in my mind. So did Beryl and Mac. Did I want what they had?

"Please don't turn away from me. I love you, Grace, from the moment I met you." He leaned closer. "I've been a bachelor all my adult life. No wife. No children. I thought nothing of it. Until I met you."

Secrets and lies. Generational decisions and curses. "I'm a married woman."

"He's dead. You're alive, with a family to support. I'd take care of all of you. Treat you like you deserve."

"I'm married," I said again without explanation. Let him believe I was still bound to my dead husband.

A loud silence followed.

"I'm sorry." I looked at him now, full on.

Jonathan's shoulders heaved. "What will you do?"

I realized, once again, that I had no choice but to stay on the path I'd plowed.

CHAPTER FORTY-NINE

My babies lifted me. Their relief and excitement upon seeing Andy, who continued to sleep despite the commotion, bubbled up and over. Esther promised to lie down with both boys. 'If either wakes-up during the night, they won't be afraid,' she assured me.

This was a huge turnaround for Esther. Her guilt appeared to inspire the behavior, and I was grateful for the change. Irene and Georgie shared my lap, while Jonathan entertained everyone with our rescue, making me the hero and keeping all the sordid bits out. It sounded like an amazing adventure and had all gasping, laughing, and Irene clapping.

The little ones were sleepy, so I tucked Irene and George in and promised to call as often as possible. Sylvie and Patricia kissed them good night. Andy lay in the bed across from George's. I stared down at my sleeping boy and said a soft prayer.

"Girls, please stay with the children for a few more minutes."

Sylvie asked, "Why? Aren't we leaving?"

"In a few minutes." I intended to speak with the Wilsons in private to learn how they intended to keep my family safe from Cleveland Creamer.

Sylvie took Patricia's hand, and the two girls sat on the floor and leaned against Andy's bed.

Once in the parlor, I spoke with Esther and Edward. "The senior Mrs. Creamer is still next door?"

"I've not seen signs of moving," Esther said.

"The children's safety and yours give me pause."

Edward said, "I understand. We have good relationships with our neighbors. I'll put everyone on alert." He spoke to Esther. "Kennedy works nights, so he'll be home in the day. A good place to hide if there's trouble." With a pivot, he faced me. "We'll keep everyone safe."

Jonathan said, "I can speak with the senior Mrs. Creamer, explain what happened. *Impress* upon her the trouble her son is in and tell her the police are looking for him."

"Are they?" Esther asked.

"No. But she doesn't know that."

Was it enough? "Thank you all so much."

Esther returned Lotus' picnic basket. "I saved two sandwiches for you both and filled the Thermos Jug with cold water."

I dug for the right words. "Andy's experience might scar him, and I won't be here to comfort him."

"What a terrible thing. Sallie Creamer seemed so nice—"

"Please keep a watchful eye on him. If he needs to hear my voice, call me… I'm only allowed to make and accept calls at dinner time."

Despite Esther's previous admonishments about phoning at that hour, she promised.

Edward walked us out. "How is Sallie doing? Did you see her?"

"She's in trouble," I said.

"I'd like to contact her. I worry for *her* children, as well as yours."

Jonathan said, "I can tell you where we found her, but she might have left."

"On my day off, I'll look for her."

"Creamer is violent. Maybe take a friend with you."

We said our goodbyes. So much transpired in one day. I longed for sleep and yet remained wide awake. Arms around both girls, we returned down the stone path to the street.

Patricia said, "Even though we worried about you and Andy, we had a nice day. Mr. Wilson is funny. He played with Georgie and his soldiers, and we all tried our hands at a game of catch."

"Mrs. Wilson is a bit harsh," Sylvie added. "But I don't think she's mean."

"I'm glad you both had a good day." So did I, in a way. At least a day that ended well.

Patricia told us the Perlmans retired early. The younger children by 7:00, the older ones by 8:00, and Cora and Noah by 9:00. So, it was too late to take Patricia to the Bronx. We drove to Pelham. The night air was cool and clean, whisking away the smoke, memories, and terrors of Jamaica Village. I shuddered every time I thought about what almost happened.

Jonathan asked, "How will you get in? Did they give you a key?"

I'd been asking myself the same question. "Ivan and Lotus live in the back. We'll knock on their door." We weren't friends, not like Mac and Beryl, but I liked and trusted both. Perhaps they sensed something good in me or worried about my children.

"Tomorrow morning, I can return Patricia."

Oh my. He was so sweet and kind. Generous. Emotions I'd never experienced before swirled. He confessed to loving me and willing to take care of my entire family. But I wasn't free, so I couldn't encourage him. Besides, I was determined to take care of myself. "Thank you, but no. I'll ask Ivan to drive her first thing in the morning, before the household awakens." I touched Jonathan's arm with the tips of my fingers. "You must work tomorrow and you're tired. I can see it in your eyes."

"Weariness is not what you see."

Heat flushed my cheeks.

We reached the Jacob's house. It was dark. I was sure they'd locked the front door.

"I'll wait here," Jonathan said. "Just in case."

I hesitated and then leaned over and kissed his cheek before scrambling out of the truck. Jonathan came around with the stepstool. He studied me. My eyes darted away. Not wanting to think about what the kiss meant or how it belied my spoken words, I busied myself helping the girls.

"Good night," he said, his dark eyes holding mine.

"Thank you so much for everything." I felt his gaze follow us as Patricia, Sylvie, and I, holding hands, walked around the side of the main house.

Ivan responded to our first knock. I explained our dilemma and Lotus promised to let us into the house in the morning and Ivan to take Patricia to the Bronx. He and Lotus shared their bath, night clothes, and made beds for us on the floor. Snuggled between Patricia and Sylvie, I thought about all the blessings in my life. A few months ago, I questioned God's existence. Now, I saw his hand everywhere. Andy rescued. The Wilsons promised to keep the children safe. Jonathan proposed marriage. Emotions rose through my body, feelings that made me squirm. What was happening to me?

Tomorrow, I'd begin my new business, start on the dress for Dahlia, and plan for an independent life, one where all five of my children were under one roof, attending school, laughing, and healing from these dark four months. This was an era for women's freedom. Magazines and newspapers published stories about flappers doing what they pleased. For the past fourteen years, I let my husband decide everything, all for the sake of comfort. And, I had to concede, for the care of my children. If there was a role for Jonathan to play in our future, it wouldn't be determined by my need for money or a place to live. But what did that mean? With my girls on either side, sleeping on Lotus' and Ivan's floor? I decided to write Jonathan in the morning, thank him for his kindness, but tell him we can't see each other anymore, without explanation, because what could I say?

I closed my eyes and tried to sleep. It was time for *me* to take care of my family. On my own. I prayed I'd find a way.

PART II

CHAPTER FIFTY

September 1924, Pelham, New York

It had been almost four weeks since we rescued Andy or anyone sighted Cleveland Creamer, or I'd seen Jonathan. He called several times after receiving my letter and wrote me, but I didn't accept the calls or respond to his note.

Ivan and Mac stepped into the hole Jonathan left and ferried us on alternate Sundays. The kidnapping and drugging of Andy appeared to leave no lasting mark. He played and laughed, spoke in his long, grownup sentences, demanded attention from his siblings just as he did before. But... there was something in his bright brown eyes that troubled me. Every Sunday, I kept a keen eye on him. I quizzed Esther and Edward. They assured me he was fine.

This weekend was special. Mac *and* Beryl were coming with their twin boys. George and Andy would be especially happy to see Josh and Nick. We'd crowd into Mac's car and have a grand reunion. It was also a special weekend for the Jacobs–Rosh Hashanah, the Jewish New Year, and the first of their High Holy Days.

On the Friday before Rosh Hashanah, Lotus and I walked into the parlor. The Jacobs expected over thirty friends and family for their holiday meal on Sunday at sundown and a smaller group on Monday evening. The servants–Lotus, Ivan, Sylvie, Cecily, and me–had to pitch in and do more than our normal duties. Sylvie's employment was a blessing, but now the Fishers were attending the celebration and planned to take Sylvie home with them. This left me sad and anxious.

I'd hoped Sylvie's contributions inspired Dahlia to make my daughter's employment permanent. News of the Fishers' return and plans spoiled that dream and sent Sylvie spiraling, begging me to prevent the Fishers from taking her.

Lotus and I stood in front of Dahlia and waited. My heart was heavy, but also excited about Sunday with Mac and Beryl. I hoped the outing salved Sylvie's angst and anger.

"Sit, sit. We have much to discuss," Dahlia said. She wore one of her many day dresses. This one was pearl gray, one of her favorite colors, with pockets and a lace-trimmed collar.

I chose a chair catty-corner to the long sofa and Lotus, draped in her oversized apron, perched next to Dahlia.

"My mother-in-law is a hard woman," Dahlia said. "Quite critical, so everything must be perfect for Sunday." She rested her hands on her lap atop the sheet of paper. "Shall we go over the menu again and each person's assignment?"

Lotus rolled her eyes, but Dahlia was looking down on notes she'd written and didn't notice.

"I will be with my friends and children on Sunday," I said. "It will be quite late when Sylvie and I return." I'd explained this to Dahlia several times earlier.

"You cannot go. No. That's unacceptable."

I settled myself. I needed this position, but I'd find another if I had to. My voice was firm and intent clear, I restated my intentions. "Sylvie and I will be gone all day."

"My parents are also attending, along with my brother, sister-in-law, and their four children. I will hear their collective disappointment in me. 'Are you pregnant again?' And when they learn I'm not, their feelings will show. Not understanding, but criticism, as if losing babies is my fault."

"It isn't," I said, my heart touched by her sadness and fear.

Dahlia dipped her head. "You must stay. I can't manage without you."

Over the six weeks of living in the Jacob's home, I'd become Dahlia's confidante, more so as each day passed.

Dahlia brightened. "The dress I intend to wear Sunday needs updating. Can you work your magic?"

I smiled my agreement.

Then one of her many mood swings descended. "But you won't stay? You'll leave me to fend for myself?"

"What else can Lotus, Sylvie, and I do for you this evening and tomorrow? We'll work on whatever you require to ensure a successful celebration."

Without a warning sound, Dahlia swooned, landing on the sofa, her dress draped around her.

"Oh no." I grabbed the Spanish fan Samuel brought her during one of his many business trips and fanned her face. "Lotus, please bring some water."

This happened several times over the last four weeks. Dahlia asked Samuel to purchase a harp for the music room. When he insisted, they didn't need one, she collapsed in his arms in a dead faint. Another time, after a fitting for her flapper dress, she asked when Jonathan and I were taking her to Harlem. I explained Jonathan might not, but I was in search of another escort. She collapsed on her bed.

Now I felt her pulse which was strong. "Shall we call a doctor?" I asked Lotus.

She sucked her teeth.

Within minutes, Dahlia came around.

"Here, sip some water," I said bringing the glass to her pale lips.

"A brandy, please."

From the sideboard, Lotus poured a glass of peach brandy.

"Would you like to lie down on your bed?" I asked. "We can help you upstairs."

Dahlia shook her head and drank. "Are you sure you can't stay and help us on Sunday? I'm not myself, as you can see." She lifted the fan and fluttered it in front of her face.

"Sylvie and I will work with Lotus tomorrow. Make sure everything is prepared and perfect, including your dress."

Another gulp. She peered at me over the rim of the glass. Piercing green eyes pleaded with me. I stared back with unblinking resolve.

She shifted again. "How is your other daughter? Cora says all is going well."

The strain on my family grew with each visit. Irene and George asked to come home from the moment we arrived. Andy clung to me, his thumb in his mouth. Esther reported several nighttime accidents. Patricia still barely spoke. "I'm glad Miss Cora is pleased," I said.

"Lotus, will you excuse us." Dahlia smiled sweetly as she said this and waited in silence until Lotus left the room.

"Do you know people... who can prevent women from miscarrying?" Her emerald eyes filled up. "A potion?"

Startled, I asked, "Are you pregnant?"

"Yes." She sobbed, flopped to a prone position on the sofa, but remained conscious. Some of the brandy spilled on her dress before I grabbed the glass.

"I've not told Samuel," she said. "He'll be angry. And I won't tell my in-laws or parents. Like ghouls, they'll wait for me to miscarry again."

"Surely not. Your parents love you."

"Yes. I think you're right." She heaved a noisy breath. "If this time the baby stayed with me... Samuel will make an excellent father."

"I'm happy for you. How far are you along?" I doubted drinking brandy was good for the baby, but many women drank throughout pregnancy. The old women of Jamaica warned against it unless one imbibed a little white rum to extinguish an ailment.

"Eight weeks. I'm not sure. The babies always leave me before the third month." A few tears slid down her cheeks. "I'm hoping you can help me."

I thought of the midwife who believed in herbal teas. Was there one to keep a child? "I'll inquire."

In another shift, she swiped her cheeks and asked in a mistress-to-servant tone, "Why should I believe you? You finished the flapper dress and we've no place to go. I kept my end of the bargain."

I had no alternative escort to a speakeasy. Only Jonathan. "I shall hold up mine."

CHAPTER FIFTY-ONE

Mac, Beryl, and the twins, drove up at 9:00 Sunday morning. Clouds hid the sun, and a stiff breeze made the fifty-five-degree air feel much cooler. I wore a black and white dress I'd remade from an old one. Mother's silver earrings shone from my lobes.

Glad for the body warmth, Sylvie and I squeezed into the back seat with Josh, who still liked to cuddle. He leaned against me, and I wrapped my arm around him. Mac put Lotus' picnic basket in the car's boot. The other twin, Nick, taller and heavier than his brother, sat in the front, snuggled between his parents. When we reached the Grand Concourse and collected Patricia, we made room for her by placing Josh on my lap and we headed for Queens.

Mac led us in a chorus of the popular song, "Does Your Chewing Gum Lose Its Flavor?"

Does your chewing gum lose its flavor on the bedpost overnight?
If your mother says don't chew it,
Do you swallow it in spite?
Can you catch it on your tonsils,
Can you heave it left & right?
Does your chewing gum lose its flavor on the bedpost overnight?

Even Patricia joined in and laughed at the chorus. We were in a grand mood when we reached the Wilsons. After climbing out, and before going inside, I hugged Beryl tight. "Thank you for this treat. It's been so long since we've had time together." She looked rested and her smile was as broad as ever.

Esther hurried us inside. Her eyes flicked back and forth while her arm waved us along. Her brown dress, indistinguishable from the others she wore, outlined her slim frame.

Once in the entranceway, the children rushed to us. Irene threw herself at Auntie Beryl and then reached up for me to lift her. I kissed and squeezed her. Georgie was already showing the twins his room. Andy trooped behind them, eager to be one of the big boys. This was a wonderful development, since just the week before, Andy clung to me.

"He's back," Esther said, the moment the little ones were out of earshot.

"Sylvie and Patricia, go mind the children." I didn't want them hearing about Cleveland Creamer.

Sylvie said, "Tell me what's happening. Are you forgetting I was here when you ran off looking for Andy?"

"I will tell you later. Take Patricia with you."

To my surprise, Patricia spoke up. "I'm old enough to learn what's wrong. Besides, I was here as well."

With seconds ticking by and urgency in Esther's voice, I gave in, and we all sat.

Esther said, "Edward saw him this morning, visiting his mother."

My hand flew to my abdomen. "Is he still there?"

Esther bobbed her head. "I've been standing watch. Edward's in the backyard, covering from that angle." She peered out the side window that faced the house next door. "I think we should call the police."

"And say what? We have no proof he took Andy, and now he's only visiting his mother."

Mac said, "What are you all talking about?"

I hadn't filled in Mac and Beryl. There wasn't a way for them to help us. But now… "A man snatched Andy and tried to sell him. His mother lives next door." Saying it aloud brought the horror back.

Beryl groaned. "Leaving them here was a mistake."

"Not helpful," Mac said.

"We've protected and cared for them." Esther sounded miffed.

I raised my hands. "Please, let's focus." I explained to Mac and Beryl about Andy's disappearance and Jonathan's and my rescue. Thankfully, Beryl made no comment at the mention of Jonathan, although I saw her eyebrows rise.

Esther paced during the telling. "There's been no trouble since," she said at the end of my tale.

A bang on the door, followed by another, sent my heart rocketing. I fingered Henry's knife in my pocket, which I now carried with me at all times.

Mac said in a deep baritone, "Who is it?"

The banging stopped. I pushed back the curtain and saw Edward standing behind Cleveland.

"What do you want?" Edward demanded.

"Girls, get the children, bring them all into one room," I said.

Beryl said, "I'm going with them and taking a cast-iron pot from the kitchen with me."

"Esther, now it's time to call the police." I straightened my back and took deep breaths.

Beryl side-eyed me and then Mac. "Do *not* let that man reach the children. No matter what or how."

Mac opened the door and the two of us stood side by side.

"The police are on their way," Mac said.

Creamer, dressed in a pinstriped suit and a white open-collar shirt, crossed his arms. "You didn't call nobody."

Mac was not tall, but he looked solid and well-muscled. I tightened my grip on the knife handle. "You stole my son. Of course, we called the police."

Edward came up behind Creamer, but not too close. Mac took another step down. "Run. Now. Before it's too late."

But Creamer didn't move. He put his hand inside his jacket.

Did he have a weapon? A gun? "Your mother is watching from her porch," I said. "And so are your neighbors across the street."

He twisted around and took in the scene.

"Jail is a terrible place. I've visited one, and it was smelly, dank, and dangerous. Leave while you're able." I moved closer so once again, I stood next to Mac. Perspiration trickled down my back. "And never come back."

Creamer back peddled. "I'd never hurt a kid. I'm not like that." He reached his roadster. "You put me in a pickle."

I did? You placed yourself. And if selling a child is not harming him, then I don't know what is. But I didn't say aloud what I was thinking.

He slid into his battered roadster and drove off. To where? Were Sallie and her children safe or still with him? Why lie about his motives for taking Andy? Might he return? We returned to the parlor. No one spoke. I clenched my shaking hands until they stilled.

. . .

The clanging of the police bell on the hood of the automobile announced the coppers' arrival. The long Packard, the department's seal on the front doors on either side, pulled to a stop in front of the Wilson home.

Edward met them, while the rest of us watched from the doorway and porch.

"What's the problem, Wilson?" A short officer with a round belly that hung over his belt asked. "Got a call from the Mrs."

The officer spoke in a booming voice. I was sure the neighbors heard him as well. After a few minutes of conversation, the officer, who'd lowered his voice, waved at us, and left.

"What did you say to him?" I asked the second Edward returned to the porch.

"Brought him up to date. He's run into Creamer on more than one occasion." Edward nodded. "He's going to keep a look-out for him."

"You've had dealings with the officer in the past?"

"Yeah. Unlike Manhattan, we're more like a small town. Police here know everyone, especially in colored parts of town. Just the way it is."

We filed back into the house. Relief mixed with anxiety kept my insides unsettled.

The rest of the visit was lovely. We stayed close to the house, but still picnicked, played games, and as the day moved along, relaxed. My anxiousness subsided, allowing me to enjoy my children and friends. Even Esther smiled occasionally.

Toward sundown, we packed up to go.

Beryl said, "I almost forgot. Your mother wrote you." She pulled an envelope from her purse and handed it to me.

My instinct was to wait until bedtime and read it at my leisure, but something compelled me to open it.

My darling girl,

I write this letter with tears in my eyes. When I received your last note, sharing your dreams of a business, and the progress you are making, I couldn't stop smiling. I'm prayerful Sylvie will return to school and enroll in college, and Patricia will recover with time, your unconditional love, and God's grace.

Your news gave me courage.

I'm quite ill with not much time left in this world. Nora and Carrie are moving to Jamaica to care for me, but I fear it will be to bury me instead. I'm tired, my sweet Gigi, and ready to join your father on the other side. The doctors tell me to take this and that, medicines that come with no promises and lots of misery. I have no interest. And now that your life is no longer in peril, I believe it's time to go.

Please forgive me, so I don't die without your blessings.

Your Loving Mother

I sank to my knees and wept.

CHAPTER FIFTY-TWO

I remember the day Father died. Not the actual day, because I was in England and he and Mother in the Congo. Rather, I recall the day I found out. Gram came for Nora, Carrie, and me at Walthamstow. This was rare. Excited, instead of my school uniform, I dressed in one of the many frocks Gram gave me. My tenth birthday was days away. Perhaps this would be an early celebration.

We gathered in the headmistress' office. A table stood in the middle of the room with a chair in front and another behind. A rolltop secretary, messy compared to the uncluttered table, held papers, pens, and several books. Silver-hammered, studs outlined the chairs' leather. Gram, on the opposite side, sat on a divan facing the door we entered.

Mrs. Ford looked as formidable as ever. With a raised hand, she kept us from running to Gram. Unsmiling, she fussed with my collar and smoothed Carrie's hair, which was more like Mother's than mine, with strands escaping its confining bun.

Gram, her crinkled skin dusted with powder, wore a long dress that covered all but the tips of her boots. Before acknowledging the three of us, she took off her wide hat–its white ribbons reflecting the sunlight slanting through the paneled windows. We waited for a signal from either woman. Carrie held my hand.

Gram patted spaces next to her on either side. "Come, children. Gather close."

From the tremor in her voice, I realized this was a sad, rather than festive, visit.

Father was gone. He lost his fourth battle with malaria. Mother tended him until the end.

Gram handed Nora, the oldest, a book–*The Life and Times of George Graham in the Congo*. It was a biography of sorts, published in 1908.

Gram said, "I have a copy for each of you, but I only brought this one with me now."

I touched the black cover. Gram opened it to a photo of Father. My eyes filled up. I missed him so and now I'd never see him again.

"Is there a photo of Mother in the book?" They were partners.

"No."

Carrie said, "Father's Black wife and brown daughters probably don't exist in the book." She sounded angry, which was rare for Carrie.

I looked to Gram for an explanation, but she closed the book with a snap.

The last time Father wrote was one month before. The letter hinted at trouble, but I didn't grasp the nuances.

My dearest Gigi,

I have already written you in reply to your long letter, and this is just a line or two, to tell you how I'm getting on, and how I left Mother. She is recovering from influenza and shall be on her feet and with me in a few more days. My bones ache, and a fever pesters me, but like Mother, I shall heal soon.

I'm sorry you had such a big fit of the "blues" just before you wrote. Young girls with your volatile spirit are often subject to them, I fancy, so yours does not appeal to me as an extraordinary case. Like your poor self, your poor father has fits of the same. My work can weigh my spirit down. Aches and pains, add to the difficulty. Your mother lifts me and Carrie and Nora will do the same for you. Go to them. They will care for you.

Say your prayers often, thank the Lord for His grace, and let the Holy Spirit guide and comfort you.

Your loving father.

At the time, I didn't wonder about his fever, or aches, and pains. Father was indestructible, and like Mother, a constant in my life.

I don't remember the rest of Gram's visit, or the consoling words she offered. In retrospect, I realize, she'd lost her son, so she was grieving too. And just like Father's Black family didn't exist in his biography, Gram soon erased us as well.

Now, so many years later, history reverberated. I'd be over a thousand miles away and unable to sit and hold Mother's hand, comfort her, tell her I love and forgive her. She had Carrie and Nora, but not me.

We arrived at Cora Perlman's late. Adult laughter and conversation greeted us when Mr. Perlman opened the door.

"Happy New Year," I said and then turned to Patricia. "Good night, my darling girl."

"I'm sorry about your mother," she said into my ear as we hugged. "I don't remember Grandmother, but I believe she was kind."

Tears filled my eyes but did not spill. Patricia and Sylvie were toddlers when we left Jamaica. A photo of Mother in a long black dress and tight lace collar, her arms around each of my girls, sat in a bag of stored treasures in my room at the Jacobs. Both girls wore a white ribbon with a bow on the side in their hair. Matching white socks and black shoes with a strap and silver bangles on their small wrists, both girls looked sad. Mother's eyes stared off into the distance. The photographer took it a few weeks before we sailed to America.

"Thank you," I said to Patricia, holding her tight. "Now you go into your room and rest. There's no requirement for you to work tonight just because they're having a party." Although I tried to whisper, I suspected Mr. Perlman heard me.

"Please don't worry," he said. "Cora only needs her to do a few things."

Patricia stepped into their hallway. "It's okay, Mama. I had a fun time today."

The door clicked shut.

With a slow step, I walked along the hall, down the steps, and out to the street. My mother was dying. Could I get to Jamaica in time? How would I plan the crossing, find the money to pay, leave my babies in foster care living next to a child-seller, and abandon wounded Patricia and Sylvie who were working instead of in school? No. A trip to Jamaica was impossible, and therefore, Mother's coming death even more devastating. I climbed into the car's back seat next to Sylvie and the sleeping Nick and tugged a shawl around my shoulders.

Jamaica was not possible, but in a few days, it would be October, and the start of my new life and business. I'd approach Jonathan about the speakeasy visit. Somehow. Without undoing my decision about not seeing him. Once I satisfied Dahlia with the adventure, I'd ask her to tell her acquaintances about my skills, the way Miss Denise spread the word among her friends. The woman at the fabric store might display some of my designs if I approached her in the right way. New frocks for Hanukkah, Christmas, and New Year's Eve parties on my request list. And just as we rescued Andy, I planned to reclaim my family by January.

. . .

The Jacob's guests were still in a celebratory mood. Lotus served dessert–apples dipped in honey, and a cake I didn't recognize. People stood in clusters of four and five and Dahlia moved among them, smiling, and chatting. She caught my eye.

"Oh, I'm so glad you're back. You and Sylvie can help Lotus."

Although exhausted, I smiled. "Of course." Dahlia was central to my plan and Lotus, my friend, in need of helping hands.

"I've promised the Fishers another girl. Not our Sylvie. She's become quite indispensable to Lotus, I understand." Dahlia tipped her head toward my oldest. "Might you stay with us and work with your mother?"

Sylvie's relief was palpable. "I'd like that very much," she said. "Thank you."

The end of a sad day, but also a good and hopeful one. Sylvie and I rolled up our sleeves and got to work.

CHAPTER FIFTY-THREE

October 1924 Pelham NY

I held up the dress. My first flapper costume. The black silk-cotton outlined Dahlia's curves rather than hid them in the more common, boyish style. Sleeveless and low cut, I decorated the front with silver beads and sparkling sequins. Black fringe hung to just below her knee and swirled with each movement. I wanted to try it on, but I resisted. The dress belonged to Dahlia, not me.

Dahlia pinned up the hair of her favorite wig, and I made a headband with a feather on one side. Black opera gloves and a bracelet with three rows of pearls finished the outfit. The war gave women opportunities while the men fought. We won the right to vote and became more independent and adventurous. Women smoked and drank in public. Dahlia and I experienced none of these things.

"It's gorgeous," Dahlia said, admiring herself in the mirror. "I wish Samuel could see me. Don't you think he'd love how I look?"

I didn't know Samuel well. He worked long hours and when home, spoke little with the household servants.

"I do," I said, unsure of my statement's truth.

We'd chosen the day for our adventure–Saturday, after sundown, October 11. The family would observe the highest of holy days–Yom Kippur, on the Tuesday and Wednesday before, and then Samuel was going away and wouldn't return until Sunday morning. Dahlia was still pregnant, wasn't showing yet, nor had she told her husband. Unsure how, I still had to speak with Jonathan. I also promised Dahlia to visit the midwife in the Bronx.

. . .

Ivan and I left on a cool October morning. The foliage was still at its peak, although some leaves, already brown, created a carpet on the grass. Wind whirled them around and covered the hood of the Jacobs' gleaming green Packard, Ivan at the wheel.

When we reached the Kline's brick house, I asked Ivan to wait in the car. It seemed prudent since he might disapprove of the numerous ways Mrs. Kline helped women, and I didn't want to cause her distress. Dahlia gave me $50 just in case the midwife could and would help.

The heavy wooden door swung open after my first rap. Mrs. Kline looked just as I remembered her from my visit months ago, short and round, with a toothy smile. Her curly red hair appeared freshly cut and styled.

"So nice to see you again, Mrs. Herbert."

She ushered me into the same sunlit room, but today, a fire flicked and snapped in the fireplace.

"Did you have a sweet and joyous Rosh Hashanah?" I asked, assuming she was Jewish, based on her last name.

"How kind of you to ask. We're not observant in any formal way but joined friends who celebrated. Lovely."

I sat on one of the Queen Anne chairs and she on the art déco sofa opposite me.

"How is Patience?"

Scents of cinnamon, rosemary, and lemons, as soft as a kitten's nose, teased mine. "Healing," I said, then reconsidered. "Slowly." The fire crackled. Its smoke pleasantly added to the aroma mixture.

"Time is the only cure for those wounds."

I nodded. Had my emotional abrasions healed? Did I believe, with time, Patricia would become her light-hearted self again? I prayed it would be so.

"What brings you to my home today?"

I explained Dahlia's situation and desire for an herbal potion to help her keep her baby.

"Ah. I wish she'd sent you sooner. The prescription works best when administered two to three months before conception." Her sad expression made me guess there was no hope.

"However," she explained in an energetic voice, "we can try. The fruit from the chaste tree is the foundation. I purchase it from my friends at the Asian market." She stood. "How rude of me. May I offer you a refreshment?"

My mouth tasted dusty from the trip. "A cup of tea, thank you." I thought about Ivan sitting in the car. Might he want a cup or need to use the water closet? "A friend, my employer's driver, is waiting outside. I asked him to stay in the car because I didn't want to endanger you."

"My dear. We've discussed the issue, so no need to worry. Do invite him in while I fix us a pot of tea."

Ivan joined us. I suspected more to find out what was going on than to use the facilities. But I trusted him. The three of us sipped tea and munched on sweet biscuits. Unlike my first visit, this time, I enjoyed both.

"Let me prepare your herbal tea. I'll be just a few minutes."

Ivan asked, "What's this about?"

"Women troubles." That often discouraged men from asking any more questions.

"Oh." He popped up. "I'll check on the car. Come when you're ready."

I suppressed my smile.

When Mrs. Kline returned, I told her about Ivan's hasty exit.

"In a social setting, my husband's reaction would be the same."

We both chuckled. What did I know about men? Father, Henry, and now Mac, Ivan, and Jonathan. I mentally shook my head. Keeping Jonathan out of my thoughts was difficult.

"Here you go. I put the ground, dry fruit in a chamomile base. Added a pinch of ginger and raspberry. Make the tea strong. Let it steep for at least ten minutes. Do you need a teapot cozy to keep the potion warm?"

"We have plenty. Thank you. When should she drink and how often?"

"Every night for thirty days. This should be enough, but if not, come back and I'll make more. You say she loses the babies in her third month?"

"Four times."

"Oh my."

Mrs. Kline's eyes looked as kind as her words sounded, filled with empathy, and understanding. I remember the overwhelming grief I experienced after losing the twins three days after they were born. I imagined Dahlia experienced the same pain each time she lost a baby.

"Has this worked for your clients? I want to reassure her and give her hope."

"It's not ideal, but yes. Last month, a woman in somewhat similar circumstances came to me. The brew, plenty of bedrest, and eating fresh fruits and vegetables, did the trick."

"I will share your story with my... friend." I wasn't sure what to call Dahlia. We weren't friends, not in the genuine sense, but I had to protect her identify.

"Good luck," Mrs. Kline said at the door. "Let me know if it works. If not, when she's ready, we'll try the prophylactic approach–ingesting the herbs months before conception."

When Ivan and I returned, Dahlia was watching us from the nursery window. I expected her to rush downstairs in anticipation, but we entered a quiet house. Sylvie and Cecily dusted and polished the parlor furniture. Lotus, humming a church song, peeled potatoes at the kitchen sink.

"Well? How'd it go?" Lotus asked as soon as I entered the room.

I'd left Ivan preparing to clean and wax the car. "She gave me no assurances the brew will work." I explained what Mrs. Kline shared without mentioning her name. "It's best used three months before, but she believes it's worth a try."

Lotus said, "I pray so. After each miscarriage, this house becomes grief-soaked and choking."

I placed the package with the herbs on the counter nearest Lotus. "There are dresses to mend," I said, but didn't add, 'to make.' I'm not sure why I hesitated to share my plan. A trip to the fabric store was on my list. I'd show the flapper dress to the owner and explain how I'd make more conservative versions for interested customers. She'd sell more fabric, and I'd make enough money for an apartment where I could also work. It sounded plausible in my head, but I needed my plan to sound that way to the store owner.

CHAPTER FIFTY-FOUR

Dahlia asked no questions about the herbs, nor did she agree to use them that night.

"Have you spoken with your gentleman friend yet?" Her face, drawn and pale, made me guess she'd been crying.

"What's wrong?"

"Samuel suspects I'm pregnant. He's angry." She flopped onto the bed and lay on her back, her legs dangling over the edge. "Do you think the herbs will work?"

"I'm unsure." With the patience I used when speaking with my girls about a problem, I added, "Mrs. Kline told me about a woman with similar circumstances, and she kept her baby to term."

"Really?" Her expression and tone were a mix of skepticism and hope.

"If it doesn't, the midwife promised to provide the tea three months before the next time you try to conceive."

"How will I know when that will be?" Dahlia sounded bitter. Still on her back, tears made their way into her hair.

"Tell me when you'd like me to prepare the potion. Bedtime is best."

Dahlia sprang up to a sitting position. "I want to go dancing, smoke cigarettes, and drink booze."

"That sounds bad for the baby. In fact, Mrs. Kline recommended plenty of bed rest and lots of fresh fruits and vegetables."

"Are you backing out of our deal?"

Just as my calm voice didn't always work with Sylvie and Patricia, Dahlia's mood stayed sour. "I will call him today."

. . .

I found it difficult to think about Jonathan. The rash kiss lingered in my mind. Suppose he said no, which is what I suspected. How would that impact my employment and future? I waited for the operator to connect us.

"Hello, Grace." His voice sounded warm and glad I'd phoned.

"How are you?"

"Surprised to hear from you." He cleared his throat. "After reading your letter, I tried you several times. Wrote to you. Did you receive it?"

Not only did I read it, but I memorized each word.

Dear Grace,

I've offended you by declaring my love too soon. I'm not young anymore, ready to settle down, and I fell for you hard. Is that my offense? Forgive me. I can wait. But please don't make me wait without being with you.

Your affectionate servant,

Jonathan.

"I apologize for not responding."

"Why are you calling now?"

This was awkward. I was calling for a favor, not because my circumstances had changed. Should I be honest and say that? I tried for a version of the truth. "I'm very glad to hear your voice."

"Likewise. I think about you every day, wondering how you're faring. How's your little boy?"

"Everyone's fine, but desperate for us to be a family again." My words spilled out in a rush. "I have an idea, and I'm hoping you will help me succeed."

"My answer is yes to whatever your need." He paused for a moment. "I'm serious about being a part of your future... when you're ready."

With the stem of the phone in one hand, and the hearing piece pressed to my ear, I paced. "I'm married."

"You said that before. Do you love him so much that even though he's dead, you can't love another? You have feelings for me. I see it, hear it."

"May I explain in person?" I wanted to share my plan. He managed his own business, and that's what I wanted to do. His experience, good and bad, might be what I needed. But that wasn't what Jonathan was asking. Why can't we be together, was his question. It was time I told Jonathan the truth, but not on the phone. "Can you come by after work?"

"I'll be there."

Hours later, Jonathan drove up in his truck. Lotus and Sylvie inquired about where I was going. My answer was vague and, by their sour expressions, unsatisfactory. Dahlia, however, seemed pleased to give me the time, hoping I'd return with a speakeasy commitment.

I was waiting for him and rushed to the door before slowing my step lest he see me acting like a schoolgirl rather than a twenty-seven-year-old woman and mother of five. I'd re-fashioned a cream-colored dress with a pleated skirt to look more modern. Its hem was now at my calf and the matching sash around my neck ended in a bow off my left shoulder. I'd left my long hair pinned up, but I'd rouged my lips a light pink and darkened my eyelashes.

"You look beautiful," he said, before even a hello.

"Thank you." He looked good. Light brown slacks, a vest over a white shirt, tweed jacket and knotted tie, gave him a man-about-town look. Although the evening air was chilly, I'd not put on a coat, nor had he. "Shall we speak in the truck?" I couldn't invite him into the house and I'm sure he had no expectation.

He helped me inside, hurried around, and climbed in. "Do you have the evening off?"

"A few hours. Until bedtime. I brush Dahlia's hair and help her get ready for bed." Tonight, I might have to brew her a potion as well.

"She can't do those things for herself? Is she an invalid?"

"I serve as her lady's maid."

Jonathan shook his head. "Never heard of that."

The late afternoon chill made me wish I'd put on a lightweight coat instead of just bringing a shawl. I felt foolish, getting all dressed up rather than being practical. What was happening to me? I wrapped my arms around my shawl-covered shoulders.

"You're cold and I'm hungry. Let's find a warm place to eat." He started the engine.

"There's no establishment nearby that serves colored folks."

"We're close to a great spot in the Bronx. Won't take us long." He pulled out onto the empty street.

"I'm not wearing a hat."

"You look perfect."

Sonny's Restaurant was an everything-store. In the front, one could purchase sundries, medicines, and household tools. A jar of candies stood on the counter, and Coca Cola and root beer signs announced the contents of an icebox. The scent of food floated from the back.

Zeb, the proprietor, a beefy colored man with thick eyebrows and a stained apron around his waist, greeted Jonathan by name.

"We go way back," Jonathan explained. "Zeb lived in Queens and ran with my brother and me."

We followed Zeb to the restaurant portion of the store. Large posters and advertisements covered the walls. I recognized Marcus Garvey and Duke Ellington, but not the baseball players of the Negro National League.

After Zeb seated us at a round, wooden table with chairs that wobbled on the tiled floor, Jonathan asked, "What's good?"

"Made ribs and fish. Got rice and carrots. The last of the peaches made a fine pie."

Jonathan looked at me.

"The fish, I think."

"Make that two." He held up two fingers. "And a couple of Cokes." He scooted his chair closer to the table.

A family of four entered and Zeb sat them at the table to my right. I couldn't remember a time when Henry and I took the children to an eatery. The idea was foreign to me. On my other side, a couple was engaged in an animated conversation. More people arrived. The buzz of conversation added to a festive atmosphere.

I placed my paper napkin, something also new to me, on my lap, and busied myself arranging and re-arranging my flatware.

"Uh oh. I'm making the lady nervous," Jonathan said.

My laugh was small and self-conscious.

"It's okay. I'm not going to propose again." His eyes were bright and held mine. "Not yet."

Our food came piled high. "I'm not sure I can eat it all."

Zeb said, "You can use a bit more meat on those bones."

"Nah," Jonathan said. "She looks just right to me."

Oh my. This was not how a lady behaved.

"Now, you're upset."

"Flustered. This is all new to me."

Jonathan raised his eyebrows. "Which part?"

Not wanting to explain, I lifted my fork and took a bite. Hints of curry, cumin, and thyme seasoned the fish. Surprised, I said, "This is delicious."

"Best in town."

For a few minutes, we ate in silence.

"So, what did you want to say?" Jonathan wiped his mouth. "Why you can't be with me?"

Afraid to start there, I asked, "Can I first tell you about my plan for getting my family back? I'm... hoping you can advise me."

He held my gaze for several moments. "Okay. Sure." Disappointment colored his words. Then he said, "I'll help you anyway I can. Take only what you're ready to give."

He offered without doubt in his voice, or condescension. As I explained my dress-making intentions, I felt more confident with each word.

CHAPTER FIFTY-FIVE

We finished our meal and shared a slice of peach pie. Its blend of sweet and tart pleased my palate. The flaky crust melted on my tongue.

Jonathan said, "Starting a business from scratch is hard, and it takes time to build up enough trade to pay your bills. Would any of your earlier clients be interested?"

I'd told Jonathan about Miss Denise and her friends. "I don't think so, but maybe. She lives in Brooklyn now."

"You dress so nice. Do you make all your clothes?"

"Yes. And gowns, curtains, and tablecloths. I can make a man's suit."

"Spooner Brothers could display and sell them."

This caught me by surprise. "You sell used goods."

"Branch out. Try something different. My pop and I been thinking about spiffing up our Harlem store and starting another one in St. Albans. It's one of the fastest growing towns. Professional colored folks are moving there in large numbers. My pops and me, found a spot with an apartment above the store we can rent."

"That sounds exciting."

"If a Black man wants to make it, he has to fashion his own luck."

"Women, too." I'd always thought that men took care of the women and children. But women won the right to vote, drank, smoked, and shed their corsets. Madam Walker, and now her daughter, helped women start their own hair salons. I could start my business and be successful. At least, I prayed so.

Zeb scooped away our dirty plates. "Get you folks anything else?"

"Tea?" Jonathan asked, knowing my preference. "Can you stay a little longer?" He pulled out his pocket watch. "It's 6:30."

I wanted to enjoy the rest of the evening sitting with Jonathan and talking about a future of safety and freedom, hear more of Jonathan's plans for his business. Would placing my dresses in Jonathan's store help me reunite my family faster? But what would Jonathan want? I knew the answer to my question.

His eyes fixed on mine and a wash of unknown emotions filled me up. We still hadn't discussed why I couldn't be with him, and he hadn't asked again. I relaxed and let the joyful sensations settle.

A sax player sat on a stool in one corner and began a Duke Ellington tune that I recognized but forgot the name. The couple to my right rose and swayed to the music.

"Would you like to dance?" Jonathan stood and offered his hand.

Without a word, I took it. We joined the other couple. Jonathan pulled me close, one hand on my back and the other holding mine against his chest. His heart thudded. Our bodies swayed until the music stopped. Still holding my hand, Jonathan deposited several bills in the man's case.

The other couple jumped and twirled to the beat of the next tune. I'd only seen this once before when Henry took me to the Rennie.

Jonathan said, "Can you dance the Charleston?"

I shook my head.

"Black folks been doing it for years, then white folks discovered it and now the Charleston is everywhere, even in motion pictures. Want to try?"

This wasn't right. My heart raced and perspiration beaded on my nose. I turned and walked back to our table. My breath came in pants. My shawl lay on the back of the chair. I scooped it up and draped it around my shoulders.

"It was just a dance," Jonathan said. He sounded hurt and... sad? Disappointed?

"I have to get back." How could I ask him to take us to the speakeasy now? I'd made a mess of things.

Jonathan settled our bill with Zeb, said our goodbyes, and we walked to the truck.

"There's nothing wrong with liking a single man who means you no harm. I'd never do anything to disrespect you. Never."

I whirled around. "My husband is alive."

Jonathan looked stunned, and I felt the same. I said aloud my terrible secret.

"Where is he?"

"Prison." Unchecked tears rolled down my cheeks. "I don't love him. I never did. But I'm still married to him. So, you see. Now, do you understand?" Sobs shook my body.

Although I'd closed my eyes, I sensed Jonathan coming closer. He placed a hand on each of my shoulders and, with tenderness, tugged me to him. I'm not sure how long I sobbed against his jacket, but I got control of myself and wiped my face with a handkerchief.

"Do your children know?"

"Sylvie does. But the rest… I told everyone he'd died. People treat a widow differently than a criminal's wife. Despite that, I lost my home and had to place my children." I couldn't speak any more or cry. Exhaustion cloaked me in a growing numbness.

"Your dressmaking will get your children back. I'm sure of it."

People walked past us, going into Sonny's. Each time a door opened, music and conversation drifted out. Streetlights blinked on.

"None of it will work if I don't take Dahlia to a speakeasy." I blurted this out without thinking.

"What?"

"She let me see and call my children in return for making her a flapper dress and getting someone to take us, and—"

"Is that why you called me?" He sounded angry.

I drew the shawl tighter.

Jonathan took off his jacket and rested it on my shoulders. "Come on. Let's get you home."

"The Jacobs' house is *not* my home."

Jonathan no longer seemed angry, just sad. He helped me into the truck, walked around, and climbed in.

We drove in silence. Every few minutes, I sensed his eyes peering at me, but I kept mine closed. When we reached the Jacobs' house, Jonathan parked. Lights glowed from the first and third floors. None from the nursery. The last of the sunset, colored gray clouds. Neither of us moved.

Jonathan spoke first. "What will you do when your husband gets out?"

"I don't know." An honest answer. I couldn't see beyond earning enough for my family to have a place to live. Henry's reappearance would upend our lives again whenever it happened.

"Won't he want to see his children?"

"He can't. Never."

"He hurt them?"

"Yes."

"Did he... hurt you, too?"

I turned toward Jonathan. "Please don't ask me anymore questions." How could I explain raping one's thirteen-year-old wife, the same age as Patricia? My hands shook. I hid them in his jacket pockets.

"I'll take you and Dahlia to a speakeasy, if that's what you need to get your kids back."

Both ashamed and grateful, I said, "I don't deserve your kindness." I pulled his jacket off and handed it to him. "But I didn't call you only to ask a favor."

The truck door was heavy without Jonathan opening it, but I pushed hard. There he was, ready to help me down.

"What you *don't* deserve," he said, "is having a husband who hurts your children, disrespects you, working as a lady's maid, losing your family." He clutched his jacket in his fist. "When did you want to go?"

"Saturday evening."

"Okay then. Saturday, it is."

I sensed him watching me walk up the path to the front door. I turned and waved, but he didn't wave back. Just stood, like a sentry on assignment. I pushed open the door, stepped in, and closed it. My heart hammered and my stomach cramped. I was unsteady and unprepared for whatever came next.

CHAPTER FIFTY-SIX

Saturday, October 11, arrived with gray skies, on-and-off sprinkles, and a cold blustery wind that stripped the mosaic of leaves from the trees. Indian summer, the wonderful fall reprieve of warm sunny days, had yet to materialize.

Dahlia was in a state. "I can't keep anything down. All day long, I throw up. It's hard to hide my condition from Samuel."

We were on the third floor in her bedroom. The flapper dress lay across the chenille spread that covered her oversized four-poster bed. Large windows and two floor lamps failed to erase the room's gloom.

"When will you tell him?" I asked. She'd not yet consumed any of Mrs. Kline's tea. At least she'd not asked me to brew it. "Soon, your condition will be apparent." Dahlia's slim figure and normally flat stomach now had the slightest rounding.

"After we return tonight, I will try the potion."

I wondered why she was taking such chances, going to a club two months pregnant, talking about drinking and smoking, since having a healthy baby meant so much to her. My face must have conveyed my thoughts.

"I don't believe the herbs will work. A baby is not in my future."

"Don't say that."

"I have little hope."

"Mrs. Kline is an expert. Other patients succeeded." I stepped closer to Dahlia, picked up the silver brush, and started brushing her hair. This often calmed her. "You begged me to find you help, and I did.

Drinking the herbs right away is important. You're to take them at night for thirty days."

She pushed my hand away. "I understand." She sounded petulant and put out, then turned contrite. "I'm sorry. You're good to me, Grace. I didn't mean to raise my voice."

"Let's get the dress on." I held the garment while she stepped into it and pulled it up over her narrow bottom, waist, and small breasts.

I stepped back and adjusted the fringe. "Stunning." And she was. Her green eyes shone and picked up the glittering green in the sequins. The dress fit and draped perfectly.

Next, we tied up her thick tresses and worked the wig until it looked as natural as possible. She slipped on the headband with the feather, which also had dashes of emerald green.

"I do look lovely, don't I?" She swung around and then back again. "I love the dress. You are magic with that machine."

A warm flush moved up my neck to my cheeks. My days held hours of free time. Often, I helped Lotus in the kitchen, but mostly, I sewed. In the evenings, I taught Sylvie. Today, I wore my cream dress again, with the bow over the shoulder, and placed a cloche hat at a tilt.

"You need a headband instead of that hat," Dahlia said. She picked up a ribbon of black velvet. "Wear this instead." Then she plucked the broach that decorated my cloche and clipped it to the headband. "There. Much better."

I peered into her vanity mirror. My hair looked nice and more appropriate for the evening.

Lotus rapped on the bedroom door. "Your *escort* is here." She'd made her disapproval clear for days–letting a stranger drive the family car, going out in the evening–a recent widow and a married woman–with a single man, a white lady with two coloreds going to an illegal establishment, and dressed in an unseemly manner. But she loved us both and promised to keep our secret.

We walked down the stairs, slipped on our coats, and waited for Ivan to tell us Jonathan and the car were ready. Sylvie walked into the entranceway. When I saw her face, I missed a step and almost tumbled.

Grabbing her hand, I dragged her into the kitchen. Lotus sat at the big worktable, polishing the silver.

"What's the matter?" I demanded.

She handed me a letter. I recognized Patricia's handwriting, languid with slated loops and curves not unlike mine. My breath felt hot as I unfolded the paper.

My dearest sister,

I want to be with you and Mama. Please get me. I work into the night. The children don't listen to me, especially the older ones. Mrs. Cora is kind most times, but she yells at us when things go bad. Mama never screamed. I am tired and sad. Why do I have to stay here? Is this my punishment for what happened?

I didn't ask how you are? It must be so nice to stay with Mama. That's what I want. Please make her come for me.

Your loving sister,
Patricia

I read the letter twice, then raised my eyes to meet Sylvie's. "A few more months."

Every payday, after sending $2 to repay Mae, Sylvie, Patricia, and I placed the rest of our meager wages in our savings box. Dahlia paid me $20 for the flapper outfit. We placed all her money into the box. I updated my dresses, using scraps of material gained from raising the hem lines. I needed to look like I understood the times if I wanted to dress others. Once I sold garments to the Pelham ladies, we would have enough money for a small apartment. Sylvie was becoming an accomplished seamstress, giving us more opportunities to earn freedom wages. That's how I thought of it. The current arrangement was our path to safety. The saved money was our means to freedom. Jonathan's offer to let us live above his store popped into my mind, but I pushed it away.

Sylvie looked skeptical. "You say that, but—"

Dahlia poked her head into the kitchen. "Are you coming? Is something wrong?"

"I will be right there." I walked into our room and tucked the letter under my pillow before turning back to Sylvie. "We will see Patricia on Sunday."

"She's unhappy. We both are. You get to have fun–go to parties and... you have friends. I don't have anyone, and neither does Patricia."

"Grace, we're ready to go," Dahlia called, her tone edged with annoyance.

Grateful for her discretion, I noted Lotus never lifted her eyes from her work.

"We'll talk tomorrow." I hugged Sylvie's stiff body and kissed her cheek. "I'm working hard on getting us out of here. Please trust me."

. . .

Ivan and Jonathan stood by the gleaming Packard, with the back door opened. As we approached, both men smiled. Ivan tipped his hat. Jonathan kept his eyes on me.

Dahlia climbed into the backseat, and I sat up front.

"Where are you taking us?" Dahlia asked. "To Harlem, I hope. That's where I want to go."

The car was warm inside, unlike riding in Jonathan's glassless truck.

"Yes, ma'am," Jonathan replied. He side-eyed me but said nothing. We both understood our place. The car rumbled onto the street and picked up speed.

"Will there be music and dancing?"

"Yes, ma'am," Jonathan said again.

Dahlia's voice sounded little-girl happy. "I've heard about The Cotton Club. Is that where we're heading?"

"No, ma'am."

"Why not? It's famous. My friend, Gladys, whispered the name to me. She's been, I think."

Streetlights and the Packard's headlights lit our way. Occasionally, we slowed to let another automobile pass, but mostly we were alone on the Pelham streets.

"Grace and I wouldn't be welcome in there."

"In a *Harlem* club?" She sounded incredulous.

"Not the high society ones. Unless you're famous."

"Gladys is from Germany. She can pass."

Now, it was my turn to be confused. "Pass for what?"

"A Gentile. Sometimes, when I'm with her, we both pretend."

How sad this all was. Passing for something, as someone, perceived as more desirable. And I was no better. Passing when it was convenient, pretending, as Dahlia said.

"The spot we're going to isn't high society," Jonathan said. "But we'll be safe and welcomed."

I'd experienced the sting of racism in my own British family, and more recently in Harlem among the police and judiciary, but never considered other races and groups who also experienced the effects. All I saw was Dahlia's wealth and comfort. I didn't know how non-Jewish people treated women like Dahlia.

CHAPTER FIFTY-SEVEN

The building was nondescript brick, with a wooden door, not unlike the factory we visited in Queens, although this door was narrower. Jonathan rapped hard. A large man with wide shoulders and short arms stepped out, his hand on the doorknob behind him.

"Yeah?"

Jonathan said, "The odds are long. Five to one tonight," providing the day's password.

The doorman let us enter.

Another gentleman approached us. "You Spooner?"

Jonathan nodded.

"Zeb told me you were coming. Didn't mention you escorting two white dames."

Jonathan didn't correct him.

"Follow me."

I assumed Zeb referred to the proprietor from Sonny's and he was the one who provided the password to get in. Jonathan seemed acquainted with so many people.

Zeb's friend led us down a dark hall to a narrow staircase. An electric flashlight clicked on, its beam allowing us to see the creaking wood step in front of us, but not much more. Jonathan held Dahlia's arm and guided her and then returned to me. My heart hammered. Being here was both exciting and scary. Jonathan holding my hand as we descended added to both feelings.

At the bottom of the steps, we turned and walked down a dark hallway. A bright red door was up ahead. The closer we got to it, the more we heard. Music. The thrum of conversation. Laughter. The scents of cigarettes and cigars reached my nose, along with colliding perfumes, and the sharp smell of alcohol. The door swung open to a vibrant scene.

White couples did the Charleston. Colored folks too, but they also danced other exuberant, choreographed numbers I didn't recognize—with feet flying and knees knocking. Women, some dressed like Dahlia, and others wearing clothes closer to mine, smoked cigarettes and sipped illegal alcohol in stemmed glasses. Smoke swirls hung in the air. Everyone was smiling and laughing, shouting over the music, and even changing partners on the floor.

Dahlia said, "This is amazing." She turned to Jonathan. "Teach me how to do that dance." She pointed to a couple with their hands on their knees, rocking their legs back and forth.

He caught my eye. "Let's find a seat first. I don't want to leave Grace unescorted."

"Oh, of course. Sorry. I'm just so excited."

He wove his way through the crowd, holding my hand while I held Dahlia's. Zeb's friend waved us over. "Gotcha a table."

We pushed forward. My head swiveled every other second, taking in the colors, sounds, and scents.

Once seated, Dahlia repeated her request, and Jonathan obliged. I watched them dance and laugh. He was so handsome. Not in a conventional sense. Jonathan's deep brown skin glistened, and his open smile, broad nose, and wide-set eyes made for a wonderful face.

The music changed to a slow waltz. I supposed to let the revelers catch their breaths, but also for the establishment to sell drinks. Women, dressed in showgirl outfits, circulated. Rounds of alcohol followed.

Jonathan offered his hand to me. I turned to Dahlia. "Will you be all right?"

"Go. Yes. I'm fine."

"We won't be far. Just here." Jonathan pointed to a spot a few tables over. He led me, then turned and held me close. "You look mighty fine tonight."

"Thank you. You've seen this outfit—"

"It's not the dress."

I rested my head on his shoulder and leaned in as we stepped and swayed only a few tables from Dahlia. He trembled, or it was I who shook.

"I love you so much, Grace. You deserve a man who'll treat you right. Your children too."

I didn't respond, just held on tight.

"You're in your thirties, right? Me too. We can't let life slip by. Soon, it will be too late."

Too late for what? Still, I stayed silent. Should I tell him I'm twenty-seven? And what about Henry when he's released? What then?

Jonathan touched my hair, ran his hand along my back, and closed his eyes. I did the same.

When we returned to the table, Dahlia was sipping a drink the color of honey in a long stemmed glass.

Jonathan spoke to me. "Is that okay?"

"I'm a grown woman and can do as I please," Dahlia said. "This is called The Bees Knees. Isn't that funny?" She pushed the glass away. "You're right. I shouldn't."

"Do *you* want a drink?" Jonathan asked me.

I repeated Dahlia's words. "I shouldn't."

• • •

A man burst into the speakeasy. "Coppers. It's a raid. Run."

Out of nowhere, Zeb's friend appeared. "Follow me."

I grabbed Dahlia's hand and Jonathan took mine.

"This way," Zeb's friend said. "They always bust in from the front, giving us a chance to go out the back."

"Payoff?" Jonathan asked.

We pushed through the panicking crowd. Some white couples stayed in their seats. Other white folks and all the colored ones made for the back door.

Loud whistles, like a siren, streaked through the club. People bumped into us. Someone stepped on my foot. They shoved and pushed. I held onto Dahlia and Jonathan, but my hand slipped. People surged between us. Jonathan spun around. "Grace."

A burly man pushed Dahlia and me up against a wall. Each beefy hand pressed against one of us very close to our breasts. "What are two fine white ladies doing with that nigger?" His foul breath filled my nostrils. "You hookers or what?"

Dahlia gasped and tried to wrench his hand away.

Without looking down and thus alerting the thug, I tugged Henry's knife out of my purse and pricked the skin of his fat gut. "You leave us alone."

"You fucking cut me." A tiny trickle of blood stained the shirt.

Jonathan squeezed through the crowd and reached us. Fists balled, he loomed over the shorter man. "Get away from them."

The fat man grunted, looked down on his stained shirt, and backed away. "Bitch." He staggered away.

Shaking, gasping for breath, I bent over. People bumped around us.

Jonathan lifted my chin. "Are you okay?"

Dahlia's loud sobs reached both of us at the same time.

I asked, "Are you hurt?

Jonathan said, "Did he harm you?"

She wagged her head.

"Come on. Let's get you both home." Jonathan put his arm around my shoulders and held Dahlia's hand. "Stay close."

Behind us, police officers continued to blow their whistles, and push the crowd toward the back door. The number of people thinned out. We followed stragglers to the exit.

One woman said, "They spoil the fun every other night."

Another commented, "Not for rich white folks. They're still there, enjoying their drinks."

I'd noticed the musicians stopped playing but didn't run either.

"A set-up and shake-down," the first woman said. "They pay the coppers."

"There's another place close by," the second woman said.

They both laughed and hurried off.

The chilly night air hit us. Our coats were still inside. We made our way to the car and climbed in.

Jonathan said, "I'll grab the coats in the morning." He covered my hand with his. "You're one brave and surprising lady." He squeezed. "A knife? Wow."

Dahlia said, "Just take me home. I think I'm going to be sick."

I asked, "Are you sorry you came?"

She dabbed at her tears, smearing her makeup. "That was more excitement than I've had... ever." She laugh-sobbed.

"Exciting, good, or exciting, bad?" I asked Dahlia.

She sniffled. Then blew her nose in her handkerchief. "Scary and exhilarating. I can't believe you own a knife and used it to save us."

"I can't either." I looked at Jonathan. "Scary, exhilarating, and grand."

CHAPTER FIFTY-EIGHT

Deep in sleep, the terror and anguish in each cry ripped through my sleep-fog and brought me awake.

Sylvie stirred next to me. "What's happening?"

I tugged on my bathrobe and tied the sash. Stepped into my slippers. "Run and get Lotus. Hurry."

Hours before, Dahlia and I wished each other a good night. Now, her wrenching shrieks filled the empty house. I ran up the stairs, following the anguished sounds, and stopped on the second floor. Oh no, no, no. The cries became loud sobs coming from the nursery.

Dahlia lay on the rug, holding a crocheted baby's blanket against her chest. Blood drips covered the hem of her nightgown and both legs. Memories of Patricia in the bathroom flashed.

I ran to Dahlia's side.

"I'm useless as a woman, as a wife. Why has God abandoned me? What have I done to make him so cruel?"

I lifted her gown and peered at her privates. Unsure what to look for or believe, I raised her hips and placed pillows beneath her, keeping her pelvis and legs elevated. "Shush, now." I lay down next to her. "Help is on the way."

Lotus yelled from downstairs. "Grace, where are you?"

"In the nursery."

She thudded up, with Sylvie behind her.

"There's a lot of blood," I said to Lotus.

Sylvie gasped. Color drained from her face.

"Ask Ivan to bring the car around," Lotus said to Sylvie. "Girl, get hold of yourself and get moving."

Sylvie spun around and ran out.

"Let's clean her up," Lotus said, exiting the room. She returned with a basin of water and a stack of towels. Together, we washed Dahlia. "Does that midwife friend of yours make trips as far as Pelham?"

"I'll call her. What time is it?" I looked through the window and saw the pale light of dawn. I hurried down the steps to the parlor and asked the operator to ring Mrs. Kline.

A sleepy male voice answered. I explained the situation to Dr. Kline, and again to Mrs. Kline, when she got on the line.

"Make her comfortable," Mrs. Kline said. "But don't move her. You're doing all the right things. See if she'll sip some water. Give us the address."

I repeated it twice.

"We're on our way."

Sylvie ran back into the room. "Ivan is downstairs."

I stood and walked to her, put my arms around my girl, and held her. Surely, she remembered her sister on the bathroom floor just months before. "A doctor and midwife are coming, so we won't need Ivan just yet." He'd volunteered to drive us to the Bronx and Queens to see the rest of the family as Mac and Beryl were taking the children to visit their grandmother. "Please get Mrs. Dahlia a glass of water."

Together, the three of us waited for Dr. and Mrs. Kline.

· · ·

Dr. Kline, a giant man with dark hair speckled with gray, lifted Dahlia, and placed her on the bed. We'd cleaned and changed her on the nursery floor. After brewing Mrs. Kline's tea potion, and giving it to Sylvie to deliver, I scrubbed up as much of the blood on the rug as possible. While still on my knees, I prayed.

Lotus found me crouched on the floor. "Are you alright?"

I managed a small smile. "It's been an exhausting evening and morning."

"Will you still visit your family? I intended to go with you, enjoy some air with Ivan, but now I can't leave her." Lotus jerked her head toward the staircase leading to the third-floor bedrooms. "She's terrified of Samuel's anger."

"Is he cruel to her?" I wondered, because she seemed to love him very much, and whenever I glimpsed them together, he appeared loving in return. He listened to her play the piano, and to the stories of her day, kissed the top of her head or cheek whenever he left the room, and spoke in soft tones.

"It's in her head, I think." Lotus made a sucking noise through her teeth. "She's a handful."

"We women know the pain of losing children."

Lotus patted my shoulder. "True enough."

Mrs. Kline joined us in the nursery.

"How is she? How is the baby?" I asked.

"As of now, Dahlia appears fine. We took a sample of her urine, and we'll have it tested."

I let a rush of emotions flood my senses. Their intensity mirrored my relief when George was born. We'd lost Olive that spring. My grief swamped me. All summer, heavy with child, I dragged around our Bronx house. Patricia and Sylvie, both toddlers, clung to each other for comfort. At night, I dreamt a recurring scene–the baby I carried was born dead. A tiny girl with grey eyes like mine. Shriveled. Lifeless. I'd wake up in a cold sweat. George's birth, easy and fast, changed everything. The girls fussed over him. He laughed at an early age, kicked his fat legs, and seemed happy to be alive. Now, he was a solemn ten-year-old with a quick mind. When did he lose his joy?

I walked Dr. and Mrs. Kline to the front door.

Mrs. Kline said, "I explained to Mrs. Jacobs and to Sylvie, bedrest is essential. Vegetable and chicken broth, lots of water, and my special tea every evening before she falls asleep for the night."

"Lotus, Sylvie, and I will help her."

"She doubts she can stay in bed. Something about her husband?"

"We'll do our best," I said, unsure of what that would comprise.

I closed the front door. Lotus stood close by. "I don't think Ivan and I will attend church today. He can drive you to your children whenever you're ready."

"What time is Samuel expected?"

"This afternoon. Ivan can meet him at the station and still get you and Sylvie back here."

Once again, how this family, two new friends, extended themselves, found me humbled.

Sylvie called from the top of stairs. "Mama, Mrs. Dahlia is asking for you."

I ran up the steps to the third floor.

Dahlia lay in the huge four poster bed, pillows under her bottom and feet, and propped to rest her head. Ashen faced, her green eyes looked dull. She waved for me to come closer.

"Please don't leave me today. I'm begging you."

I sat on the edge of her bed. "You're going to be fine. Just a scare."

A sob turned into a burp. "For now." She bit into her lower lip. "I don't want to be alone when Samuel comes home. He's going to be so angry with me."

"Lotus and Ivan—"

"You're my only friend. This is how best friends help."

I'm your paid servant. "Might I call someone from the synagogue? You've mentioned Gladys."

"She's not a genuine friend." Dahlia closed her eyes. Her lips trembled. "Please."

My worry was Patricia and Andy. Irene and George appeared adjusted to our situation–always happy to see me, but no longer crying or looking forlorn when I left. But Patricia's letters came daily, filled with pleas and anguish. And Andy... what happened to him? He seemed drugged and since then, troubled in a manner I couldn't articulate, but sensed. Did they touch him? Or worse? With only one day to visit, it was essential I do so. On the other hand, Dahlia was fragile and indeed promised to help with my business, make introductions, start an account for me at the fabric store. Wasn't that friendship rather than employer-servant behavior?

"May I ask you a question, a private one?"

Her eyes searched my face. "Yes."

"When a man and woman lie together, share a bed, the woman often conceives. Why is the pregnancy your fault?"

She stared at me for several minutes without speaking. I understood the army gave men protection during the war so they wouldn't contract terrible diseases from having relations with prostitutes. And everyone was aware of Margaret Sanger's scandalous determination to give women lawful ways to prevent pregnancies, but so far, she only had a clinic to help women with medical problems tied to pregnancy.

Dahlia said, "It's my fault that I lose babies."

"This time, you're keeping her. Rest and the tea. Your husband will understand and be happy for you both."

"Stay with me." She sounded like Patricia's insistent pleas.

My heart melted, and I gave in. First, I had to tell Sylvie she must visit the children alone. Then find Lotus and Ivan and offer a similar explanation. Dahlia held a lot of my future in her hands and her fear, although irrational, felt real to her.

CHAPTER FIFTY-NINE

Samuel arrived home and Ivan turned the car around to collect my children. What a good man Ivan was. I didn't know Samuel well enough to make a judgement. All our previous interactions consisted of 'Good morning,' and 'Good evening.' My impressions came from the few stories Lotus and Ivan shared, and Dahlia's fear of his anger concerning her miscarriages. Now, as he hurried into the master bedroom, I was unsure what to call him or if I should stay.

About the same height as Dahlia, Samuel's curly brown hair, round face, and bushy eyebrows gave him a plain, scholarly appearance–in direct contrast to Dahlia's beauty.

"Babe, what happened?" Samuel, using a popular term of endearment, knelt by the bed. He shrugged out of his suit jacket and let it fall to the floor. "Ivan told me you had an accident."

Dahlia, still pale and fragile, smiled and touched her husband's face. "I missed you."

"And I you. But how did this happen? Where are you hurt?"

On tiptoes, I eased toward the bedroom door.

"Grace, don't go," Dahlia said, her voice low and weak.

Samuel whipped his head around, his eyes wide and eyebrows raised. From his expression, I guessed he hadn't noticed me before. "Good afternoon."

I dipped my head in response and stayed by the door.

Dahlia said, "Grace has been taking care of me. She called a doctor and spent her entire day off tending to me."

Samuel said, "What kind of doctor?" He sounded cross. "Ours or hers?"

"Don't be like that. Anyway, he's Jewish." Dahlia lifted a limp arm and waved me over. "Come sit next to us."

Mollified, Samuel stood. "Thank you for looking after my wife. Please tell me what's wrong with her. What did the doctor say?"

It was not my place to tell him about the baby. "She needs bedrest, lots of fluids, and they… he left medicine for her to drink every evening before sleep. I'll fetch it now." This conversation required privacy, even if Dahlia didn't believe that. I slipped out the door, walked down the stairs, and took my time brewing the potion.

When I returned to the bedroom, I heard weeping and low voices from behind the closed door. I knocked.

"Not now," Samuel called in response.

I returned to the kitchen. A seldom used buzzer to summon servants hung on the kitchen wall. Perhaps Samuel would activate it when they were ready.

Lotus made us both a cup of tea. She'd gone with Ivan in the morning to pick up Patricia and drop the sisters off at the Wilson's. Then she and Ivan left for church.

"Thank you so much for today," I said. "I don't know how we'd manage without your kindness."

"Phish." Lotus flapped her hand in my direction. "You'd do the same for us." She blew to cool her drink.

Radiators, warming the house, hissed, and coughed. The light from the many windows disappeared. I turned on the lamps. Still nothing from the Jacobs. Lotus and I chatted. She asked me about sewing and offered to tell the ladies at her church about my talents. I asked after her son and daughters, and she brought me up to date on their lives. One was pregnant with her second. Ivan and Lotus planned to visit them the weekend after Thanksgiving. I promised to make a baby bunting, a hooded sleeping garment, as a gift. Before spending all my free time sewing dresses for display and hoped-for-sales, I'd started a crocheted baby blanket to give to Lotus' daughter as well.

The front door slammed shut. Sylvie dashed into the kitchen with Ivan a few steps behind.

"Mama, we have to get out of here. Now." She looked flushed and her voice screeched.

"What's wrong?" My eyes swept over her body, looking for injury. I raised my glance to Ivan and lifted both my hands.

"Your boy, he's having a hard time," Ivan offered in response to my raised hands. He tugged off his coat and hung it on a peg next to my bedroom door.

"Andy threw himself on the ground and screamed and cried when I told him you weren't coming." Sylvie said. "Those men terrorized him. He's so scared."

It had been weeks since the abduction. Why was this happening now? "What did Esther say?"

Sylvie's yellow dress looked crumpled and stained, as if she'd been rolling on the ground. Her short hair, loose and curly, swayed with each word. "It started a few days ago. He'd been having bad dreams, but she decided not to tell us. Then, on Thursday, the fits started." Sylvie sank into a chair around the long kitchen table. "He must be with us. And Patricia too." She scrubbed her eyes with her fists.

"Tell me everything. From the time you arrived until you left."

"Irene and George were their happy selves. They rushed to Patricia and me. But Andy, with his thumb in his mouth, held back. I hurried to him for a hug. He pulled away and asked for you. When I said you couldn't come today, that's when the fits began."

"Fits? More than one?"

"Yes. On and off all day. 'I want Mama. The wicked men are coming.' It was awful. Irene started crying for you as well, and Georgie disappeared into his room and shut the door. Patricia... she... it was such an awful day."

Ivan said, "When I arrived to pick them up, it was obvious things were bad. Everyone looked teary. And Mrs. Wilson, she seemed real upset."

I covered my mouth with both hands and tried to think. How could I fix this, accelerate my plan, and get my babies back sooner? I squatted down next to Sylvie in the same manner Samuel did with Dahlia. "Okay. We'll figure something out." With both arms around her, I held her tight. "I'll find a way."

Lotus brewed tea for Sylvie and Ivan and served slices of chocolate cake leftover from Saturday. Sylvie sipped the tea but didn't touch the sweet.

A buzzing noise summoned me upstairs. The box on the wall had a button for each room in the house. The master bedroom lit up and droned again.

Lotus said, "Go on. Sylvie and I will be fine." She lifted the porcelain pot filled with Mrs. Kline's herbs. "Let me know when Dahlia wants this and I'll re-heat it."

"I'll be right back." I kissed the top of Sylvie's head, nodded my thanks to Lotus, and strode out the door and up the stairs.

This time, they left the bedroom door opened. Dahlia sat propped up with pillows. Samuel removed his tie and rolled up his shirt sleeves. Upon seeing me, he said, "Dahlia is ready for her medicine, and I'd like a brandy."

I turned to go.

"Wait," Samuel said. "Staying in bed is going to be hard for my wife. Your attention will have to increase. I'll send for our family physician in the morning, and we can work things out."

Sylvie's report filled my mind. I needed more time, not less, to make enough dresses to sell. I'd have to find outlets and speed up finding an apartment. Jonathan and Spooner Brothers. Was that an answer? I forced myself to focus. "A nurse might—"

Samuel cut me off. "We have enough servants in this house. There are only two of us, and I'm gone all day. I don't think we'll require a nurse."

"Of course," I said. From his tone, I'd overstepped. "I look forward to receiving instruction from the family doctor. Now, if there's nothing else, I'll get the medicine and brandy."

Somehow, Sylvie and I had to take care of Dahlia and start our business by Thanksgiving, my new deadline. Would Andy get worse? Was the end of November too late?

CHAPTER SIXTY

Monday morning, Samuel left for the train station at 8:00 a.m. with Ivan at the wheel. Dahlia lay in bed with books and magazines to read. I brought her breakfast on a tray.

"I need music," Dahlia said. "It's too quiet in here and I can't leave my bed to play the piano." She scooted back and patted the bed linens flat before I placed the tray on her lap. Among her many clothes was a collection of nightgowns, some warm cotton, and others lacy and light. Today, she wore pink, cotton polka dots.

"You should ask Samuel to buy a Victrola." I told her about ours and the stacks of records. "Hours of company, like a good book." I pulled up a chair next to her. "Lotus made your favorite." Coffee with cream accompanied a plate full of blueberry crepes. Lotus included a tall glass of water.

Although I listened to Dahlia's conversation, and made what I hoped were appropriate comments, my mind was far away. I planned to accept Jonathan's offer to sell my dresses. Sylvie and I sewed nine garments between us–six from me and three plain ones from Sylvie. Plus, if I could persuade her, Dahlia's flapper dress. Even if I could only borrow it, shoppers would stop at the window and look. I felt confident it would pull in customers. An idea flashed.

"Dahlia, Jonathan's store sells Victrolas. Ivan and I could fetch one for you this morning and by this afternoon you'd have music."

She dabbed the corners of her mouth with a linen serviette. "Does he have George Gershwin's *Swanee*? Or his newest, *Rhapsody in Blue*?"

"I've not heard of Gershwin."

She swallowed a mouthful of crepe. "He's a Jewish composer and lives in Brooklyn and has been on Broadway. Gladys saw him in person."

I doubted Gershwin's music would be in Jonathan's Harlem store, but I agreed to search for it.

"Samuel leaves me cash in case I want to go shopping." She clapped her hands like Irene. Or how Irene used to before I broke up the family. "An excellent idea."

It was wonderful to see her excited and not fading in bed. If only my children had an equal transformation. "May I ask a favor?"

"Of course. We're best friends."

"May I borrow the flapper dress? I want to show it to... potential customers."

"What customers?" She gulped her coffee from a porcelain cup edged in silver and took another bite of crepe.

"Jonathan offered to display my work in his shop's window whenever I'm ready."

She frowned. "That's why you want to buy me a Victrola?"

My annoyance must have shown on my face.

"Well, it was my idea to have music." She tilted her head and smiled, a winning look that I'm sure worked well on Samuel. "You can have the dress. My present. I have nowhere to wear it and..." She patted her abdomen. "If I carry this baby to term, I'll have no desire."

With all the sadness and struggles in my life, I was grateful for the blessings as well. Although a servant, I accepted that Dahlia and I were friends.

Sylvie helped me pack the dresses. I gave her careful instructions about caring for Dahlia and asked her to remember everything the family doctor said should he arrive before I returned.

Lotus said, "I almost forgot. Your friend Beryl called. She told me she has a package for you from Jamaica."

"A letter from my mother?"

"Like I said, a package."

Ivan brought the car around. Lotus wished us good luck, and Ivan and I set off in search of music, news from home, and my family's future.

. . .

I stood in the entranceway of Spooner Brothers, my satchel filled with dresses and Ivan at my side.

"Grace." Jonathan looked surprised and worried. "What brings you here?" In a few strides, he was by my side, taking the packed dresses from my arms and placing the satchel on a sofa with a price tag pinned to a cushion. "Ivan, it's good to see you."

The men shook hands. "Same here." Ivan looked around. "I like your place."

I still hadn't spoken, just stood there frozen, which was ridiculous.

"Thanks." Jonathan turned back to me. "Are your children well? Are you?"

"Yes, and yes," I said with a nervous laugh.

"In that case." He made a bow, like he did the first day I met him. "How might I be of service, Lady Grace?"

This elicited another silly laugh from me. My face flushed. He's just a man, I told myself. Get a hold of yourself. After a deep breath, I said in a normal voice, "You offered to display my dresses, and I'd like to try it. Plus, Dahlia wants to buy a Victrola."

"What's going on here?" Vincent, Jonathan's father, approached us. He wore a brown suit with a vest and a hand-knitted brown and black, stripped tie. I'd not seen him since I sold our belongings, nor had I noticed back then how much Jonathan looked like him.

"Pop, you remember Grace."

"Nice to see you again." His voice was rough and intonation southern. "Jonathan told me you make fancy dresses for sale."

"Plain ones, too," I said.

"Didn't remember your accent. You British?"

271

"Via the Congo and Jamaica." Although I often stressed my British side because it made life easier for me, for a reason I couldn't articulate, I wanted Jonathan's father to know more.

Jonathan introduced Ivan to Vincent.

"What brings you both here on this fine day?" Vincent asked, moving his gaze away from me and towards his son.

"I have wares I'd like to sell and a purchase to make." And I think I've fallen in love with your son. The thought startled me, but I knew it was true.

Together, Jonathan and I unpacked the dresses. Jonathan made room in the store display area that faced the street by moving an electric ice box, and we hung several dresses, including a prominent spot for the flapper frock. Then, in the store's section set aside for used clothing, he hung the rest.

"Need to make some signs," Jonathan said. "Indicate these are original designs by Lady Grace." He flapped each dress, shaking out the wrinkles. "Do you have any children's church clothes?"

Vincent said, "That's an idea."

"No, but Sylvie and I will get to it." Excited about the possibilities, I thanked them both. Everything was coming together. "Do you have a style in mind?"

We examined magazine and newspaper advertisements, and I made sketches on a pad Jonathan gave me. We sat side by side at a kitchen table for sale. His father watched from over my shoulder as I drew. Ivan strolled around the store, looking at everything.

"Oh, I almost forgot," I said, lifting my head from my work. "We want to purchase a Victrola." I looked around from my seat. "Is mine… the one I sold you, still available?"

"Yeah—" Vincent began.

Jonathan cut him off. "No." He looked at his father for several seconds. "But I'm sure we can find one for you."

"I promised Dahlia music," I said, more to myself than to Jonathan. Bed ridden and lonely, the Victrola was a brilliant answer. "Where might you look?" Perhaps I could go there now.

"Don't worry about it," Jonathan said. "I'll solve this."

Still worried about the music, I rose. It was time to go. Beryl was expecting us, and I was eager to open the package she mentioned in her message.

Jonathan stood close and reached for my hand. "Pop, I'd like to speak with Grace in private. We'll just be a few minutes. Can you check on Ivan?"

"Suppose." After looking both of us up and down, he walked over to where Ivan examined a set of tools on sale, along with a wooden carrying case.

Jonathan pulled me into an alcove. A floor mirror leaned against the wall. Shelves along the opposite wall stored miscellaneous items–dusting cloths, mending paraphernalia not unlike my sewing basket's contents, and a measuring tape. He stood in front of me for several seconds and then leaned in and kissed my cheek. "I'm glad to see you," he said in my ear and kissed my other cheek.

I stood frozen, quivering, wanting, afraid.

His mouth brushed mine. I closed my eyes. He pressed gently, and I parted my lips. When his tongue slipped into my mouth, I shuddered. Misunderstanding, he pulled back and stared into my eyes. With brazen purpose, something else I'd never experienced, I stretched up on my tiptoes and leaned into him, pressing my lips against his. When his tongue slipped into my mouth again, I met it with mine.

My breath turned hot, and shivers moved through me from my toes to my breasts. My nipples swelled against my brassiere and camisole. The store bell jangled. We broke away.

Vincent said to a customer I couldn't see, "Good afternoon. How might I help you this morning?"

We stepped deeper into the alcove and Jonathan kissed me again. "I love you so much." He kissed my cheeks, my nose, my neck and fumbled with my hair pins. Several fell to the floor and much of my hair tumbled down. He dug his fingers into it. "You are glorious. Everything about you."

He pressed his body against mine and we kissed. I couldn't breathe.

With both palms on his chest, I pushed him back. "We're in a public space." I tried to catch my breath. "Your father might come looking for us." I still tasted Jonathan, smelled him, felt him, even though he now stood a few steps away.

He reached down and helped me gather my hair pins from the floor. The rest of my waves tumbled down.

"You look swell with your hair all loose and around your shoulders." He laughed. "And I intend to kiss you again."

"This is not why I came to see you," I said, trying to restore decorum. "Only to take you up on your offer." The quaver in my voice matched the one in my belly.

"My offer to marry you?"

The way he asked, with a lilt to his tone, I was unsure if he was joking. "You know, I can't." After fastening my hair, I smoothed my dress. "Ivan and I must go."

"I saved the Victrola for you. Put it aside for the day you'd be able to play it again."

Oh my. "Thank you. Thank you so much, but Dahlia needs it. I have money to pay you."

He nodded his head, showing understanding. "Then I'll find you another."

I had no answer to his kindness. Nor did I see a future for us.

"One more kiss." He leaned in, but I turned my face. This wasn't right. And yet... I turned back and kissed him on his lips, pivoted, and walked out to find Ivan.

With his father watching, a perplexed expression on his face, I paid Jonathan with Dahlia's money, and he loaded into the car the Victrola, Henry's and my jazz records, and the coats retrieved from the speakeasy. Once again, I was grateful, and a little sad. We waved goodbye, climbed into the Packard, and headed for Beryl's.

What an amazing day. I closed my eyes and licked my lips, tasting him again, and not caring if Ivan noticed.

CHAPTER SIXTY-ONE

Beryl welcomed Ivan and me. My equilibrium returned the moment she opened her door. This was my life before. Spontaneous visits with my dear friend, sharing news from our families in Jamaica, helping each other raise our children. My life with Dahlia, and the imagined one with Jonathan, were foreign and frightening.

Beryl wore a rust-orange house dress that complimented her coppery complexion. Like Lotus, a colorful scarf wound around and covered her hair.

"What smells so good?" Ivan asked, his nose raised and sniffing the air.

"I prepared lunch. I hope you're hungry."

Rice and peas, pan roasted chicken, and stewed tomatoes sat in individual bowls on the table with serving spoons. Steam rose from a round teapot covered with a knitted cozy.

Beryl said, "I baked cassava bread. Let me get it." She stood. "There's a new Caribbean store on Amsterdam Avenue up the street from where you used to live. They carry cassava flour. Just like home." She returned with a warm loaf and butter dish.

The conversation hummed along. Beryl shared news of her boys and their missing teeth. I told her George grew two permanent ones. Sylvie made yarn hair for two of Irene's bald dolls. Ivan ate two helpings, listening to our chatter but not chiming in. When we got to Andy's nightmares and dresses on display at Spooner Brothers, Beryl's expression turned somber.

"I hope this works," she said.

Ivan sipped his tea. "It's gonna. Jonathan is a good sort and I like the father's style."

This surprised me.

"Yep. Good people," Ivan said, taking a third helping of meat and bread.

Beryl rose. "I'll get your package," she said, her face still in a deep worry frown.

I was worried too. Wary. But also, hopeful. I touched my lips with two fingers and smiled. Henry destroyed the anticipation young girls experience, dreaming about the man who would love and marry them. So much loss at every stage. Today, I felt my life turning around, escaping the downward spiral, and rising.

The box Beryl placed in my lap was square and wrapped in brown paper, tied with string. When I examined my name and Beryl's address, I recognized my sister Carrie's handwriting. I tugged off the string and paper. Inside, I retrieved a book with a black cover and a letter from Carrie.

August 26, 1924

My dearest sister,

I write to you today with a heavy heart. Mother passed in her sleep last night. As you know, she'd been sick for some time, and she was tired and ready to join Father and our Lord. Gram gave me and Nora a copy of Father's biography. I want you to have it. There are photos and memories to comfort you.

I pray you and your children are well and that your heart is healing. Nora and I will return to England once we settle Mother's affairs.

Do you ever wonder what became of our home in Bolobo? There is a photo on page 145. I will write again soon and please do the same.

Your devoted sister,

Carrie

Mother was gone since the end of August. All the time we lived with Dahlia, all those times I thought about Mother and sought her image for comfort, remembered her embrace, heard her voice encouraging me to keep going, she was already gone.

I opened the book and saw they published it in 1908. A photo of Father dated 1902 graced the first page. I searched for a picture of Mother and found it. Carrie's prediction that there'd be no caption under her likeness turned out wrong. There Mother was, staring at the camera, her silver earrings, the pair she gave me, visible in her lobes.

. . .

I was alone. Of course, I'd been alone for a long time, but Mother's death felt like a marker in my life. Ivan and I drove to Pelham in silence. I clutched the book and letter to my chest.

Ivan stayed with the car to polish and do whatever he did to keep it running. I walked into the bright kitchen.

Lotus' expression was grim. "What's happened?"

"Esther Wilson called. Frantic." Lotus came over to me and grabbed me into an awkward hug, the book between us. "It's Andy."

The tears I didn't shed for Mother earlier now poured down my cheeks. I waited for Lotus to explain, to break my heart beyond repair.

"Esther began by begging for forgiveness. Said it happened at a weak moment, a breaking point."

"Tell me."

"She's giving Andy up, back to the state, for a new placement."

I gasped. Did I also scream? Cry out? I don't remember.

Lotus rushed on. "He's been having terrible nightmares, and wets his bed every night, and jumps at every bang or thump. Plus, she said, she's terrified Creamer might show up again and she won't be able to protect Andy."

How could this happen? Esther had changed so much over the last weeks. Kinder. A friend looking after my frightened boy.

Lotus eased me into a chair. "I asked her to wait and speak with you, but she said it's done. She'd already contacted a Mrs. Barker. They're going to—"

I found my voice. "No, no, no." I jumped up. "Where's Sylvie?"

"With Dahlia. She's been asking for you."

"Ivan has to take me there." I started for the front door.

"He can't. The Mr. needs him, but—"

"I'll take the train, and trolley, and run…" I pulled opened the front door. There must be a mistake. Esther wouldn't do this.

"Let me finish. Slow down."

I faced Lotus. What else was there to say? Esther and Edward… did he agree to this? Such a kind man. Worried about Sallie's children and mine. They had no right to give Andy to another family without my permission. They wouldn't.

Lotus said, "Ivan can't take you, but I phoned Jonathan and he's on his way here."

"Bless you, Lotus. Bless you and Ivan." Tears choked my words. "Please speak to Sylvie and Dahlia. We've bought her a Victrola and records. Ivan can set it up for her." Jumbled words rushed. "Did the doctor come? Explain an emergency came up."

Ivan hustled into the house. "Jonathan is here." He said it like a question.

"Go," Lotus said.

"What the heck is happening?" Ivan asked, but I was out the front door before Lotus answered.

Jonathan drove as fast as the law and car allowed. We breezed through the empty streets of Pelham and slowed when we reached the congestion of Manhattan. Carts, cars, trolleys, bikes, and pedestrians clogged the streets. We inched forward until we reached the East River and crossed the bridge into Queens.

At various times during the ride, I thought I might throw up. I trusted Esther. How could she betray me like this? Betray my children? Why did Edward go along with this terrible act? Andy's going to think bad people are taking him again. Oh, sweet Jesus, please help us.

We arrived at the Wilson's home at 2:30 p.m. Irene and George were still in school and Edward at work. Only Esther was home. Without Andy.

She stood on her porch with both arms crossed under her small breasts. A brown and green dress hung to her shoes. Her make-up looked marred, as if she'd been crying. "I'm sorry. You're too late," she said as Jonathan and I approached. "There's nothing to be done."

"Where is he?" I asked.

"He cried all night, and wet his bed, and I was exhausted. Irene had a fever and George was sniffling. I lost my mind. I'm so sorry."

"Where is he," I asked again. Esther's apology meant nothing. She gave my child away.

"With Mrs. Barker. She's trying to find him a placement. I called her to tell her I changed my mind, but there was no answer."

I spun around. "Jonathan, please take me to Manhattan."

CHAPTER SIXTY-TWO

We arrived at Mrs. Barker's office breathless. Both Jonathan and I panting as we ran down the street from where we parked his truck and scrambled up the narrow steps of The Foster Home Department and New York Children's Aid Society. We found Mrs. Barker sitting behind her desk, a thick sweater wrapped around her shoulders. The office was unheated and cold.

"I know why you're here," she said, without a hello or offer for us to sit down. She eyed Jonathan. "The police will come the second I call. They're just a few blocks away."

"I'm Jonathan Spooner and Grace is my wife. You're in no danger."

What was he saying?

"Oh," Mrs. Barker said. "That's quite a different matter."

"May we sit?" Jonathan asked.

"Mrs. Wilson made no mention of a marriage." She waved us to the two chairs in front of her desk, the same ones Reverend Copes and I sat in when I made a pact with the devil. "Are you here to take responsibility for your children and remove them from the dole?"

"Yes," I said, still not seeing how this would work. My heart hammered, and I found it difficult to breathe.

She pulled out a sheath of papers. "As long as you're married and have a place for them to live. We'll need to inspect... Well. There are very few of us working here. You'll have to prove you're married and... Do you have a marriage certificate?"

I said, "There was no time to grab it. Once we learned about Andy's removal from the home, we came directly here."

"I will need your certificate. Come back when you have proof. I understand you're working. Who will care for your children while you're away from home? You must satisfy me you can make a decent home for all three children." She tugged her sweater tighter around her shoulders. "Barging in like this is unacceptable."

I rose and walked around the desk. Mrs. Barker shrank back. "What is not acceptable, is you allowing a three-year-old to be kidnapped and sold to villains."

"What are you saying?"

"A crook stole and harmed Andy." My voice rose with each word. "I've already spoken with my lawyer, Mr. Booth, and he said I can prosecute you. Hold you responsible for child sellers and molesters snatching Andy. *You* placed him in a home next door to a criminal. Now we're taking all three of children to protect them, and you're not stopping us."

Color drained from Mrs. Barker's face. She stammered something unintelligible.

I leaned in even closer. "You will give me my child now, or I will call Lawyer Booth back and have the police arrest you."

Jonathan, a bemused expression on his face, came around and took my arm. "She's quite serious, Ma'am." He guided me back to my seat. "Scares the heck out of me."

Mrs. Barker, with pursed lips, drew herself up.

"Where is Andy?" I held her gaze.

"He's napping in our nursery down the hall. We keep foundling infants and toddlers there until we can find a placement." She paused and her voice dipped in volume. "The nun who runs an approved orphanage is coming to collect him." More confidently, she said, "But now that you're here, well, of course, after you sign your papers, you can take him home."

I stood. "Show me. Now."

Mrs. Barker rose and came around the desk. She grabbed a set of jangling keys that shook in her hands. Her voice quaked as well. "This way."

Jonathan and I followed.

My legs almost buckled. Jonathan grabbed me and kept me upright.

Andy sat on the floor playing with a wooden train and a ripped rubber doll. "Be good, or off you go to bed." He tilted the train upright as if it were another a character in his story. "And Mama will be sad if you're not good."

"Andy."

He jerked his head, dropped his toys, and ran into my arms.

. . .

Jonathan, Beryl, Mac, and I sat around the kitchen table. Josh, Nick, and Andy played in the twins' bedroom.

"We can keep Andy for as long as you need us to," Beryl said.

Mac said, "The boys love him and so do we."

Lamps lit the kitchen. Beryl pulled the curtains closed against the night sky. Warm air pumped from the radiator.

"I can't ever leave him again," I said. Flashes of Mother holding me in Henry's house, comforting, bathing, and making me soup. Andy's ordeal seemed much worse. He was so young and vulnerable, and I still didn't understand what the men did to him. "He's wounded and needs his mother's love."

Jonathan cleared his throat. "You can all stay with me. Patricia and Sylvie too."

"She can't," Beryl said.

He ignored her and turned toward me. "You're a widow. No one knows anything different. We'll say we're married."

I opened my mouth to protest, to add sense to this conversation. I couldn't fake a marriage and live in sin. But Jonathan spoke first.

"We'll not share a bed, just a home. You can work in the shop and sew your dresses. The children could go to school. No one needs to know our business."

Memories of his kisses and touch filled me up. This wouldn't work. "Thank you, but I cannot."

Jonathan's eyes filled up, and he ducked his head, stood, and turned away.

A thought came to me. "What about the store in St. Albans, the one you're trying to open, with the apartment on the second floor?" We had talked about it during our meal at Sonny's. "My salary could be the free apartment, and we could share the money made from my dresses in both stores."

Jonathan faced me, his eyes still wet.

"I'd open the new store for you, manage it, earn my keep until... I'm free."

The silence that followed left each of us uncomfortable.

Finally, Beryl said, "I think Irene, George, Andy, and you should stay with us until you and Jonathan decide what you'll do."

Jonathan nodded but said nothing else.

"Yes. Thank you." Sylvie and Patricia would be fine for a few more days with Dahlia and Cora, but not Irene and George. Andy disappeared again. That must be frightening. Besides, I was furious with Esther, no matter how much she regretted her actions. Suppose something else happened, and she did this again. My children were no longer safe with them.

"We three will squeeze into the front seat. Be back in an hour," Jonathan said to Beryl. He sounded sad.

I called Esther. She was still weeping and begging for forgiveness. "We'll be there shortly. Please have my children ready."

"What about the state?" she asked.

"Mrs. Barker has decided not to fight us." I hung up and hoped that was true. We never filled out the papers, but how closely did the government check on colored children? All the orphans sent to the Midwest never received follow-up visits and Mrs. Barker implied she didn't have enough employees helping her, so I stopped worrying about what the government might do.

Andy, Jonathan, and I drove to Flushing.

. . .

We stood on the Wilson's lawn. Stars and planets, crowded together, dazzled in the night sky. In Harlem, we saw only the brightest. I stood for a few moments pointing out constellations to Andy–the big and little dipper, Venus, and the North Star.

The Wilson's door swung open, and Irene and George scrambled down the steps and into my arms. Andy squealed with joy.

"You ruined my life." A male voice screamed from across the lawn. "I wouldn't let them hurt him."

Cleveland Creamer stepped into the diffused light coming from the Wilson's house. He waved a gun. "Lost everything. Police after me. Lucky Strike gunning for me." He pointed his pistol toward me. "Sallie and kids gone."

From the corner of my eye, I saw Jonathan charging toward Creamer. I grabbed all three children and pulled them against me. The truck was closer than the front door. We stumbled toward the vehicle. A shot pierced the air, and then another. I covered my children with my body, squeezing them together with all my might. Another boom, followed by a searing pain, scorched my back and right shoulder.

Oh, please Lord, don't let him hurt my babies. Don't let me die.

Edward yelled from the house, "The police are on their way."

Jonathan, covered in blood, stumbled toward me. "Grace, Grace."

Everything turned black.

CHAPTER SIXTY-THREE

I opened my eyes. Pain zipped through me. Jonathan lay next to me covered in blood, still, as if asleep.

"Grace. Take this." Edward pressed a white towel against my shoulder. "I have to help Jonathan."

I tried not to look at the blood flowing from Jonathan's gut or the blood oozing from my shoulder. "Are the children safe?"

Edward used another towel to pack Jonathan's wound. "Esther's got them barricaded in the house. Creamer, the evil coward, ran."

The Wilson's neighbor, Kennedy, ran up to us. "I called the police and asked for an ambulance." He knelt beside us. "You okay, ma'am?"

I wasn't, but I moved my head in the barest nod.

Time crawled by. Every few minutes, Esther peeked through the front room curtains. Blood saturated the towel against my shoulder, seeped between my fingers, and dripped down my arm.

A white Studebaker, with the word Ambulance printed in large letters on its side, whirled onto the Wilson's front lawn. I couldn't think or breathe. Lightheaded, and terrified for Jonathan, I fought to stay conscious. My eyelids drooped and my head listed left.

The screech of a police car brought my head up with a jerk. Two officers, pistols drawn, approached us. The medic stayed in the ambulance. Why wasn't he saving Jonathan?

One officer, pointing his pistol, yelled to Edward, "Step away. Drop your weapon."

"I'm staunching the blood from his wound," Edward said. "The shooter is getting away."

"Drop your weapon, boy, or you'll be down next to him."

Edward lifted Jonathan's hand and placed it on the towel. "If you can hear me, press—"

"I'm not gonna tell you a second time, nigger."

Edward raised his hands and stood. "I'm unarmed, officer. This man needs medical attention now. As does the lady." He lifted his chin in my direction.

A second officer standing over me motioned for Kennedy to raise his hands, and for me to stand, but when I tried, my head swam. I sat down hard on the brown grass.

Still pointing his gun, he patted down Kennedy and then let him lower his hands.

The first officer banged on the Wilson's front door. "Police. Open up."

Where was the friendlier officer from the day we rescued Andy?

Once he finished investigating who was in the house and terrorizing my children and Esther, both police officers listened to Edward's account of the shooting and took Creamer's description.

The medic finally approached Jonathan, who was unconscious and still bleeding.

Kennedy said to the medic, "Help the man."

Edward agreed. "He's lost a lot of blood."

"We can take them to the Negro infirmary," the medic said to the officers, ignoring both Kennedy and Edward.

Hospitals were for whites only or segregated with a poorly staffed and financed colored wing. A group of Black physicians ran an infirmary near the Wilson home.

Neighbors stood on their porches and steps and watched.

Under the supervision of the medic, Edward and Kennedy put Jonathan into the ambulance, and then returned for me.

I rose, swayed, and tried to steady myself. Kennedy grabbed me and with his help, I hobbled over and into the vehicle.

Was Jonathan going to die? Was I? What would become of my children?

The ambulance thumped over trolley and train tracks and rocked through ruts in the road. Each bump sent pain shooting up my right arm and shoulder. Blood continued to seep and drip.

When we reached the infirmary, Edward and Kennedy carried Jonathan in. The medic stayed behind, watching, and waiting. Kennedy returned. With one arm around my waist and the other under my knees, he lifted and carried me into the infirmary.

I'm not sure how long I waited, sitting on a wooden chair, my head resting against the wall behind me. A nurse replaced the towel with a bandage. "Hold it tight," she said and then returned to Jonathan's side where a Negro doctor bent over Jonathan, tending his wound. I prayed Esther would comfort and reassure my children, and I prayed God would spare Jonathan.

. . .

The next week passed in a blur. I drifted in and out of consciousness, slept, and roiled in pain from the bullet wound until someone stuck a needle filled with morphine into my arm. Sometimes I saw Beryl and Mac. Other times, Lotus was there, fussing. Mae seemed to speak to me, but I didn't understand what she said. Was I still in the infirmary? Where were my children? Last night, Sylvie slept next to me. Was I back in Dahlia's house? Did I imagine it? Patricia's sad eyes were close to my face. She had a spoon, filled with a liquid, in her hand. Everything went black again.

I opened my eyes and looked around. The room was large and saturated with light streaming in from tall, paneled windows. My sewing machine stood in one corner, a chair in front, and my basket on the floor. A vanity held a wash basin and pitcher. Calla lilies in a vase graced a table next to the wide bed. A note on white paper lay next to the flowers.

"Well, look who's awake."

I couldn't place the rough male voice with a warm southern accent.

"Thanks to pain-killing drugs, you were sleeping on and off for a week. Lost a lot of blood, but the doc fixed you up."

I peered at him. Vincent. Jonathan's father. "Where am I?"

"You're in our apartment above the store," he said.

"My children?" Several times, I remember Andy cuddling up, but when I next woke, he wasn't there.

"Everybody's in school except Andy. He and Miz Beryl are playing a game in the back."

"School?" I had many other questions, but I forced myself to ask one at a time. My throat was dry and scratchy.

"Yep." He sat on the edge of the bed. "Your girl, Sylvie, she's a feisty one." He chuckled. "She enrolled them. Ivan, a good man, got permission from the people he works for and helped Sylvie collect everyone's things." He nodded, as if agreeing with his own assessment. "You've got good friends. Plenty of folks care about you."

"May I have some water?"

"Sure, sure." He reached for a glass next to the vase of flowers, placed his hand on the back of my head, and lifted it so I could take a sip. Someone braided my hair in long plaits. A bulky bandage covering the wound caused by the bullet, made it hard to move my right arm or shoulder.

"Jonathan?"

"Down the hall. One of the Negro nurses from the infirmary is here. Once I tell her you're awake, she'll be by."

"Is he... okay?"

Vincent made a noise close to a groan. "Touch and go." He pressed the glass against my lips again, and I drank. "You two are something. Edward Wilson said Jonathan tackled the lunatic, and you used your body to shield the kids." Vincent shook his head. "Saved everyone."

"I thought I saw Esther here."

"You did. She helped Sylvie settle your family in their rooms."

He picked up the note by the vase. "Miz Lotus brought this for you, along with the flowers."

Dear Grace,

Lotus told me about the shooting. I couldn't believe it. Suppose the killer accosted us at the speakeasy? All three of us might be in the hospital. Well, not in the same one. Ivan explained the system to me. Dreadful.

I'm still bedridden under doctor's orders, otherwise I'd ask Ivan to drive me to see you.

I pray for a quick and complete recovery for both you and Jonathan. Your friend,
Dahlia

I re-folded the note. The flowers were beautiful. When I felt stronger, I'd write her and tell her every night I pray for the birth of her healthy child. I returned the paper to Vincent who placed it beside the vase again.

My list of questions wasn't complete, but a brown-skinned nurse, dressed in white with a white cap perched on her head, walked into the room. "And how are we today?" She had a cheery, sing-song voice. "So nice to see you awake."

"How is Jonathan?" I tried to push myself up to a sitting position but sagged against the pillows in defeat.

She helped me sit, propped against several pillows. "Jonathan is as well as expected," she sang. "Let's look at you."

Vincent said, "I'll leave you ladies to it."

"Wait. My sister-in-law, Mae?" A fuzzy memory of her tending me prompted the question.

"Sylvie invited her, and she came. Nursed you when Beryl and Lotus couldn't stay. Like I said, you got good people on your side."

Mae must have forgiven me for not being a friend to her. She loved her nieces and nephews.

"Enough questions," the nurse said.

"Yes, ma'am." Vincent left the room.

"I'm Nurse Jacqueline." She took my pulse and blood pressure, peered into my eyes, and recorded her findings in a notebook. "Your color is back. A good sign."

"May I see my family?"

"After we bathe you and change the dressing." She pulled back a corner of the bandage. "Coming along."

My mind flashed on Mother washing me in the tub and removing vomit from my hair. I smiled at the memory, but then remembered. Mother was gone.

EPILOGUE

November 1925, Harlem, New York

I swept in front of Spooner Brothers' Harlem store. Filled with dresses and the latest haul from a young widow who was moving to Georgia, the window behind me gleamed from my washing and polishing. Jonathan and his father were due for dinner, driving from the new store and apartment in St. Albans.

It took a month for Jonathan's prognosis to turn positive. Although he credited me with saving Andy, Irene, and George, Jonathan saved *all* our lives and almost lost his. After another month of convalescence, he could hobble around. The young ones took to him. By the third month of us living with Vincent and Jonathan, even Sylvie and Patricia liked and trusted both men.

My wound mended, but the trauma my children experienced lingered. Andy's nightmares still occurred. I allowed Patricia to drop out of school and take up dressmaking. Eighteen months wasn't enough time to heal. Both Patricia and Andy still had sad days. The "blues," as Father called them. Irene and George appeared happy at the local public school, but they, too, had blue days. Sylvie applied to Hunter College, and we waited for her acceptance letter. The school offered free night classes, and she decided to work with Patricia and me by day and study evenings. We all wanted to pay our way and never again be at the mercy of others. My dreams for her life included falling in love with a decent man like Jonathan. But she shunned the boys who came around.

I pushed the last of the dirt and debris over the curb. The street cleaner came on Fridays. I'd already scrubbed the interior of the establishment. The store would shine as brightly as the front window for Saturday customers. But now I had to prepare after-school treats for my brood, and dinner for everyone.

Every Friday, father and son returned at supper time, and every Wednesday morning, Jonathan came alone to spend the day with me and the evening with the children. He slept in the room with Andy and George before returning on Thursday to the smaller apartment in St. Albans. Sylvie and Patricia shared a third bedroom. Vincent converted a storage room into a playroom. A patch of grass behind the store became a place for family activities.

A little more than a year passed since the day Creamer, now jailed, shot us. Thanksgiving was fast approaching. Jonathan, Vincent, and I planned a big dinner for the Friday after the holiday so Lotus, Ivan, Beryl, Mac, Mae, Esther, and Edward could join us. We included Kennedy, who helped so much that awful day, but he was traveling to see his family in New Jersey.

Dahlia's baby boy, due last April, was born a month early. I'd finished knitting a pink and blue blanket decorated with intricate flowers. Jonathan drove me to Pelham and waited for me in his truck. The young maid, Cecily, opened the door. Laughter and chatter greeted me. The big house was full of family and friends.

"Who are you?" an older woman who looked a lot like Samuel asked.

"A friend," I said. "Grace Herbert." I wore a cloche hat and my pearl-grey dress, one of Jonathan's favorites.

Cecily said, "I'll tell Mrs. Dahlia you're here."

The look-alike woman stared at me. I held her gaze, head high.

"How do you know my daughter-in-law?" she asked. "To which synagogue do you belong?"

Dahlia stood in the archway behind the woman. I couldn't see her expression, but she raised her palms and made an apologetic shrug. In acknowledgement, I tipped my head before Dahlia turned, and walked away. I understood. How could she explain me or our relationship, especially to her judgmental mother-in-law?

"Please give this to Dahlia." I said, ignoring the senior Mrs. Jacobs and handing my gift to Cecily.

Senior Mrs. Jacobs sniffed and retreated.

A striking woman, as tall as a man, approached me. "Are you, speakeasy-Grace?"

That made me laugh. I covered my mouth.

"I'm Gladys," she said.

"Cotton Club, Gladys?" I asked, still suppressing my laughter.

"Yes," she said, grinning. She shot a glance over her shoulder. Her expression turned serious. "You saved her baby with your tea. Thank you."

I nodded, accepting the gratitude for Mrs. Kline.

"She has many friends now. Other mothers fussing over her."

"I understand." I was happy for Dahlia. This is what she prayed for.

Gladys held the heavy door open for me.

As I walked down the path to the truck, I reflected on Dahlia's lack of courage in front of her disapproving mother-in-law. My mind slipped back to the two maids who worked for Henry during our years together in Jamaica. Class, colorism, and other remnants of colonialism, looked a lot like my adopted country's prejudices. My parents taught me to be kind and polite to everyone. But it was clear who held lesser stations in life. No matter what roles I'd played for Dahlia, and she for me, we were never genuine friends. I was her servant and not her equal.

In April, Jonathan gave me a Victrola for my twenty-eighth birthday, and I admitted my actual age to him. A few days after the celebration, I approached Lawyer Booth about securing a divorce. New York law required proof of infidelity, and I would not use Henry's rape of Patricia as evidence. So, we continued to live as a family, and as husband and wife who didn't share a bed. He managed the store in St. Albans, and I managed the Harlem enterprise. Sometimes... often, the longing in Jonathan's eyes, his touches, and kisses, made me desperate to yield. What was the harm? Beryl and Mae knew the truth, but would they still judge? What stopped me was Sylvie and God.

I pushed these thoughts away and, satisfied with my outdoor cleaning, walked into the store. The insistent ringing of the phone greeted me.

. . .

I lifted the stem and receiver. "Good afternoon."

"Is this Mrs. Henriques Herbert?"

My forehead crinkled. I hadn't used that name in two years. "Who is this?"

"Officer James Sullivan, the Chaplain at Dannemora State Hospital for Insane Convicts."

"I'm Grace Herbert."

"I'm sorry to report Mr. Herbert... Henry died last night."

"Oh." I sat down on the nearest chair. Pressure against my chest made it hard to breathe.

"My condolences. The mortician of your choice can arrange transportation for his body, and you can pick up his belongings here. Is that something you can manage?"

What belongings? He had nothing I wanted or required.

"You live downstate. Is that correct? Will traveling here be a hardship?"

I never visited him, not even once, or wrote, phoned, or sent a package.

"Are you still there?"

"Yes. I don't mean to be rude, but—"

"I sat and prayed with him. He'd been sick for a year." I heard the accusation in his voice. He cleared his throat. "Volunteers from the local Methodist church help relatives secure remains and belongings."

"Throw them away," I said, surprised by the emotions surging through me. Like a pen on a solid surface, tapping came over the line. "What will you do with his body?"

"If you don't claim him?" His voice carried a blend of surprise and disapproval. "A pauper's grave."

I found it difficult to think.

"Is that what you want us to do? What about a decent burial, a service? Henry told me your family is Episcopalian."

Thoughts of Mae flashed in my mind. We'd mended fences and became more like family. Not sisterly like Beryl and me but tied to each other through the children. And what about them? I told Patricia and the little ones, convinced everyone, Henry died two years ago. As far as anyone knew, Jonathan and I were married. I'd have to tell my children the truth. What would they think of me?

Snippets of memories, sounds, and smells swirled. I couldn't catch my breath. "Please give me a moment to collect myself. May I call you back?"

"Of course." He paused and cleared his throat again. "Henry expressed great remorse and sought God's forgiveness. I thought you'd appreciate knowing."

He never asked for my forgiveness, never apologized to his daughters. "Thank you."

I didn't wait for another response, condemnation, or urging to be a better wife.

Henry was dead. Did I ever love him? I don't remember a single day when I missed him. If Mae wanted to bury him, then so be it. I wasn't interested but would respect her choice.

I searched to name the emotions filling me up. What were they? Relief and...? Deep breaths quieted the banging of my heart. My shoulder muscles eased.

The first time Henry died, I was afraid and shrouded in shame. This time, I experienced joy.

I was free.

THE END

"Confront the dark parts of yourself and work to banish them with illumination and forgiveness. Your willingness to wrestle with your demons will cause your angels to sing."
–August Wilson

ACKNOWLEDGEMENTS

With gratitude, I thank Black Rose Writing, Reagan Rothe, and his talented team for this opportunity.

Thank you to my early and beta readers for their keen eyes for details, patience, and encouragement–my husband Robert, my friends Willa Hogarth, Dorin Hart, Marianne Haggerty, and my writer-son Robert, Jr.

Thank you to author Russell Rowland and the band of workshop writers who weighed in.

A special thank you to my daughter, Alicia, for her research assistance.

And another special thank you to writer and coach Kathie Giorgio.

As always, I'm grateful for my family's love and support and for all the readers who read this and my earlier novels.

ABOUT THE AUTHOR

Karen E. Osborne is an award-winning, and Amazon Kindle best-selling author of four women's fiction/suspense novels. Karen's author life followed a career traveling the world as a trainer, and motivational speaker.

Getting It Right, Akashic Books, June 2017, was featured in Essence Magazine and Poets & Writers. *Tangled Lies*, Black Rose Writing, is a murder mystery, chosen as a 2021 BestThriller.com finalist, 2022 Maxy Awards finalist and Amazon's Kindle Top 100. *Reckonings*, Black Rose Writing, dropped June 16, 2022, is a Maxy Awards finalist and Indie Reader Discovery Awards winner." BestThrillers.com. *True Grace* is her latest project.

Karen hosts a weekly video podcast on her YouTube Channel, *What Are You Reading? What Are You Writing?*

OTHER TITLES BY KAREN E. OSBORNE

NOTE FROM KAREN E. OSBORNE

Word-of-mouth is crucial for any author to succeed. If you enjoyed *True Grace*, please leave a review online—anywhere you are able. Even if it's just a sentence or two. It would make all the difference and would be very much appreciated.

Thanks!
Karen E. Osborne

We hope you enjoyed reading this title from:

BLACK ROSE
writing™

Subscribe to our mailing list – *The Rosevine* – and receive **FREE** books, daily
deals, and stay current with news about upcoming
releases and our hottest authors.
Scan the QR code below to sign up.

Already a subscriber? Please accept a sincere thank you for being a fan of
Black Rose Writing authors.

View other Black Rose Writing titles at
www.blackrosewriting.com/books and use promo code
PRINT to receive a **20% discount** when purchasing.

www.ingramcontent.com/pod-product-compliance
Lightning Source LLC
Chambersburg PA
CBHW050140120726
47903CB00002B/429